Murmurs of Insanity

A MORIAH DRU/RICHARD LAKE
MYSTERY

MURMURS OF INSANITY

GERRIE FERRIS FINGER

FIVE STAR
A part of Gale, Cengage Learning

GALE
CENGAGE Learning·

Farmington Hills, Mich • San Francisco • New York • Waterville, Maine
Meriden, Conn • Mason, Ohio • Chicago

GALE
CENGAGE Learning®

LIBRARY OF CONGRESS CATALOGING-IN-PUBLICATION DATA

Finger, Gerrie Ferris.
  Murmurs of insanity : a Moriah Dru/Richard Lake mystery / by Gerrie Ferris Finger.
    First edition—pages cm
    ISBN-13: 978-1-4328-2858-5 (hardback)
    ISBN-10: 1-4328-2858-4 (hardcover)
    I. Title.
PS3606.I534M87 2014
813'.6—dc23   2014006959

First Edition. First Printing: July 2014
Find us on Facebook– https://www.facebook.com/FiveStarCengage
Visit our website– http://www.gale.cengage.com/fivestar/
Contact Five Star™ Publishing at FiveStar@cengage.com

Printed in the United States of America
1 2 3 4 5 6 7 18 17 16 15 14

To the memory of my mother, father, and brother.

CHAPTER ONE

The object of my loathing sat at the defense table, ogling his attorney as she presented her closing argument. By the expressions on the faces of the elderly judge and the besotted male jurors, I didn't think her words were sinking in as she high-stepped before the court in red peep-toe heels. Those three-inchers certainly set off her navy pencil skirt and red-trimmed bolero jacket. Add the natural blond hair and big blue eyes and who would bet against the defense?

Having testified to my part in the police operation authorized by the juvenile court, which I represented, I itched to get out of the overheated courtroom. Instead, I squirmed on the hard bench determined to stay for the verdict.

The prosecution's case against Devus Dontel—Big DD—McFersen began to fall apart when the judge agreed that juveniles need not testify to video evidence showing that they acted as dealers, spotters, and runners for McFersen. The ruling was one of self-incrimination since the juveniles admitted to police, and me, that they'd purchased drugs from Big DD for clients—thus becoming dealers themselves. The prosecution went for the lesser charge of corruption, but without the video, my testimony and that of two narcotics cops didn't appear to sway the jury quite like Miss Peep-Toes.

I anticipated a short closing argument and got it. She summed up by saying, "Mr. Devus Dontel McFersen didn't solicit those kids. They were sent to him by law enforcement, by a purported guardian and finder of children." *That was me.* "Shame on you Atlanta Police Department and Moriah Dru. We are in moral decay when the protectors of children send them into harm's way." More yackety-yak and then she raised her finger to the ceiling as if personally affronted. "Be that as it may, my client is innocent of the charges and any implied wrongdoing. Not one child testified against Mr. McFersen. It's only fair and just that accusers face those whom they accuse. We have only the words of those who sought to entrap my client—" voice rising. "—those who sought to sully innocent children by exposing them to crime rather than protecting them from it. Shame!" She half turned toward me, and I felt the eyes of the spectators—most of them there for the defendant—crawl over me. She tapped heels back to the table, saying, "Thank you, Your Honor." With that, she sat.

The judge, who I knew, observed me like he was sorry for what was going to happen. Then he addressed the jury and read the instructions.

The thirteen members of the jury—the regulation twelve and one alternate—glanced at their watches, most likely thinking they could wrap this baby up and get home before the traffic. I felt myself sagging just as someone sat beside me.

Lake.

Lake in his sharp Burberry. Lake—my love—still the man who could, by simply showing up, have my heart strumming. He removed his black felt fedora and perched it on his knee.

He nodded hello, rather stony-faced I thought, and faced the bench. The judge noted his presence by adjusting his glasses as if wondering why a detective lieutenant in homicide would come into his courtroom. And, as if to avoid witnessing a possible dramatic arrest, the judge rose quickly. Lake and I stood. Bliss stretched the soreness of the wooden bench from my backside.

Lake took my arm and led me through the double doors into

the anteroom where I fetched my black cashmere coat. In the broad hall, he said, "Buy a poor city servant a cup of coffee?"

"There's better day-old coffee at the cop house than what's in those machines downstairs."

"I could use a cruller, too," he said, his hopeful grin shimmering in his dark eyes.

The man and his sweets; cops and their crullers. "I don't think this verdict is long in coming," I said.

"I saw and heard. Quite a performance." He put his hand at the back of my waist and urged me toward the elevators. "Too bad. A scumbag is a scumbag, no matter the letter of the law."

"Or the defense lawyer's curvy calves."

His expression droll, he said, "Juries want accusers to face the accused. It's only fair and just."

"It is?"

"Learned counselor said so. I went up against her last year. Her client's hair and weapon wasn't enough, she argued. She wanted an eyewitness to the murder. She wore fetching black. We lost that one, too."

Crowding in with ten people, we rode the elevator to the lobby in silence. Outside, on the cracked sidewalk, Lake placed his fedora on his head, angling it ever so slightly against the crisp wind. "What's on for the rest of your day?"

"Office," I said, thinking of sitting at the computer doing what was once real paperwork. "Pearly Sue's in Florida on the parental abduction I told you about. Dad just wanted to take his son to see his new girlfriend, which mama didn't approve of. Neither did Portia since she wouldn't give permission to take the child out-of-state. The real mom is still bonding with the boy after getting out of prison."

"Isn't it nice of these citizens—keeping us in business?"

"What a cynic."

We came to the Superior Coffee Shop where the crullers

were superior—calorie-packed, but superior. Carrying our cardboard trays, we found a round table and sat knee-to-knee. Nothing was said as I drank coffee and he ate. Chewing his last bite, Lake chased it with a gulp of coffee. Wiping his mouth, he said, "I'd like you to do something for me."

I raised my eyebrows. "Your plants don't need watering. They froze last week." Winter in Atlanta can be a bitch.

"Next time you're at the nursery, buy me something in an evergreen. But that's not the favor." His intense stare told me this was serious.

Nevertheless, I said, "Okay, you can have my donut."

He picked it up. "Did you know that Linda has a brother?" He bit into the sugary dough.

"Linda Lake? A brother?" Linda was Lake's ex-wife. Her pert blond persona popped into my mind as I sipped coffee. "I had no idea."

"Half-brother actually. He lives in Athens."

"Athens is a long ways away."

"Georgia."

"Lake, my dearest. I like your ex-wife, but I don't keep up with your ex-in-laws." Had I sounded snarky? Lake's expression told me I had. "I take it a problem has arisen."

Lake had lost interest in the cruller and laid it on the plate. A meaningful indication. He drank the rest of his cooling coffee. "Linda called me," he looked at his watch, "about forty-five minutes ago. Her half-brother's name is Baxter Carlisle. He owns several restaurants in Athens." He paused, as if not knowing how to go on.

"Baxter Carlisle is Linda's half-brother? I've been to his restaurants with Portia and friends many times."

Portia Devon is a juvenile judge and my lifelong friend. She attended the University of Georgia. During my community college days, I spent more time in Athens than Atlanta. "So, what's the problem?" I wadded up my napkin. "I've got to get back."

"Young girls, I would say," Lake said.

"How young?"

"At present, eighteen."

"How old is he?"

"Fifty-two."

"Dangerous age, but she's of consent."

"That's not the point." Lake looked up, his eyelids half-closed over dark brown eyes. "I never knew. The family kept it a secret."

"A Lolita complex? Linda just told you?"

"Out of necessity."

"How much necessity?"

"Athens police brought Bax in for questioning in the disappearance of Damian Hansel, a student at the University."

"Damian?" I asked. Lake nodded. "Is there a gender problem, too?"

"According to Linda, Damian is the boyfriend of the object of Baxter's obsession. She is also a student."

"Baxter Carlisle's got himself mixed up with college kids?"

"Hansel's disappearance is going public, like, *now* probably."

"How old is he and how long's he been missing?"

"He's nineteen and was last seen Thursday evening." He paused as if to stare across time. "Four days now."

"What's the name of the object of Baxter's obsession?"

"Cho Martine."

"Interesting name. So he's obsessed with her and offs her boyfriend? Is that the thinking?"

"Too early to off Hansel just yet."

"What's Martine, the teen, saying?"

"She saw Hansel on Thursday evening. They studied together for exams at their usual internet café. He went home. She went home. They live near the campus."

"Is there an Atlanta connection that could bring you in?"

"Martine is from Savannah. Hansel's an out-of-state student from Tallahassee, Florida."

"We need a Gretel in here."

Lake explained that Hansel didn't show for his exam Friday. Nobody saw him over the weekend. When he didn't show this morning, a friend called Hansel's father who came to Athens and eventually filed the missing persons report. The father also told Athens police that Damian was something of a traveler and been known to disappear to museums and internet cafés, although he never missed exams. Lake ended by saying that was all he got from Linda, and that the Atlanta Police Department hadn't received any more information.

I thought about Linda Lake. I met her before I knew her husband was a cop. Linda was the fire department's spokeswoman before she gave birth to her and Lake's daughter, Susanna. She's the opposite of me. Think of your ideal Junior Leaguer: tiny, blond, pert, gabby, and currently engaged to a real estate tycoon. And, no, Lake didn't leave Linda for me. When I met him—at the same time I was assigned to partner with him in Atlanta Police Zone Two—they had already agreed to an amicable divorce.

I asked, "Why is Carlisle suspected in his disappearance, and who said he's obsessed with this Cho Martine?"

"Martine filed three complaints against him—all stalking related."

I'm a sucker for missing persons' mysteries. "It could interest me," I said, "but Hansel isn't a case for Child Trace. Too old." Child Trace is my specialty private investigative agency, and I consider anyone past eighteen a full-fledged adult.

"You had a seventeen-year-old last year. Two years isn't that different."

"You're right, but Hansel sounds self-sufficient. He goes off on his own, but returns. He still might." Standing, I said, "I got to get back."

He threw two dollars on the table with me wondering, once again, why he tips when we stand in line to get our donuts and coffee and then bus our own table. I looked around. Nobody to tip. I picked up the two bucks and waved it at him. "Thanks."

Outside, we hurried back to the courthouse, huffing lines of condensed air. He said, "Linda is beside herself. Her name could be linked to his. Inevitably, would be, depending how the case goes."

"Has Carlisle ever been arrested for anything relating to his little . . . complex?"

"I ran his sheet. A DUI in Clarke County eleven years back. The recent stalking charges haven't hit the system."

"Why not?"

"Complaints days apart. First one Friday, second Saturday, third Sunday."

Starting after her boyfriend goes missing. "Did Martine get a restraining order?" Lake shook his head.

I asked, "What form do these complaints take?"

"Two peeping Toms and a stalking by automobile."

"She can prove it was Carlisle?"

"One grainy photograph of a face in the window."

We walked up the courthouse steps. I already knew most of what he had to say about the public Baxter Carlisle. He was well-known because of his restaurants. He owned three—a sports bar where college kids hung out, a steak joint where college kids take their parents on visiting weekends, and an upscale faux French for locals.

"I've been to the ersatz French," I said. "I went with Portia and her mother a couple of times. Porsh and I spent a lot of time in Carlisle's sports bar, too."

We passed through courthouse security and walked down the hall toward the elevators.

I said, "So you think if I trace this Damian Hansel and find him lurking in a library, starving, thirsty, unshaven, having forgotten about his classes and exams, that will clear Baxter?"

"I think you will find out he's dead and that Baxter is a suspect."

"Linda thinks that?"

"She's . . ."

The babble of heavy voices reached me. The elevator doors had parted and Devus McFersen led his followers out. His six-foot-five, two-hundred-seventy-five pounds came barreling at us. He stopped, spread his legs, pushed his coat open, and propped his fists at the sides of his waist.

My eyes met his. "I see you were acquitted."

His gold-toothed smile took up half his cheeky face, but it wasn't pleasant. "Not guilty!" His voice hurt my head as it echoed throughout the lobby. His glance shifted to Lake, who would not be mistaken for anything other than what he was. Devus bestowed a trademark smirk. "Well, the lady got herself a copper for a bodyguard." He wagged his head. "In case ol' Devus beats the rap."

"You were acquitted, Mr. McFersen," I said. "There wasn't enough evidence. That's how the law works."

"You wanted to put my ass in jail."

Lake warned, "Watch your tongue here."

Pulling his coat closed, Devus said to me, "And you watch who you try to put in the box."

"Is that a threat?" Lake asked.

Although a man of agility and speed, Lake's six-foot-two, one-eighty was no match for Devus's mountain of muscle.

Devus laughed and so did the minions standing behind him. Then he leaned into me and spoke in a whisper. "I jes be sayin' you be smart being careful."

He moved around me. So did four men who could be

linebackers for the Atlanta Falcons. Following was his mother, who'd obliquely accused him on the stand, but apparently the members of the jury didn't think a mother's accusations amounted to much.

Nor a child finder's.

CHAPTER TWO

After a few hours in my office computing expenses in the McFersen trial, Lake's request put me on Northside Drive in my antique Bentley, heading for Linda Lake's house. I would do anything for Lake because he would do anything for me. But this situation held particular interest. For all the time I spent in Athens, a city that makes me feel good just being in it, I'd never even laid eyes on Baxter Carlisle.

I knew what time Linda picked up Susanna from kindergarten because I'd been put on the list of people authorized to fetch her after school. Linda took me up on my offer to do so on the days she had a Junior League charity function or tennis. I'm always happy to do it. I live in the neighborhood—Peachtree Hills—and love that little girl like she was my own. I sometimes think of her as mine. I've never married, although I know that's no precondition—either to childbirth or loving children. I was engaged once, but my fiancé died in a drive-by shooting handing out flyers for Big Brothers in neighborhoods desperately in need of Big Brothers.

I turned from Northside Drive onto West Wesley. A shot or a backfire startled me. I quickly recalculated. Small caliber. Tires squealed. Something had come for me while I was lost in thought.

Who?

I looked in the rearview mirror. An old battering ram of a Cadillac headed straight for my rear end. At least two large people loomed inside. I hadn't considered being followed. Why hadn't I foreseen this? I should have driven the used Audi I purchased and drove on road trips. I floored the Bentley's gas pedal. Pickup was solid. The car lurched into acceleration gear. I flew ahead—dear God don't let someone decide to cross the street without looking.

Another shot split the air. And another.

In the rearview mirror, on the Caddy's passenger side, I spotted the hand holding the gun. The shooter was firing into the trees. He wasn't going to kill me, and he wasn't going to slam me from behind. This was scare-back time. I'd scared Big DD with prison. No bad deed gets forgiven. It only gets even. The Cadillac revved and lurched around my car. I swerved onto Argonne Street. From the passenger window, the hand holding the gun wavered and fired into the sky again as the car disappeared up the street. With my heart beating a rumba, I reversed and got back on West Wesley. I didn't see the Cadillac when I crossed Peachtree Street and entered Peachtree Battle Shopping Center. God forbid I should lead the bad guys to Linda Lake's place.

I needed to let my pulse get back to simply racing and sat in a parking slot and thought about what had happened. What should I do? Call Lake? He had enough to do without looking for a car that was, by now, hidden in some ramshackle garage. After two or three minutes, I started the Bentley and pulled into a gas station. Doug, the day manager, had finished with a customer buying a lottery ticket. "What gives, Dru?"

"Thirsty," I said and went to the cold Coke cooler and fished out a wet bottle.

"On me," he said. "You sure look hot."

Although he flirted a lot, I knew he didn't mean sexy. My face must have been aflame. I opened the bottle on the side of the cooler. "Nearly wrecked," I said and heaved a deep breath.

"You drive Peachtree Street enough, you get used to it.

Defensive driving that's what you got to do. The Bentley okay?"

"Close, but not a scratch."

"I ever tell you I was here when Portia's mother used to drive that car down Peachtree Street?"

"Yeah you have."

"She caused many an ol' boy to swerve into bus stops and parking meters."

When Portia's mother could no longer drive anything, and when my car was bombed, Portia had insisted I buy the Bentley for the princely sum of five hundred dollars.

"Thanks, Doug," I said, leaving.

My cell phone played Haydn's Piano Sonata No. 52 in E-flat major. Lake. Probably wondering why I wasn't at Linda's. I let it play out and drove to my street, parked the Bentley in my one-car garage, and got into the ten-year-old Audi, new by the Bentley's standards. If I was followed, I didn't detect a standout among the silver cars and SUVs behind me. I took a circuitous route to Linda's and parked for ten minutes on a side street a block over. The first of the school buses came down the street.

Linda wore a slacks outfit that likely cost more than my clothing allowance for the season. Although her face showed stress, her hair and makeup were flawless. Before she gave birth, she'd been the media spokeswoman for Fire Protection Services and spoke in front of the camera every chance she got.

Linda pulled me inside, saying, "I knew Rick would get you for me." She held out her arms. "Let me take your coat. Oh my, what lovely cashmere."

Giving up a coat that's older than the Audi, I said, "Lake told me a little of the problem."

With me following, Linda swayed through the minimalist, but stylish, living room, into a study. Red leather and books gleamed in winter sun slanting through plantation blinds. "It's not five o'clock, Dru, but I think a toddy is in order."

Toddy. For the body.

At the recessed bar, she prepared two gin and tonics, gave me mine, and held hers up. "For the body."

I held mine up. Clink. "For the body."

"And the mind," she said, swallowing. "Let's sit."

"Where's Susanna?" I asked, cozying into a leather armchair.

Linda said she was at Lozetta's, the part-time nanny, because she knew Susanna would want to talk about her day at school, and her new friend, and her kitten and her new exotic fish. By the time she finished saying this, I could have talked to Susanna. Linda finally wound down. "I knew you'd want to know about Baxter, and all."

I nodded, deciding not to talk about my visits to his restaurants. "Tell me about Baxter." *And all.*

She sipped at the glass rim. I have to give her credit for self-control. Lake thought she was falling apart, but I didn't think that possible. I put the drink on a crystal coaster. After the Cadillac scare, if I took a sip I'd probably go after the whole bottle.

Linda, too, placed her glass on a coaster. "Lordy, he's all I have since that drunk took Mama and Daddy away from us. I didn't know where else to turn. Me and Rick, well you know, we stayed friends. It's all we ever were really. He loved his job more than me. I always knew that, but he was so dedicated. I love a man who's dedicated to what he believes in. He believes in Atlanta and justice . . ."

My mind wanders when chatty people go all nervous to avoid a painful discussion, and I thought of my own daddy getting killed. Involuntarily my mind went to Daddy in his coffin. Then I saw Mama in the nursing home, in a rocking chair, her big blue eyes as blank as Daddy's would have been had they been open. *Stop this introspection. It gets you nowhere. You'll be reaching for a bottle like your daddy.* That was another subject: Daddy's alcoholism.

I brought my mind back to what Linda was saying.

"Susanna, the apple of his eye, and you, Dru, but I'm not the jealous type. I want Rick to be happy."

"Me, too," I broke in. "He's more than happy to help you, and so am I."

"You are?"

"That's why I'm here."

"I'm so glad. I don't know which way to turn. I can't tell you . . ."

"Let's go over what I know so far." I recounted what Lake had told me and ended by saying, "Sounds like your brother has a Lolita complex."

"Huh? Oh. Lolita, yes. Daddy was so het up when . . ."

"When what?"

"Well, we'll save that for another day."

"No, if it's about his character, we need to have it out, and now."

"Oh, you're so like Rick. Facts and more facts."

"Why was your daddy so het up?"

"You know Baxter is my half-brother?"

I nodded.

"Daddy . . ."

"Let me get the connection straight. Whose son is Baxter?"

"Mama's by a previous marriage. She married a Carlisle when she was sixteen; had Bax when she was seventeen and divorced Tommy Carlisle when she was twenty-five. Then she married Daddy when she was twenty-seven, a Hanover. If you ask me, a better marriage than the Carlisle one."

These society marriages might as well be arranged by a matchmaker, and arranged again, and again. Incestuous, that way. "You were saying your daddy, who is Baxter's stepfather, was irate. When—why?"

"Such dirty laundry Baxter's gotten us into." She hooked strands of silky blond hair behind an ear. "Bax was thirteen, fourteen—and I was little then, but I knew something bad had happened . . ." She looked at the floor and rushed into speech. "Baxter diddled the little girl next door."

"How old?"

"Nine, I think." She looked up at me. "It wasn't bad, more like playing doctor, or, you know . . ."

"It was bad," I said.

"Oh, Dru, don't say that."

"What did your daddy do about it?"

"Well, Mrs. Marx came over to our house and raised the holy roof."

"Rightly so. What happened to Baxter?"

"Daddy took a strap to his bee-hind. They were in the basement but I could hear . . . Oh, Dru, it was horrid. Bax's real daddy came and got him for the summer. Then, when school started Bax came back. It was never the same, I don't think."

I guess not.

"Any more incidents?"

"Baxter went away to the Georgia Military Academy."

"Any more incidents?"

"It was in the town, a girl, fourteen, she said Bax assaulted her."

"Raped her?"

"Well, that's the harsh term."

"It's a harsh deed."

She sighed. "Yes."

You so desire to keep people like Linda in their fairy castles, but I couldn't. "I understand the need to keep skeletons closeted. Once it's over, no use dwelling on it. But it didn't get over, did it?"

"She recanted. The girl said she consented. She didn't go to the police or anything."

"How much did your family pay?"

"Bax's daddy paid, I heard. I don't know how much."

"I can see why you're upset."

"Well, yes. When we hadn't heard anything more after the college thing . . ."

"College thing? Where was this?"

"He went to college in West Virginia. Same thing, only the girl got pregnant. Bax paid support until the boy was raised."

"Do you know this boy?"

She shook her head no. "I can't remember his name, but it'll come, maybe."

"So, back to the present, you hadn't heard anything else until this problem in Athens with Damian Hansel."

"It's not the same. The girl is in college."

"No, it isn't the same. The thinking is Baxter could have done something to Damian so he could have his girl."

She gasped, jumped up, and ran from the room, returning with a box of tissues and a handkerchief. This took thirty seconds. Sitting, dabbing at her blue eyes, she said, "I'm so glad Susanna's not here. I hate for her to see me cry. I hate for you to see me cry. This is just so awful. These girls, they throw themselves at Bax. He's so good-looking, and then they—they say awful things about him."

"Have you told me everything there is to tell about Baxter and his problems?"

"Honest, I have. Bax left grad school and his daddy set him up in a different town than Atlanta." She laid her hands in her lap. "You know what I think?"

"I'd like to know."

She lowered her head and looked through her mascaraed lashes. "His daddy did that so he didn't have to be bothered with him anymore. Tommy Carlisle was like that. Everything was about him."

I let a few seconds slip by. "If you really want me to help you, I'll have to talk to Baxter. Will he talk to me?"

She grinned. "Oh, he'd love to talk to you. He's not always after—after the young ones. He's had girlfriends, older ones. He's brought them to Thanksgiving and Christmas. That's probably what Rick remembers about Bax. You better be careful. Baxter might take you away from Rick, and I wouldn't want to be responsible for that."

There was really nothing left to say, so I had her scribble Baxter's address and phone number on a slip of monogrammed note paper, then let her cry her thanks on my shoulder in the living room and sniff back grief at the door.

This *older one* was happy to be outside, taking a breather.

CHAPTER THREE

I wish Linda's story was unique. I know firsthand it's not. I don't understand the vagaries of human sexuality, although I wish I could grasp and forestall the grosser anomalies before they ruined and took lives. I know Linda to be a superficial person, a good person, but the depth of her mental acuity went no lower than the meningeal sheaths holding her brain together. Yet, she was as disturbed as her personality allowed. Theirs is not an uncommon story in our culture. The family had bought out and covered over Baxter's proclivities as if they were nothing more than shooting out streetlights with a BB gun. The boy and man appear to have needed psychiatric help. I may not understand the urges that drive people, but I know that most obsessions are never cured. There are drugs and there are programs if one wanted to try them. Baxter Carlisle either failed or didn't sign on.

I put my Bluetooth ear bud on and called Lake. "He's been into nymphets since his teens."

Lake almost choked. "Linda said that?"

"More or less."

"With Linda, it would less. It's the Junior League in her."

"The *incidents* were paid for."

"Rich people do that."

"If he's involved in Hansel's disappearance, he jumped the shark, diving into a place where money gets wet and sharks drown."

Lake said he had just spoken to an Athens cop. Nothing, no leads, no Hansel.

Hansel owned a Jeep that was still parked out back of his apartment. His bicycle was missing, but his Harley was parked in the garage. His father, Henry Hansel, was in Athens, going from hangout to hangout trying to find someone who might know something. Hansel's father was an attorney and his mother was very ill and not with the father.

"I bet the Athens PD love him going from hangout to hangout asking questions," I said.

"The sergeant didn't sound happy. People like Henry Hansel mess with people's memories, insert thoughts into their minds."

"That makes him a good lawyer."

"What's next?"

"Dinner with you, get a good night's sleep, and then, tomorrow, Athens, G-A."

"Ah, you're on the case."

"And without a fee."

"Linda didn't offer?"

"Linda hasn't married her real estate tycoon yet. He'll pony up for Saks' slacks, but he doesn't know about Baxter's past is my bet."

"Keep track of your expenses; I'll see you get reimbursed."

"I'll see that you see."

"Where's dinner?"

"My place. Your heater is lame, thus your frozen Wandering Jew and Marginata."

After sweet nothing 'byes, I called Portia Devon. Portia and I go back to second grade at Christ the King Catholic School. Portia's clerk said she'd be right with me. While waiting, I drove onto lovely Peachtree Street, an asphalt ribbon with potholes covered by iron squares.

Portia is the senior presiding judge of the Superior Court's

Juvenile Justice Division. When I was on the verge of leaving the Atlanta Police Department, she urged me to start a child finding agency, going so far as offering to fund the enterprise. Fortunately—or unfortunately—I got more clients than I could handle that first month, though half were courtesy of the Juvenile Justice Division.

Portia came on the line. "Moriah. Sorry about that scum McFersen. You keep up with that son-of-a-bitch. He'll be selling to children by this weekend."

"I'm assigning Pearly Sue to monitor him."

"Poor bastard."

"As a mistress of disguise, he won't be able to distinguish her from all the other junkie prostitutes that come seeking his wares," I said, then paused because I was about to change the subject and wanted to give her a clue. "Listen, Porsh, I've got a different kind of case."

"You need something from me?"

"You're clairvoyant."

"You're obvious."

"A student is missing in Athens."

"That! I heard it first from Lake, but now it's hit the media."

"Baxter Carlisle is Linda Lake's half-brother; the restaurateur in Athens."

"How could I forget? We spent enough money in his establishments to pay for his pony farm."

"Linda's upset."

"I can see why."

"She told me some things, and I wondered if . . ."

"Moriah."

"I know about confidential." As many cases as I've handled for her, she never breaks confidentiality. Bends sometimes, but never shatters. "If I ask anything specific, you could not answer. That way . . ."

"No."

"What if I know he likes adolescent girls?"

"According to the cops and the reporters, he's smitten with a girl of eighteen."

"But his past . . ."

"No."

"If Damian Hansel doesn't show by tomorrow, I go to Athens to talk to Carlisle, the Martine girl, and anybody else I can find. First, I thought maybe you could give me some insight . . ."

"Insight I can give you. Do not fall prey to anyone's charms. Got that?"

I thought about Linda's saying Carlisle was good-looking. Good-looking guys are usually charmers. "Got it," I said.

Portia hung up. No insult. That's how she ends conversations. You should have her walk out of the room when she's finished talking to you. Turns, waves backhand, and departs. And I love her to death.

My brain trotted down memory lane as I turned onto Peachtree Hills. After she graduated from the University of Georgia, Portia went to law school at Emory. I'm a different story. After a two-year course in police science, I went to the Atlanta Police Academy. That career choice had little to do with civic zeal and a lot to do with money, as in: I had none. Daddy was a marginal stockbroker turned insurance salesman. We lived on an edge carefully hidden by Southern gentility, and then one day I realized that Daddy wasn't going to work any longer, and that he lay around the house nipping at a quart of Jim Beam or Old Crow. It didn't stop me from loving him, though.

I pulled into my white gravel driveway and—*what the hell?*

My white fence had been flattened. I shifted into park and jumped from the car. Piles of trash started at the flattened fence and strewed over the back garden to the neighbor's fence, even covering the birdbaths. Hanging bird feeders had been slashed or flung to the ground. I couldn't move and felt something pressing against my ribs, making it impossible to breathe. I heard a shout and willed my feet to turn so I could look down the driveway.

My neighbor across the street, Carol, ran up, glum-eyed, and said, "I didn't know what the truck was going to do. I thought maybe you'd ordered a load of white gravel, but you just redid it last month, so I . . ." She stared at my unbelieving face. "I'm sorry, I should have called police."

"That's okay," I said, rubbing my forehead to clear the daze. "Tell me about the truck . . . who drove it, all you can remember."

She rushed into speech like she was guilty of something. "It was a dump truck, not like a city garbage truck. It was old and beat up. It was a dark color. A black man drove. There was two of them. I didn't see the passenger. They didn't get out. I couldn't see them knock down your fence, what they did in the back. They left and I came over . . . Oh Dru, I'm sorry. I was just going to call you and see if you wanted me to call the police. What with Lake and all . . ."

"How long ago?"

"Half hour, twenty minutes. I didn't know . . ."

"That's fine, Carol. I'll call police."

"Lake?"

"Patrol, then Lake," I said, dashing to my car for my cell phone. I noticed the garage door was shut, the garage intact from what I could see.

The woman manning dispatch said she was sending a car, so I went back to Carol, who watches my place when I'm away, waters my plants, and fills the bird feeders. She said, "Don't go inside."

"I'm not," I said, walking toward the back door with Carol on my heels. I heard her gasp at the same time I saw the writing on the wooden slats. WHITE TRASH.

I heard the squeal of tires and saw the unmarked squad car brake behind the Audi. "How did he get here so fast?" I asked, but not to Carol specifically.

She answered though. "He's always looking out for you, Dru. You're so lucky." I held out my arm in case she swooned.

Lake sprinted the few yards toward us. Carol said, "He's so handsome."

He stopped in front of me, leaned to give a kiss to my forehead, and said, "Didn't take long to get retribution."

Twice.

"No," I muttered.

Carol looked from Lake to me. "You know who?"

"Excuse us, Carol," Lake said. "We're going to check inside."

"Oh," she breathed out. "Yeah, well, if you need me for anything . . ." She backed off and gave a small wave. We waved back.

"Son-of-a-bitch," Lake said, taking the Sig Sauer from its shoulder holster.

"DD didn't do it," I said, wishing I had my gun. It was locked inside my house. "He'd have sent one of the brothers." I put my arm on Lake's to hold him in place. "He sent two in an old Cadillac. One fired several shots. Into the trees."

"Where?"

"West Wesley."

Lake looked ready to explode. I hastily explained, "I didn't go to Linda's until the coast was clear."

"Bastard." He radioed Zone Two to send a car to check on Linda. Linda and Susanna had once spent a lot of time with her relatives in the north Georgia mountains until a case was resolved.

He looked at the WHITE TRASH scrawled on the side of my cottage.

I said, "I take exception to that. I drink fine wines and brush my teeth."

Keying open the lock and deadbolt, I stepped aside to let Lake enter the little hall that held a small chest freezer, a coat stand, and a six-tier baker's rack for household cleaning products, birdseed, and a few tools. Nothing looked out of place. In the kitchen, nothing appeared disturbed until Lake went to a side window that had been broken, the screen torn away. Lake held up the weapon—a fist-size rock, painted blood red. "Son-of-a-bitch. We'll see whose heart gets torn out first."

I felt tears push against my eyelids and turned my head. But he knew. Gun ready, he led us through the rest of the cottage. Nothing else was amiss. Lake holstered the Sig. "Just threw the rock in the first handy window."

"He must have used a sling shot," I said, kneading the back of my neck to ease the tension. "It's double paned."

Two beat cops appeared at the door. "Saw you were here, Lieutenant," one said. I knew him. "You okay, Dru?" he asked, eyes full of concern.

I mumbled, "You're here. I'm okay."

He smiled shyly. I love cops. He said, "We got someone at Linda Lake's house now, Lieutenant."

Lake nodded and indicated the window. "Painted rock through it. I'll initiate forensics."

"Antique car in the garage untouched. A mess otherwise."

"One he'll wish he never made," Lake said.

Devus Dontel McFersen, who came to Atlanta from Houston by way of New Orleans when Katrina hit, should have been here long enough to know cops have their own special justice when it becomes personal. I didn't envy Big DD.

"Let's get out of here," Lake said.

"Which hotel do you prefer," I said, thinking of the below normal January temperature. "I'll get the bill."

"No need, lovely, rich girlfriend. The heater guy said he'd be by today sometime. Lou said he'd be home to let him in." Lou was a photographer who lived in Lake's warehouse building, one of the few near the railroad tracks in Atlanta that hadn't been turned into expensive loft-living condominiums.

From experience, I'll always have doubts about repairmen arriving on the day and time specified, but I acquiesced with a shrug and said, "I'll drive the Bentley in case they come back with more trash. If I go to Athens tomorrow, I'll drive the Audi, but I want to leave the Bentley behind your security fence. Then I'm calling Webdog and get him researching."

"Sounds like a plan."

But first we stopped by Linda's. The cop said she'd just left for her mother's place in the north Georgia mountains. And wasn't happy about missing her morning tennis match. The kitten and the exotic fish were gone, too.

CHAPTER FOUR

From Peachtree Street to Marietta Street, then onto Forsyth Street, I followed Lake to his Castleberry Hill community, a few blocks from the railroad yards that split Atlanta north from south. Back when the city was a rail depot in the wilderness, they called it Terminus. As the population grew, the citizens didn't cotton to the name. A doting father renamed the city Marthasville, after his daughter. That name didn't quite capture the imaginations of townspeople, either, and, a couple of years later, a railroad engineer suggested the name Atlanta. The fabled name stuck.

Most of the warehouses, like the John Deere I passed, had been gutted and rebuilt, but the century-old cotton warehouse of our destination was like Lake—original, sturdy, and rare.

He drove through the chain-link gate into the parking lot across the street from his building. Until recently, the asphalt lot wasn't surrounded by a high security fence, but when my Saab was blown up by the suspect in a string of suburban girl murders, Lake got the city to spring for the fence and an ID monitor.

I gathered my briefcase, backpack, and laptop and joined Lake at the gate.

Crossing the street, I looked up at the third story. The high, double-hung windows were shut tight. In summer, green burlap curtains would be flapping out because Lake didn't have AC to conk out.

My head brushed the cord that hung from one of the windows. His doorbell was an old cowbell that he'd mounted on a curtain bracket. The cord was strung through a hole he'd drilled in the windowsill. He also had a mirror set up where he could see the street and anyone standing where I stood on the single-step stoop watching him unlock the wide loading door. Like I said, Lake and his loft were originals.

Inside the cold hall, the tenants' mail was piled on a table made from concrete blocks and boards. Lake flipped through the day's offering and took his. We labored up the narrow, steep steps to the beat of live rap music, and my spirit lifted, not at the quality of the music, but of Lou's way of relaxing after his day of shooting—photographs.

Inside, Lake hooked his hat on the hat bracket and went to the big brown heater stove that had been installed sometime in the 1940s. He turned on the gas. The gas worked fine; it was the circulating electric fan that didn't work. If you sat close to the thing, it would roast one side of you while the other iced. I kept my distance with my coat on. Lake turned. "Sorry." He removed his lined Burberry and hung it next to his hat.

With the exception of a small, walled bath area in the southwest corner of the room, the loft was one long room. The bath area had been built in the 1950s. It had a claw-foot tub and a hose sprayer for a mini-shower and hair wash. Lake had partitioned the rest of the loft into two halves. Smack down the lengthy center, he'd laid an oriental runner over the heart pine floor. Moveable screens separated *rooms.* In the sitting area, leather sofas and chairs crouched around a stone coffee table. He'd mounted a big screen television on the brick wall. I'd never seen it on unless Susanna was in residence. Susanna had her own partitioned room across from the sitting room. Her mama wasn't happy that her precious slept in an unrefined loft for two days every other week, but Suze loved the place, especially the two cats, Max and Remy. As working cats, they kept the rats away.

Lake had taken off his tie and was laying blue jeans and a polo shirt on the bed.

I plopped my things on a leather sofa, shooed Remy from the chair, and sat. I looked at the laptop and set about calling Webdog, my computer genius.

"Yo," Web answered. "Sorry that your gangbanger walked."

"There's always a next time for Devus. I got a few people I need info on."

"I'm your guy."

"Damian Hansel, student, University of Georgia."

"I heard about him. Gotcha. Who else?"

"Cho Martine, a student at Georgia as well. Girlfriend of the aforementioned."

"She's the one signed a complaint against . . ."

"Baxter Carlisle. See what you can find on all three. Start with the students."

"Will do." I could hear the keys rattling and envied his warm hands. "Over and out."

I signed off. A strange current in the air caused me to go to a window. When a silent crackle crossed the back of my neck and I shivered, I rubbed my coated arms. What was happening at my cottage? Where had my mysterious cat, Mr. Brown, hunkered when the trashing began? My cottage wasn't the house I was raised in. That house on Morningside Drive probably sells for half a million now. After Daddy took too many pills with too much bourbon, Mama had to sell fast and cheap. She lived with me until I came home and found my cottage hot as hell and Mama standing on a chair with a scissors in hand, about to cut the electric cord on the clock. "It stopped," she said. "I need to wind it."

The nursing home is a beautiful and expensive place, and

Mama hates it. My Saturday visit loomed, and, though I'd never admit it to a soul, I plain didn't want to go. Often she didn't know me, but I didn't mind that. She'd call me by her sister's name, Bella Louise. Mama's name is Anna Lee. Bella Louise died ten years ago from a freak fall down the steps. Between that and my father's suicide, we (the doctor and I) believe it hastened the onslaught of Mama's Alzheimer's. Oh, horrid disease that affected so many of my ancestors. Lake thinks I take risks because I fear if I take care of myself, I'll end up like Mama. Lake thinks a lot of things about me that I could take issue with. I'd never tell him I detest going to see Mama. He'd think less of me. I try in vain to feel the deep compassion of a dedicated caregiver. Lake thinks I'm compassionate because I'm a child finder. The truth is, I don't interact that much with kids. They're gone, I find them, I give them to whom they belong, and move to the next case. But I cherish our time with Susanna and hope she and Linda got to the mountains just fine.

Behind me I heard Lake make a noise. It was the kind borne of futility. "Friggin' fan won't come on."

Facing him, I sighed. "Sorry, I'm no help."

"You appeared deep in thought."

"I was."

"Baxter?"

"No."

He put his arms around me. I touched his cheek with mine. He said, "Don't beat yourself up, darling. You know you can confide in me."

Had I been thinking aloud? "Okay, I'm freezing."

He drew his face away and brushed hair from my forehead. "I want you to know I'm here for you when you get into your moods."

"Jerk."

He laughed. "Where do you want to eat tonight?"

"Let's do the I-don't-care-where-do-you-want-to-eat, before you impose your will upon me."

He reached for his jeans. "I don't impose my will upon you." One leg in, he said, "Chinese."

"Thai."

"Italian."

"Vietnamese."

He hopped around. "German."

"Sushi."

He zipped up. "I thought you'd never get around to it."

"Let's go someplace different for a change."

"Nakato."

"Buddha's Temple."

"Steel's."

"MF's."

"Sushi House."

"Arata."

He snapped his fingers. "Arata's. Let's go there. We haven't been there in . . ."

"Two days."

Arata is a small sushi restaurant tucked between an upscale antique shop and a hairdresser on West Peachtree Street. Faux Japanese statues and wall hangings add to the atmosphere as soft oriental music plays. We sat at the bar where the owner, Arata, makes everything fresh to order. For starters, Lake went for the Copacabana rolls—scallops, mango, and scallions. The man do love his wasabi straight. Not hungry, I ordered a sashimi salad with the citrus wasabi dressing.

Then came sashimi plates of red snapper and shrimp with a side of wasabi-mayo sauce. After that, came the *oh-toro-nigiri* with lime juice sprinkled on top. I nibbled on the buttery tuna, but couldn't conjure an appetite. "You're going to be hungry later," Lake said, chewing tuna.

"Don't think so."

"You didn't eat your donut, and I bet you didn't have lunch."

"I had a gin and tonic at Linda's."

"You're going to waste away, and don't forget we're doing the 10K before you leave in the morning."

"I'll carb up. You always have leftover spaghetti in your fridge, and a half a cake."

"Pie tonight."

Arata listened while he watched inscrutably and prepared. He sat a plate of *nigiri* spread and raw veggies in front of me. A favorite. "My pleasure," he said.

Half an hour later, and bloated, we left.

Back in the cold loft, Lake dug out more quilts and I went to soak in a hot bath. While I toweled dry by the stove, Lake's landline rang. "Butch, what's up?"

He listened. I listened. Butch was phone watch tonight. He wouldn't call unless . . .

"Okay then. I'll be there." He hung up.

"They can't solve it without you? Nutter brandishing a toy gun at Waffle House? The underwear bandit pilfering Superman drawers at Macy's again?" I asked.

"Nothing so hazardous. They picked up your trash man. I'm going to the interview."

I don't know if I was disappointed or not. Tired, guilt-ridden, spooked, love-making didn't have its usual allure, but I like to snuggle. I asked, "You won't be in on the interview, will you?"

"No, I won't be where that lowlife can see me." He looked at me. "Would you rather I stayed here?"

"Oh no," I said quickly, and realized I was relieved to see him back in his jeans.

Some nights are not made for love.

Chapter Five

Devus's main goon had bonded out at three in the morning, and Lake crept in half an hour later, taking care in case I was sleeping. I wasn't, and he summarized the lowlife's words. "He didn't do nothin' for nobody."

My sleep was restless and I heard downpours in the night. A warm front had moved into Georgia bringing with it serious rainfall. The next morning, after our bodies relaxed and breathing became normal, Lake and I rose and ran our usual 10K route to Piedmont Park; after which we ate at our favorite breakfast place, Fanny's on Sixth.

When I checked my email, Linda had sent more information on Baxter's premises. He lived in an historic home on Prince Avenue. Some of those historic register homes could be pretty run down, but being related to Linda and the owner of three popular restaurants told me Baxter Carlisle's historic home wasn't one. Linda et al. would have kicked him out of the family for that alone. Linda wrote that he owned several condominium complexes. She also said he was expecting me.

I was correct, his historic home was quite handsome, all two stories of the Federalist with six columns across the front. The door opened before I rang.

Baxter Carlisle looked like a blond-haired movie star who I won't name, lest the comparison conjures up and attributes to that star Baxter's sexual anomalies. The Atlanta morning newspaper reported on Damian Hansel's missing status along with a photograph of the young man. It didn't run a photograph of Baxter, nor was he mentioned.

Baxter's smile was knockout. The dimples, the dentally enhanced white teeth and not overly full lips. Wisps of blond hair strayed onto his forehead, the way Lake's dark hair often did. Hands outstretched, he said, "Miss Moriah Dru, welcome, welcome." I thought he was going to hug me, but he swept one hand aside like the courtly gentleman he appeared—longish frock coat and silk morning ascot folded crossed-band and held with a stick pin.

I almost asked if he planned to attend a wedding, but refrained. "Good morning, Mr. Carlisle."

"Baxter, please. I'm not really this formal. I'm off to a brunch at the Athens Polo Ground." That explained the ascot.

He took my navy peacoat, the warmest coat I own, and hung it on a quilted hanger in the foyer closet. I stepped over polished wood floors into a small sitting room with tall ceilings, set off by fifteen-inch crown molding. White wainscoting met pale yellow, silk striped wallpaper. It was a lovely room and not at all masculine.

On a marble coffee table, a tea and coffee service waited for a deft hand. The china cups had the kind of thin looped handles I can barely manage. "Coffee or tea?" Baxter asked.

I ached for a mug. "Coffee," I said. "No cream, no sugar."

He sat and pulled at the creases in his pants so that they hung just so. Then he laughed. "These little niceties we do as preludes to grand overtures are humorous, don't you think?"

I frowned, thinking silence was best, then grinned and nodded at the charming man.

He said, "I prefer Rachmaninoff's Prelude in C-Sharp Minor." He raised his hands like a pianist. His left hand rode down the imaginary keys. "Boom, boom, boom." His low voice hit the base note forcefully yet harmoniously. He looked up and grinned. "Then we're off into the heart of the matter."

Indeed, and it was me to go first. "I assume Damian Hansel hasn't turned up."

"You assume correctly, Miss Dru. And, before you ask, I will be interviewed by the police this afternoon. I believe the Georgia Bureau of Investigation is involved."

"Inevitable," I said.

"Linda told me you hunt for children and that you are very successful at it." He sat back in a chair that must have cost thousands. His body language said smug, but his mouth said amused.

"If that's all she said, I have some 'splainin' to do."

He projected an aura of genuine tenderness. "You do not. I made up my mind the minute you walked in the door that I can trust you."

"Yet, you're wondering why I'm here to find Damian Hansel, age nineteen, a young man considered to have left childhood at least a year ago?"

His smile bloomed. "That had occurred."

"I find young people who have disappeared through no device of their own."

He appeared puzzled. "You don't know that about Damian Hansel, do you?"

"From what I hear, and that's from an Atlanta police detective and Linda Lake . . ."

He held up a finger. "That police detective wouldn't happen to be Rick Lake, would it?"

"One and the same."

He beamed; then looked serious. "I don't often bond with men. I attribute it to a daddy thing. I didn't live with mine, and my stepfather was a nice man, but not my daddy. He made sure I knew that."

"So you bonded with Lake."

"As have you. I saw it in the mention of his name. Lucky Rick. His common sense and dedication to what he believes in speaks for him as words cannot."

"Let's talk about your relationship with Cho Martine."

By the small twitches in his facial muscles, this was the part he was hoping to avoid. "She's not missing," he said.

"How did you come to know her?"

"I came to know Damian."

"We can start there if you'd like."

"Damian Hansel started hanging out in Carlisle's. He came in with his father the first time, then started coming regularly by himself. I didn't know quite what to make of the young man. He's quite an aggressive boy. Some would say upbeat, I say aggressive."

I waited an upbeat or two myself. "And?"

"He wanted to redo the interior."

Baxter explained that Damian was in the fine arts program at the university, and that he'd brought back grand ideas from artsy European trips and was eager to remodel Carlisle's.

Baxter said, "To my taste, he's a ham-handed young man. I'm happy with my impressionists, thank you. He wanted me to take on the classicism look, Diana the Huntress, and all that. Said it implied grander fare for the restaurant, rather than light stuff. Bunk, of course. Who eats deer any longer?"

"Is he a good artist?"

"For one thing he's an artist in search of a specialty, and what he has created so far is bad."

Baxter tried explaining what he meant, then gave up and said I could see for myself at the art school's gallery.

"Baxter, Cho Martine?"

He lifted his chin. "I must take myself off to brunch, Miss Dru."

41

"I've come to help you at the request of Linda Lake." I paused and leaned forward as if to stand. "If you don't want my help, fine."

He hesitated, then spread his hands palms down. "I don't know that I'll need it, but anyone can use a sympathetic ear."

"My ears are open to all facts, observations, and emotions, sympathetic or not. I do not judge." I wish that were true.

He got up and so did I. "I'm not dismissing you, Miss Dru, but I must be on time. I'm a known punctuality freak."

I held out my hand. "Nice to have met you, Mr. Carlisle. I wish you luck."

He snapped his fingers like he'd had a brainstorm. "Why didn't I think of this immediately?" I leaned my head to one side. "Come with me to the brunch. I chose not to invite a friend, but I can certainly change my mind. I contribute enough to the organization."

I looked down at my sensible shoes and wool slacks. My turtleneck came from Saks, but it was old. I said, "Peacoats aren't polo attire."

He waggled a finger. "Never a worry with me. I have the proper attire for you." I was about to dissent when he said, "I'd say size six." He looked at my booted feet. "Shoes, eight?"

"Correct, but . . ."

"No demurring."

I followed him to the straight staircase that divided the entrance hall and led to the second floor. "Upstairs, on the right, two doors down, is a guest room with a guest closet. You will find a costume that will be perfect."

Costume. "I don't know about this," I said, one foot already headed for the steps.

His white smile dazzled. "Call it a bribe. If you say you'll go, I'll answer your questions about Cho Martine."

"Bribe taken."

The room contained four closets with male and female costumes for any occasion.

The wind had picked up and a light mist sprayed Baxter's Lexus. As Baxter chatted I felt as if I'd known and loved him all my life. He explained that today's affair was the kickoff to the upcoming polo season and for a charity sponsored by the Athens Polo Ground. Angel Dreams Care Center, he told me, was a nonprofit charity established for children with physical or emotional disabilities. It had been shown, he said, that their interaction with horses had a beneficial effect.

My own interaction with those magnificent creatures has never been positive. I believe they think I'm too tall and awkward. They see me check out their skinny legs and take offense. How can they run on them?

"Do you ride?" I asked. "Play polo?"

"Heavens no. The beasts had no use for me when I was growing up. Linda rode like the wind, though. She was truly fearless."

Our Linda Lake, fearless in fashion and fearless on a horse?

He said, "I am a charity case. I belong to every charity and civic organization from Atlanta to Augusta."

"Good for business."

"Can't say it's not."

I asked if we could cruise by Damian Hansel's place, and he readily agreed since it was on the way. There was nothing to see but a two-story brick apartment building with green-painted doors looking as forlorn as Cinderella before the ball. Food wrappers drowned in gutters while plastic cups frolicked in the wind. Damian's apartment looked familiar. When Portia attended the university during her first couple of years, she'd lived a block away on South Milledge Avenue, and lot of partying went on between those buildings. I wondered if I could get into Damian's place for a gander into his life. Probably not, but then I had an idea. "Baxter, how well do you know the cops in this town?"

He grunted, an inelegant sound coming from him. "Not well enough for them to believe I'm incapable of doing something to Damian."

"All the years you've lived here . . ."

"Different time and state of affairs. The ol' boy guard was thrown out and the new regime was sworn in. Our present gendarmerie consists of ex-GBI agents and Atlanta tough guys. Don't you know—they're going to shape up the city? We've had our share of murder and mayhem in the last four years."

"Maybe there's a connection."

"To the missing Damian?"

"The cops don't tell everything they know."

"They're not telling me anything, and I've told them everything I've told you."

"I doubt you've told me everything."

"You've asked me different things, but at least not over and over."

I thought about the things I didn't ask him—about his Lolita complex. Tough subject to bring up to so charming and sensitive a man.

We arrived at the hotel in the Historic District. I got out and stood tall in black suede three-inch heels. I smoothed the velvet pencil skirt that fit me like my skin. It was a luscious shade of violet and matched the barely pink silk blouse. The cutaway jacket caressed my arms and back, and I tried to think how I could steal it when Baxter put his hand at my elbow. "You must have that ensemble."

I hadn't realized I was preening. "Thank you, but I can't think when I'll attend another polo luncheon."

He laughed. "You are gorgeous, you know. That black hair, so wild. You must be the envy of women who spend countless hours trying to look like they just got out of bed."

"Not so. When I pass a hair salon, the personnel rush out to drag me inside and start in on my wild black hair."

We sat at a $32,000 table. Eight people filled the seats, so, if everyone paid, these brunchers ponied up $4,000 for a buffet featuring caviar, smoked salmon, sushi, champagne flowing from a fountain, eggs Benedict made to order, crepes, and desserts rich in fat and sugar. Lake would be in heaven. Bax introduced me to my tablemates, and that's when I started thinking of him as Bax. Everyone called him Bax.

One man, I noticed, avoided looking at Bax for the entire meal, and I wondered if word had gotten around town that Bax had a connection to a student's disappearance. The man, name of Edwin Hardy, played polo. Probably around thirty, he had the look of a young Prince Charles—the eyes and nose combination with dark hair hiding wide ears.

I met father and grandson attorneys, Anthony Desmond Du-Plessy, Sr. and Anthony Desmond DuPlessy, the Third. Senior was mid-seventies. He looked like his hair started to recede in his twenties and left permanently in the next decade. Anthony Three Sticks was a handsome man with a full head of blond hair and assessing gray eyes that fastened on me. I knew I looked good, really good. Today made up for the times I don't, really don't. As Baxter noted, I have thick, black hair that curls naturally. I stay slender because I run every day that I can and work out at the Y. My skin is my best feature. My nose is rather long and narrow, but my eyes are large and blue, thanks to my Irish ancestry. A man who once hired me asserted that I was a descendant of the Druidha—my last name being Dru—the ancient Irish religion that put enemies in baskets, hung them in trees, and burned them alive. If Devus McFersen continues to harass me, I'm taking up basket weaving.

The younger Anthony, who had told me to call him Tony, interrupted my thoughts. "I know you by reputation," he said. "You're a godsend to foster children in this state."

Granddad Anthony, who I continued to call Mr. DuPlessy, said, "How would you like to defend the scum she goes after for abusing children?"

"I don't take losing cases," Tony said, adjusting the knot in his perfectly tied tie. "That is why I don't do criminal law."

Baxter inclined his head toward the older lawyer. "Anthony has been my attorney for decades. Now that he's retiring, Tony will handle my affairs. I'll be the elder and expected to act like it." He smiled, giving his dimples permission to delight.

I looked at Anthony Senior. "Retiring to a life of golf?"

"A little golf, but mostly boating."

Tony said, "Granddad has a sailing yacht he keeps in Savannah. He and Grandmom plan to see the world via the seven seas."

"Your grandmom is not so delighted as all that," Anthony Senior said. He turned to me, "Our Baxter here just returned from Europe, touring from Moscow to the Baltic States. The last time I was on the Baltic Sea there was a force nine storm."

"Nothing so dramatic for me," Baxter said. "Rather calm." He showed off his white teeth again. "Would you like to come this evening and view my slides?"

Granddad and grandson laughed at the same time the president, F. W. Lord Buttonworth, rose to open the meeting. It became obvious, the difference between those who came as boosters and those who played in the matches. Edwin Hardy gave Bax a couple of black looks when Bax made comments during Buttonworth's rundown of meeting dates and regulations. When Bax put his hand on my shoulder or took my hand, which he often did, Hardy stared at me. I interpreted Hardy's sly stare to mean I was way too old for Baxter.

We, like the DuPlessys, ducked out early. While we waited for the valet to bring the cars from the underground garage, I asked Bax if he'd paid for me, and he said that he'd given a healthy donation in my name. When I began to object, he said, "It's a write-off. Ask Anthony."

Anthony confirmed that it was a legitimate deduction. After the DuPlessys' cars arrived and they departed, I asked Bax, "Where's Anthony Junior in the DuPlessy family tree?"

"Sad to say his branch was cut short by a storm. I'm speaking literally here. He was parked, waiting for Tony, when a tree limb crashed through the windshield. He lived for a few days then passed. The old man's been my lawyer from the day I arrived here. Junior was a fine man, determined to get elected to Congress, but . . ."

"No more stalling," I said, smiling at him so he wouldn't think me obnoxious. "Cho Martine."

Bax's car arrived. Saved by the brake and shush of tires. The minutiae of getting on the road gave him time to gather his thoughts—slipping into seats, buckling up, starting the engine, reversing, looking both ways, finally pulling into the street.

"Bax?"

"I wonder . . ." he began and glanced at me. "Will you be shocked when I tell you . . . ?" He halted. Stalling.

I said, "That you're in love with her?"

For a classy man, his guffaw sounded like a dandelion smiting a rose. "No, my dear Dru, I loathe the woman."

I thought it odd to refer to a female student as a woman, especially in the South where middle-aged men and women were often called boys and girls.

He breathed in slowly, and then sighed out. "Fascinated by her, yes. So fascinated, I can't stand to be around her."

"That's why you stalked her."

"A very bald statement. And untrue." He sucked air into his

lungs and let it out slowly as he spoke. "I walk, you see. I am fifty-two years old." He looked straight ahead as he spoke. "I hope to reach a hundred. Therefore, I walk."

He vowed he didn't peek in her windows or follow her in his car. That, quite the reverse, she appeared to be following him. "If she persists in nonsense accusations, I'll file slander and throw in libel for good measure."

"Are you saying she stalked you?"

He put a closed fist over his mouth and coughed into it. "Now, understand I can be quite vain, but I'm not being vain now. She seems to be as fascinated with me as I her. I've wondered if she doesn't loathe me, too."

He explained that he'd met her when Damian brought her to Carlisle's to bolster his idea of remodeling the interior to reflect romantic classicism. Cho waxed enthusiastic, but Bax had, he avowed, politely told her that he intended to stick with the Impressionists.

We'd reached Baxter's garage. The door opened without prompting. We didn't speak and I went to the stairs. Interrupting me in my climb, he said to keep the suit. I shook my head no.

He grinned. "I shall have to enshrine it then."

I turned and looked down the steps at him. "The photographer at the brunch took our photograph. That should suffice."

He waved. "Be aware, I shall box the suit and send it to you."

I realized as I changed clothes, I'd never been more drawn to a man, his world, and his way of speaking as I had been to Baxter Carlisle. I also realized I wanted to save him. There was vulnerability about him, a trait he'd hidden deep within his core, yet so carefully that the care he'd taken showed.

He stood at the bottom of the staircase as I descended. "Cho Martine," he said, taking my hand and leading me toward his beautiful parlor. "As promised."

I sat on the edge of my chair, holding a glass of fine Chardonnay. He had me enthralled, yet I expected to be disappointed. He wasn't going to tell me everything, just what he considered essential.

He said, "Cho Martine's mother is Japanese and her father is French. The family makes its home in Paris and Savannah. Why Savannah, you might ask?"

I might, I thought, but didn't.

"Viktor Martine is a naval architect. Renowned throughout the world. He travels—as a consultant."

"What is Cho majoring in?"

"Mathematics. She also plays violin."

"Any good."

"Adequate."

"How did you come to hear her play?"

"How?" he laughed and pulled at his right ear. "Don't look so serious. I couldn't resist."

"I got the how. Where?"

"At Damian's apartment."

"Why were you there?"

"He pestered me until I went to see his art. Montages of human bodies are not appealing. Neither is Craft Art or Idea Art. He showed me a mess of colored ribbon and threads on canvas he called 'My Soul.' "

"Where does Martine live?"

"A place on Willow."

"You take your walks on Willow?"

He raised his eyebrows. "And have for thirty years." He rose to refill his wine glass, but I put my hand over mine. He said that he owned a lot of property in Athens and Clarke County—from rentals to farm land. He employed property managers, but occasionally checked things out himself. "Spot checks are part of the lease agreement. You never know how a group of male students, or females for that matter, are taking care of your property."

"Do you own Martine's apartment?"

"The entire building, yes."

"Does she have roommates?"

"She's not that kind of . . ." He shrugged. "Inevitably you will meet her."

"Inevitably. Do you know her schedule?"

"Schedule?" His question was meant to buy thinking time.

"Her class schedule, do you know it?"

He looked at his watch. More thinking time. "I believe she's in a math class now. She's in the honors program."

I looked at him and instinctively believed he knew what I was thinking. "You know entirely too much about Cho Martine."

"For a man of my age, you mean?" He put his wine on the coaster. "Let's go."

"I don't have to change clothes, do I?"

CHAPTER SIX

I knew the streets of Athens almost as well as I knew Atlanta's. Besides visits to Portia, I'd had a brief affair with a UGA football player before he turned into a brute. From Oconee Street, Bax turned at Wilkerson. Crossing East Broad, we were on Willow, soon passing the Sandy Creek Nature Center. Bax chose silence as he steered and braked, so I reflected on losing my virginity to a brute football player, and how they call Athens the Classic City, although it bears no resemblance to the Athens of Greece and mythology.

He parked the car and we walked in step, my being as tall as he, for almost a quarter of a mile, heads bare in the chilly haze. Baxter halted before we came to the newish, trendy condominiums. "Am I looking at Cho Martine's unit?" I asked.

"First floor, end, yes." He indicated the unit by raising his chin toward it. "You can see I couldn't hide in shrubbery that's not there." The bushes weren't three feet tall and were sculpted into round balls. "She said she saw me twice and took a photograph once. I saw the photograph. It could have been anyone, male or female, looking into a window at night. She said I followed as she drove through Athens trying to get me off her tail. It's not true. She said I left my calling card under her windshield wiper when she went into the grocery store to call police. That's not true, either."

"Doesn't she have a cell phone?"

"I've never seen her use one."

51

"Not much in the way of hard evidence," I said. "How did she get the calling card?"

"I'd given her one on the day she came into Carlisle's with Damian."

I looked at Baxter when suddenly his quiet gasp told me something abrupt had happened. I turned to look at the same time he said, "Here she comes. Beware the fire-breathing dragon."

A tall black-haired girl had come out of the condo, stopped, and stared our way as if her radar eyes had scoped us out from inside her apartment. She flounced down the steps. When she hit the walkway, she ran. Despite a long coat, she loped with the grace of a deer scared by a twig breaking. She slowed as she neared us. Her olive face looked like massed black clouds ready to unleash their energy. A sweet Lolita, at this moment, she was not.

I heard Baxter say softly, "Cho."

She glared at him, and her almond eyes appeared crossed. If she saw me, she didn't show it. "You are despicable," she said, her long hair flared by the whimsical wind. "You are making my life unbearable. You will be punished for this intrusion into my private space." She'd clenched her fists. "Why do you stalk me, old man?" Her breath was vapor pouring from her mouth and nose.

Baxter stood stone still, his lips pressed tight.

"Miss," I said.

She didn't so much as glance at me. She said, "I look out on the street and there you are, all the time. It is tiresome to call police so often. This time I file for a restraining order."

"Miss Martine," I said.

She shook her fist at him. "The police, did you hear. I have to go every day."

"That is—" Baxter started to say.

I interrupted—with force. "Miss Martine."

She didn't appear to be finished beating up on Baxter, who was unaccountably mute, when, suddenly, she looked at me. "Who are you? And how do you know my name?" I identified myself. She didn't care who I was. She curled her lip at Baxter. "You have gone too far." I told her I wanted to talk, and she said, "I do not need to talk to you, or him." She backhanded hair that had blown into her face. "This man hounds me day and night."

I heard the squeal of brakes and tires halting. A marked police car pulled into the curb.

That's how I came to be in the Athens-Clarke County Police Station, sitting across the desk from the sex crime unit's Sergeant Perry Thomas—middle-aged, weathered, and looking more like a tired farmer than a cop. Certainly not Baxter's description of an ex-GBI agent or Atlanta-toughened cop.

Thomas said, "Now let me get this straight. You are a child finder, located in Atlanta. You are here at the request of Baxter Carlisle."

"To consult on the stalking and peeping charges."

"I don't suppose you'll tell me what he told you?" He grinned, and I noticed the gap in his two front teeth.

"He didn't do it."

Thomas smiled without cracking his lips. "They all say that."

"I used to be police."

"You don't say? In Atlanta?" I nodded, and he asked, "Why'd they let you go?"

I told him I resigned to start Child Trace, my agency.

"You're tracing kiddies here in Athens, Georgia?"

I was wrong. He's an ex-GBI guy. We weren't going to get along.

"What can you tell me about Damian Hansel's disappearance?"

He sat back like I'd asked him to climb the Eiffel Tower in his bare feet. "Well, ain't that something."

I raised my eyebrows but didn't reply.

"I don't know if you know this, Miss Moriah Dru, but Damian Hansel is not a child."

"Teenagers get lost, too."

From behind, I heard one word. "Dru!"

I turned to see a familiar face standing just outside the open door. It had been a while and I'm bad with names, but his popped into my head just in time. "Felix."

I stood, and he came in and hugged me. "I saw your name on the sheet," he said. "I couldn't believe it might be you." He looked at his superior, stood at attention, and said, "Miss Dru and I were at the Academy together."

"Happy to hear it," Thomas said, looking neither happy nor unhappy. He made a shooing motion with his hand. "Officer Kona, you got business somewhere, I suspect, so you and Miss Dru can catch up on your gossip later. On your own time."

Chastised, Felix Kona, one of the nicest men ever to wear a uniform, said, "Yes, sir, I do." He bowed at me and turned to leave.

"Kona," Thomas called. Felix faced him. "No speaking out of school on our cases, you hear?"

"Don't have to tell me that, Sergeant."

Thomas wasn't talking out of school on their cases either. I got up, thanked him for his information, and left him to his sneer.

When I got to the duty desk, I didn't see Baxter or Cho. Baxter and I had ridden in the squad car. Cho drove her own car—a spiffy Mercedes. I asked the fresh-faced desk officer, "Has Mr. Carlisle left?"

"No, ma'am," he said. "He might be a while."

"I'll need to call a cab. I got my cell. If he comes out, and

I'm gone, will you let him know I've gone for my car, and that I will call him later?"

"I will do that, Miss Dru."

I smiled. "You know my name."

"I know your work. You saved those two little girls."

He'd made my day. "I might need you for a reference."

He lowered his voice. "You got friends here."

"Felix Kona and I were at the Academy."

"Felix said." He motioned his head toward the door leading outside. I knew then that Felix awaited me.

Coincidences happen, but Felix being an Athens cop wasn't a noteworthy one. It could have been any police officer who got fed up with Atlanta and moved to a smaller, friendlier force. As to Perry Thomas, he might have been a good cop, even a friendly one, but he apparently didn't like women ex-cops or private investigators. I'd dealt with bias before. My way was to work hard, make men look good, and let them take the credit. Unless they were hardcore buttholes, my way usually won them over.

Felix was in an unmarked. I glanced toward the building. Perry Thomas's office was on the other side. Now, if I were Thomas, I'd sneak around to see if his Atlanta recruit met up with his former colleague out in the parking lot. Maybe he had, but I didn't get the feeling I was being watched.

Felix reached over and opened the door. I got in. "Living dangerously," I said, motioning my head toward the cop shop.

"The sergeant's all right," Felix said. "He doesn't like this case."

"Don't blame him."

Felix pulled the car onto Lexington Road. "How's Lake?"

"Lake's good."

"You two pulled off some hummer saving those kids."

"I guess Perry Thomas didn't get the word."

"He did. He's envious, but he's all right. Work with him here, you'll win him over."

"So how's it going with you?"

"Good. My wife and I like it here. Best place to raise our kids."

"Kids now. You'd just gotten married when I left."

"Two, going on three, come spring."

"Your wife's a teacher, isn't she?"

"Subs now, with the kids."

"What can you tell me about the Damian Hansel case?"

"You heard the sergeant."

"Then don't say anything."

"Heck, there's nothing to tell. He's still missing. No signs of foul play. Thomas is pissed at that girl. She files reports, makes accusations, a regular pain in the ass."

"You meet her?" I asked.

"First time she came in. Loose cannon."

"An angry loose cannon. What about Baxter Carlisle?"

"Everybody knows Bax."

"How well?"

He took a deep breath as he turned onto Broad Street. "There's rumors."

"What rumors?"

"Girls, but not in this town. Citizen hotline says he goes away."

"It's a smart man that doesn't poop in his own nest. Where's he go?"

"They say Thailand."

"Ah, the virgin capital of the world."

"And Costa Rica."

"Where they sell six-year-olds to old goats."

We arrived at my car parked in front of Baxter's place on Prince Avenue. I noticed the Mercedes as I got out. I said to

Felix, "Thanks for the lift, I won't tell a soul if you don't want me to."

"Never lie, if they ask point blank. I won't."

"Good advice," I said.

"Say hey to Lake for me."

I had a feeling Lake might be saying hey to Felix, face-to-face.

I watched him drive away and walked over to the Mercedes. She sat behind the wheel staring at me. I started to come to the driver's side when the passenger door sprang open. "In," she called.

I leaned in. "Maybe we should meet at a café."

"Why?" she asked, suddenly smiling as if sugar were melting in her mouth. She looked beatific for a moment, then pressed her lips together. "You don't trust me?"

"I don't have a recorder."

She reached into her console and brought out a tiny model. "I do."

"That doesn't do me any good."

"Are you afraid of me?"

"It's the conflict thing."

"You and Baxter against me."

"Not against."

She rolled her eyes in a typical teenage gesture. "All right. Where do you want to meet?"

"In the café where you last saw Damian Hansel."

Somber-faced now, she lowered her eyelids. "Since he's missing . . ." Her voice was low and quiet. "I don't go there."

"Miss Martine, I'm going there. I'd like to talk to you about Damian, but if you don't want to go there, some other time then." I stepped back.

She pulled the passenger door inward and said, "Call me Cho and follow me."

I have a healthy respect for strong people. At eighteen she'd already tapped into a well of strength. I cocked my head. "Sure."

The café was located on College Avenue. It was small, ten tables, and only one was unoccupied.

"Where did you and Damian sit?" I asked, unbuttoning my coat.

She pointed to a square table at the end of the coffee bar. A young man sat there engrossed in his computer work. Cho stood quite still, staring at him with such intensity I bristled. He looked up. His mouth parted and he adjusted his glasses. Several seconds went by. I've never seen people not blink for as long as Cho didn't. The knot in the young man's throat bobbed, whereupon he surrendered. Gathering his books and computer, he moved to the empty table.

That was quite a performance, I almost said.

Cho took off her coat and tossed it on the bench. Black jeans and a black mock turtleneck added to her height and slimness. Nothing said Japanese petite about her. She slid onto the bench, and I pulled out a chair and sat. "This is the way we were," she said. I asked questions and she readily answered. Damian wasn't studying for a big exam, more like a quiz, but Damian studied hard because he was a perfectionist and didn't want to get anything wrong. Damian was his usual self that night—fun, happy, witty, and obsessive over his paleontology quiz. Cho paused, made a moue of a smile, and then continued, "He was focused on the inner body as art, for an art class." She studied my hands as I wrote in my particular shorthand. When I glanced up, she looked like one of Raphael's Madonna's, and I considered why. Her nose was long for her face, her eyes only slightly slanted owing to a round-eyed parent. Her lips were downturned, sad. I couldn't make up my mind whether she was beautiful or not. She wasn't in any sense of today's perfect face.

There was a mature quality about her. I chalked it up to living in sophisticated places. I asked, "You are pursuing a mathematics degree, is that correct?"

"Is that what *he* told you?"

"Mr. Carlisle, yes."

She shuddered dramatically. "I'm pursuing math right now, but I don't know where it will lead me. There are all kinds of disciplines in math studies. As an artist myself, I see the finite in things, too."

As I do when I question people, I go over the facts and conversations a second time. Police training. When asked, Cho insisted that Damian was happy at school with his professors, his advisors, his friends, and that he wasn't worried about anything that evening but passing his exam the next day. He hadn't said anything about going off by himself. In fact he was anxious to meet his best friend on Saturday, and pursue . . .

"Who is his best friend?"

She smiled her Madonna smile. "Arne Trammel, an art major, too."

She said that Damian and Arne were supposed to meet up for an art project on Saturday. Damian was quite excited about it, but secretive about specifics. Also, Damian and Arne were planning a trip to Spain in the summer. Damian wanted her, Cho, to travel with them. She hunched her shoulders and said she wasn't sure that she could.

I asked "Have you talked to Arne Trammel about Damian's disappearance?"

"When Damian didn't show at his place Saturday, Arne called me, clearly upset. He has no clue where Damian could be, except that . . ." She paused and narrowed her eyelids.

"What?"

"He believes Baxter Carlisle . . ." Saying the name hardened her jaw. "That man did something to him."

"What makes him believe that?"

"Damian loathed Baxter Carlisle."

When I asked, she denied it was because Baxter wouldn't consider changing the décor at Carlisle's Restaurant. "It was Baxter's attitude that made Damian angry. But even that wasn't the main reason." She twisted her fingers together like an anxious child.

"The main reason was you, wasn't it?"

She looked like she wanted to whimper. "I did nothing to encourage him," she said in a whisper. She could assume so many guises from instant to instant that her face was like liquid plastic and her emotions just as fluid. I found it hard to fathom her.

"When did Baxter start paying special attention to you?"

"He always did." She waved like swatting at a fly backhand.

For a man who loves nymphets, it was hard to see Baxter developing a passion for Cho. She looked too wise for a man attracted to carnal innocence. Certainly the shrewish side she showed when maddened would be enough to have him running for cover.

Cho's eyes often strayed from me when we talked. This time her expression froze. "He's here." The words burped from the back of her throat.

I turned. Baxter weaved through tables toward us.

Cho looked like a kamikaze zeroing on a target. "He will not let me alone."

Bax stood above Cho, his expression beseeching. "What do I have to do to keep you from filing these ludicrous complaints?"

"You followed me here."

"I saw Miss Dru's car."

"You're using her as an excuse to stalk me again." Her words were like breaking crystal.

I noticed heads had risen from computers and books.

60

"Shhhh," I cautioned. "We're in a public place."

Baxter whispered, "I'm not stalking you. I hope never to see you again."

Her narrow eyes focused on his face. She reminded me of a Japanese samurai as depicted in their war art. All of a sudden, she rose and swept past him.

He shrugged at me. "Guess she's off to the police station to fill out another form."

"Baxter," I said, standing, "why did you come in here?"

"I live in this town. She is not going to harass me out of it." We walked out the door. "Let's get out of here. I'm thirsty; it's four-thirty. No one in this town complains about rushing the cocktail hour."

On the way, I called Lake. His cell went to answering, and I left a message that I was having a drink with Baxter at Carlisle's.

CHAPTER SEVEN

The tables were clothed in linens the shade of lightest pinks and violets. Years ago, they'd been stark white. Impressionist paintings still hung on the walls—the play of natural light off pastel ladies with parasols and large hats, graceful birds, rivers with curvy waves, airy butterflies in fields of green.

I followed him across the light hardwood floor, through the empty restaurant where square tables lined walls and round tables filled in the center. The bar was built of sumptuous rosewood. I settled onto a velvet barstool and let my shoulders fall into a relaxed pose. I wanted to give him a sense that I was easy, although I wasn't.

"What's your pleasure?" he asked.

"Gin and tonic."

He told the bartender, "Make it two, light on the tonic, two twists of lime." He considered me. "You look tired."

"Up early to meet a day packed with surprises."

He tapped an index finger on the bar. "The authorities think I did something to Damian."

"What have they told you?"

He shook his head as the drinks were set on coasters. Bax immediately lifted his and sucked in the liquor like he hadn't had water in a week. He said that the Georgia Bureau of Investigation would head the case. He chugged the rest of the drink, his first sign of nervousness. He signaled for another. I hadn't taken my first sip yet.

I nearly smiled at his bashful grimace. "Will you be my very own exclusive, private investigator?"

I thought about the Devus McFersen case. "Exclusivity I cannot promise. But I will handle your case with a little help from my colleagues."

"Good enough. I'd like to keep this out of the press."

"Can't promise that. The GBI might have other ideas." He finished off his second drink. "I have a few more questions, Bax."

He raised his eyebrows. "Is this a test?"

I looked at the bartender who tried hard not to listen. "I'd like a tour of your restaurant."

"Got it," he said, rising.

"I'm not a pedophile," he said, motioning toward the comely young ladies that were framed on the walls.

"Linda told me a little," I said, pausing a beat before saying, "The nine-year-old next door. You were a teen, she was a child."

I followed him through French doors leading into a smaller dining room. He closed the doors and we sat at a square table for four. He began, "I'm assuming that Linda does not know the entire story, one which you can learn. She was there when I was soundly thrashed and banished to Alabama with my hateful father for an entire summer." His gaze skimmed my face. "However, I will admit that I fell in love with my nine-year-old next-door neighbor, and she fell in love with me."

"She was nine. You knew better."

"It was whispering in each other's ears, laughing and joking. I was her babysitter."

My stomach began to grind. Surely he wasn't going to absolve himself with some mealy-mouthed justification.

"As I said, you will learn the truth if you care to." A tuxedoed man—early thirties—brought two glasses of water then left.

Baxter picked up where he'd left off. "I told my beautiful neighbor that I was going to marry her when she turned sixteen. I'd be twenty. She said she was going to marry me when I turned thirty, after she got out of college and became a doctor. She was quite a brilliant child, and is today a brilliant doctor in Savannah. We keep in touch."

"She ever marry?"

"No." He flicked his eyes at me. "I ask her every year on her birthday. She says no every year on her birthday." He took a deep breath like he was going to have to say it again.

"Then why did you get strapped?"

"Because her mother started asking her questions, and touching came up. My lord, touching her arms, rubbing her back and cheeks, and her hair, that wonderful golden hair she had. There was no unnatural touching."

So many times I'd heard this. Sometimes it was true.

"What is her name?"

"I thought you'd never ask. Kirin Littlefield, a neurosurgeon."

My turn to take a deep breath. This was not pleasant. "What about the fourteen-year-old?"

"I didn't know her age. We both did it for the money. I gave, she received."

"She was a prostitute?"

"That surprises you? How about that her uncle was her pimp. They were in the bar and she kept hitting on me. No kidding. I asked how old she was and they both said she was eighteen. I learned different in a hurry. After the deed, she said she was fourteen, and that I was going to be in trouble with the law. I gave him eighteen-thousand-dollars, one for each year they lied."

Males and their loins. "What about the girl you got pregnant?"

Baxter twitched his nose. "Linda was her usual chattering self, I see."

"She was. I asked you . . ."

"The girl was fifteen going on twenty. I met her in a bar, too. I was drinking a lot in those days."

"That's no defense. Why were you drinking?"

"Everybody did. Get drunk, pass out, wake, have a hair of the dog and start over."

"Where is your son?"

"You know that, too?"

"As you said, Linda was her usual chattering self."

"I would have married his mother." He studied my surprised look. "When I informed Linda of my intentions, she almost vomited. My mother and stepfather about had twin heart attacks. She was eighteen and the boy was two. Darla was pretty in a cheap way. I had visions of reforming her. The Pygmalion syndrome."

"She give the boy your name?"

"No, her name. Gilmeath."

"You were already a black sheep so why didn't you go ahead and marry her?"

He spread his hands. "She married someone else. End of love affair."

"Before she married, did you continue to have a sexual relationship with her?"

He nodded. "Why do you look so shocked? She was pregnant with my child. She wasn't a virgin."

"Jesus."

His lip twisted. "Did you go to Catholic school or something?"

"As a matter of fact . . ."

He laid his palm on his chest. "Episcopalian here. Unlike Catholics, no stipulation of fornication for procreation only. Unlike Baptists, no admonishments against drinking and dancing." Was he trying to make me not like him? "I was an early bloomer. I had my first taste of rubbing and touching sex when I was ten years old."

"By whom?"

"My new nanny. She was from Russia and did delicious things. I thought it was what nannies did. Then Mama fired her."

I shook my head. "Baxter, Baxter."

"I'm sorry if you hate me now. Do you still want to work for me?"

"I want to find Damian Hansel, but you should know I'm expensive."

Sometimes I work for free, or in the case of Devus McFersen on a state stipend, which is saying the same thing. Did I intend to ask for a ridiculous sum because I didn't want this case after all?

Bax spread his hands. "I, fortunately, have deep pockets."

The tuxedoed man knocked twice then slipped into the room. For the first time, I heard the murmurs of patrons. He addressed Bax. "A gentleman here, sir. To see you and Miss Dru."

"Thank you, Oliver."

Lake entered. Baxter and I stood. Seeing him was like coming up for air after a deep dive into cruddy waters.

Baxter frowned. "Rick."

"Hi, Bax. Dru."

"Good to see you," Baxter said, extending his hand.

I said, "Baxter and I are formalizing our working agreement."

Ending the handshake, Lake spoke gravely. "Sergeant Perry Thomas said he thought you two had some kind of agreement. He said he didn't know where I could find you, but I imagine he's not far behind me."

Baxter looked ready to break into a million pieces.

Lake said, "A cell phone belonging to Damian Hansel was found on the banks of a creek in Atlanta."

"Atlanta?" Baxter looked stunned by this bewildering news.

I blurted, "Cell phone? That all?"

Lake's eyes bore into Baxter's. "The last call in the call list came from you."

"When? I never called him. Never ever."

"We'll get to that later. GBI and Atlanta PD are dragging the creek."

Baxter's face drained of color. He sagged onto the chair.

"Which creek?" I asked, knowing Lake had not named one of the major tributaries of the Chattahoochee River for a reason.

Lake sat across from Baxter. "Peachtree Creek, near Northside Drive."

I sat next to Bax. His lower jaw lost definition. Linda grew up off Northside Drive; so, presumably, did Baxter.

Lake said, "With recent rains, the creek is at flood stage. You know how fast it runs there."

Baxter surfaced from wherever his shock had driven him. "Why there?"

Lake reminded him that Perry Thomas would be walking through the door shortly and that he had a few questions. "When were you last in Atlanta?"

My intuition told me Bax wanted to lie, but thought better of it. "I went Friday."

"Isn't that the first day Miss Martine filed one of three stalking complaints against you?"

"It isn't true."

"Where were you at the time she alleges?"

"I had gotten things settled here and . . ."

"Quickly," Lake said. "No need to set the scene."

"I wanted to get away and went home to pack a bag. The police came. I went with them and they took my statement. I came back here, closed up at the usual time, and drove to Atlanta."

67

"Where in Atlanta?"

"I have a condominium on Peachtree Street, near Piedmont Hospital."

"Not far from Peachtree Creek."

"Ten minutes." His eyes looked ready to bleed. "I didn't do anything to Damian Hansel. This is crazy. Somebody is setting me up."

"Why would *somebody*?" Lake took out a notebook.

"Cho Martine."

"You think she had something to do with Hansel's disappearance?"

"The only thing I know for sure is that I didn't."

"Hansel have problems with anyone else here in Athens?"

"Not that I know of. I don't know the kid that well. I told Miss Dru all I know."

"Okay," Lake said, glancing at me. Back at Bax, he asked, "You go anywhere in Atlanta? Someone see you?"

"An after-hours bar."

"That's most bars in Atlanta."

Baxter shook his head. "I don't want to say."

Uh-oh. Here we go.

"Private club?" Lake asked.

"You might say."

"Where?"

"Cheshire Bridge Road."

Lake ticked off on his fingers, "Porn shacks, lingerie shops, titty bars, gay clubs, massage parlors. You care to say which one?"

"Massage."

"You call that a bar?"

"They serve wine."

"These places have names."

Baxter glanced at me. I nodded. He had to give in. "Relaxation."

"I know it," Lake said. "Age problems." Lake didn't blink, didn't screw up his face in disdain. "Who's the girl?"

"Her name is Tiffany."

"That's an unusual one," Lake said, sliding his mouth sideways. "I'll have to talk to her. She give you a blow job?"

"Uh, that's . . ." Baxter's face reddened and he looked at a picture on the wall. "Yes, but you'll find she's well into her twenties."

"We'll see what her birth certificate says. Then what?"

"I went to my condo. Slept until ten Saturday morning, then came back to Athens."

"All relaxed, huh?"

"I know what you think," Baxter began.

"No, you don't."

"I hate you're involved in this, Rick. We always had a nice relationship."

"Still do," Lake said. "Unless you did something to Hansel."

"I didn't." Baxter blinked a couple of times. "Listen," he said, "I've been thinking about the last time I had anything to do with Damian. Couple of weeks ago, he and his friend Arne came in and sat at the bar. We'd just opened. It's unusual for students to come into Carlisle's. It's pricey and caters to older folks. They drank beers and then started bickering."

"What about?"

"My bartender said it had to do with art. They fussed over perception, concepts, statements, that kind of thing."

"So?"

"It got loud, and I had to come to the bar and ask Damian to keep it down. We could hear them cursing in the entryway. When I walked up, I heard Arne say that he wasn't doing insanity. He drank off his beer and left. So did Damian."

"Where does Arne live?"

"Two doors down from Damian."

Lake gave Baxter the hard stare, the no nonsense, if-you-lie-to-me-you're-dead stare. "I'm going to say something harsh, Bax, so listen good. If you're lying, I'll find out, and if you're hiring Dru to cover up anything illegal, she'll find out. You'd probably rather I found out than Dru."

Baxter's eyes didn't know where to settle, on me or Lake, but he knew damn well what Lake meant. "I'm not lying, Rick." He twined his long fingers together. "I wish Linda hadn't involved you. She means well. I don't know how I came to be involved in this mess. That obnoxious boy came into my restaurant and wanted to change everything, and I didn't go along with him. He brought his girlfriend and I've been caught up in something ever since. And I have no fucking idea what."

There was a commotion at the front of the restaurant. "Well, that's that," Lake said. "The local and state gendarmerie has arrived."

Baxter looked at us. "Have dinner here on me. I'll tell Oliver."

Sergeant Perry Thomas and Felix Kona stood in the doorway. A GBI agent thrust through them. I knew Joe Hagan of the Athens Bureau. He nodded at Lake and me, then said to Baxter, "Mr. Carlisle, please stand." Which Baxter did. Joe motioned Felix forward. Felix had his handcuffs at the ready. Lake stood. "Are you arresting him, Joe?"

"Taking him in for questioning that might lead to charges. Standard protocol."

"No need to embarrass Mr. Carlisle. He has agreed to talk to you willingly. This is his business establishment."

Joe Hagan motioned Felix away. "Go with Sergeant Thomas, Mr. Carlisle. I'll be around to talk to you."

Baxter nodded and walked over to Thomas, who had his

hand on his gun holster like Baxter was going to take off like a jack rabbit or whip out a knife.

As for Baxter, he might as well have been handcuffed. People were arriving in the vestibule for cocktails and dinner as Baxter walked through. I gave it five minutes to get all over town.

Joe said to Lake, "Overlapping jurisdiction going on here."

"Yep," Lake said. "Working with you, Joe, is always a pleasure." Joe is one of the few staties Lake likes.

Joe said, "Same here."

Oliver, the maître d', brought in two couples and led them to a table across the room.

Joe, Lake, and I sat and huddled across the table.

Lake asked, "You found a body yet?"

Joe shook his head. "Last I heard, twenty minutes ago, divers quit. Dark. You hanging out here?"

Lake looked at me. "For a time."

Joe looked at me and winked. "Carlisle hire you?"

"You got here before I could get a check."

His grin was pleasant. "Timing was never my strong suit."

I said, "Baxter says he had nothing to do with Hansel's disappearance."

"No surprise he said that. There's his phone call on Thursday night, the last call in Damian's call list."

Lake said, "Bax said he never called Damian."

"Somebody did . . . using Baxter's cell phone," Joe said.

"Can I ask you something?" I said.

"Fire away."

"Any trouble with Baxter since he's been in Athens?"

He thought a moment. "Not while I've been in the bureau here, and I haven't heard anything against him. No police record. But lately there's been trouble at his bar, Power House."

"What kind?"

"Rough trade. Fights. One fatal last week."

That surprised me. "It's been a long time since I was in Power House, but I don't remember rough trade."

"For a couple of years now, locals, skinheads, have taken over from students. There's a lot bigger TV sports bars where students go."

"Did Damian Hansel hang out there?"

"Not his kind of place. Also, in case you don't know, there was a burglary here ten days ago."

"What came of it?"

"The alarm scared the burglar off. Stupid. There's nothing to take in a restaurant except the silverware. Carlisle's safe is in the basement and weighs ten tons. Athens PD said it looked like the scum was looking for something behind the bar, like a cash register. Since when do restaurants have cash registers?"

"Not since the stone age," I said.

"Ten days ago," Lake said. "Maybe looking for something else. Baxter Carlisle's gotten into a world of trouble in that time. What do you know about Cho Martine?"

Joe shook his head. "About as much as you. Filed complaints against Carlisle with the PD; now her boyfriend's gone. She was questioned. Knows nothing, she says. Can prove she was in Athens from Friday through the weekend. I ran her down on her way to class."

"Who found the cell phone?" I asked.

"A runner. It was laying on a pine tree stump. Plain sight. He ran by it again on his way back. No one was around so he turned it over to a patrol cop."

"Interesting," I said.

Joe made a move to stand, and I put my hand on his arm. "Baxter said there'd been several killings lately. I didn't pursue it. I was going to talk to Athens PD about it, but I'm not in Thomas's fan club."

Joe thought a moment. "Can't see how it fits in. One kid got killed a month ago. Used his apartment as a chemistry lab. We got onto him right before he was murdered. Made MDMA laced with caffeine. One of his buyers apparently objected and knifed him, or his boyfriend did it. It's still open."

"Could it be related?"

Joe shrugged. "Nothing I know says so now."

"What about the locals at Power House?"

"Two drunken losers with guns." He stood and so did Lake and I. "I got to go," he said. "Lieutenant, it's possible we'll find the body in your jurisdiction, so you want to sit in?"

"I'd like that," Lake said.

The look on Joe's face told me I wasn't going to be sitting in. I said, "I got an inside track."

Joe, the big winker, winked.

Leaving the restaurant, my cell rang out Haydn. The number on the face was an Athens number. No name. "Hello," I answered.

"It's me, Baxter."

"What's going on, Bax?" I asked. Joe and Lake paused to listen.

"Call my lawyer," Bax said. "Go to my office. You still at Carlisle's?"

"Just leaving."

"Have Oliver take you in there. I still use a rolodex. Anthony DuPlessy, whom you met, will be listed in it. Tell him to come here. Also, in my top drawer is a ring of keys. Tell Oliver to give you the key and garage door opener to Lionell Place. He'll know which one I mean. It's yours. Stay there. Alarm code is 81962, my birth date . . . which you can find in a biography of me on the Internet if you forget."

"I may do that, Bax. I've made no plans."

"One more thing. What is your fee?"

"Ten thousand for a five-day week, plus expenses."

"You got it. Tell Oliver to write you a check." As if he understood my silence, he said, "Oliver is my business manager. He masquerades as a maitre d' to keep the help honest."

"Lake and Joe are on the way," I said. "Has Thomas questioned you?"

"Some. Mostly sitting on my butt, waiting for the big, bad shoe to drop."

"You'll be out soon. No body yet."

He laughed, and I could hear the sarcasm. "That cheers me."

"Did they ask you about the cell phone call to Damian?" He answered "not yet," and I asked if he was positive he didn't make the call, and he said that he never had a reason to call Damian. "You lose your cell phone, or was it ever out of your sight?" I asked.

"I have several devices. What number was it from?"

I told him I didn't know yet, and that he should ask the cops questioning him and right away, that they may or may not tell him, but he needed to ask. With a promise that he would, we ended the conversation.

While walking with Lake to my car, I told him where I'd be staying. I didn't ask him if he was spending the night in Athens. I hoped he would continue as APD's presence here, but a detective lieutenant in Major Crimes had many duties and usually hung out at the shop divvying out murder and mayhem cases to the men he supervised.

CHAPTER EIGHT

Oliver either was born with or was a master at copying Baxter's elegance. He handed me the keys and garage door opener and drew me a map to the condos. Also, he wrote a big fat check, which meant I had to go to work in earnest, not that I didn't always, but it's a bonus when you get one of Georgia's richest men for a client. Webdog had informed me of that fact.

"Baxter Carlisle is listed in Georgia's Richest. Real estate, baby, real estate. Wasn't it Bob Hope who said go out and find land nobody wants and buy as much as you can, and they will come?"

"I don't know, Web. I'm not a movie buff."

"He bought in Palm Springs before there was a Palm Springs, and, for sure, they came."

"Maybe it had something to do with him being Bob Hope."

"Might be right, boss. Anyways, this Carlisle slid out of the womb onto a pile of money. His ancestor started one of the first insurance companies in Atlanta. It's undergone several name changes, but started out as Dime Assurance for Life and Home."

"I can see the reason for the name changes. Dimes for dollars."

"Baxter Carlisle is also one of Georgia's most reclusive gazillionaires."

"Wouldn't do for our Bax to run for office."

"All would be revealed."

"You mean his taste for teen girls?"

"Maybe that's why he collects dolls."

"What?"

"He has one of the most extensive doll collections in the world. Every Barbie ever made, and lots of old-fashioned, expensive dolls. Travels all over the globe to find them."

"Is this supposed to be a secret?"

"The dolls are housed in one of his homes in Augusta. His caretaker's grandson was a college classmate of mine. Last year the guy flunked out and went to Mexico, but we stay in touch."

"No spoofing attacks needed?"

"Nope."

"Speaking of spoofing, can you spoof a cell number?"

"Easy, breezy."

"What else did you find on Baxter?"

"He's never been married. He has a son, thirty-two in a month."

"What's his name?"

"Oliver Gilmeath."

"Ah, all is revealed."

"All?"

"Father and son together in Athens. The maitre d'-slash-business manager. Wonder when they got together?"

"He always supported the boy and let the kid visit in summer. Oliver went to Duke University. Is gay. Has a partner who resides in England most of the year. They commute."

"Expensive commute. Name of partner?"

"I'm going to spell this. U-l-i, Uli. Last name van U-u-m."

"Lot of U's going on there. What kind of name is that?"

"Born in Prague of Belgium parents. Educated at the Glenn Paullus Art Institute in New York. Lives in London. A sculptor, of some note."

"Lots of art in this case."

"He seems to specialize in private parts." I asked what private parts. "Penises. And not of your average Joe."

"You've seen?"

"On the net. When he applied for a grant he had to submit work. It makes 'Piss Christ' look heavenly."

"Nice. You get to Damian Hansel and Cho Martine yet?"

"Dirk's is digging." Dirk's is a general private investigative agency with whom we contract out routine stuff. Web said, "With young people who obey the law and pay their bills, they don't have much of a public history to track. Hansel's never been in trouble with the law, has two paid-up credit cards, owns a Jeep in his name, both parents living, mother's ill." He took a breath. "If there's anything deeper, I'll find it when I hash his plaintexts and compare it to the input hash."

For the deep stuff, we don't hire Dirk's. "Hash away. And Cho Martine?"

"An enigma. I'm going to have to consult John the Ripper's dictionary for her."

"Haven't I heard of John the Ripper in some underworld context?"

"You don't want to know the brute."

"That all you got for me now?"

"Yep. I'm gone."

He'd caught the phone hang-ups from Portia.

I don't like using Web's cracking expertise, but when you need info fast, you got to do what you got to do.

I decided to take Bax up on his offer of dinner and went from Baxter's office to the maitre d's dais. I wish I had taken his offer of the lovely suit. I'd have to tackle dinner and Oliver Gilmeath in my working clothes. The restaurant was full to capacity, and the woman who registered reservations told me that there was nothing available for one. I told her I needed to talk to Oliver. She said Mr. Gilmeath would be with me shortly.

He came from the bar with a steady smile—the unthinking,

practiced smile of an expert in public relations. When he saw me, his eyes brightened and he came up holding out an exuberant hand.

"You have decided to join us for dinner," he said.

Glancing around him, I saw the reservationist's pressed lips, which told me that Mr. Gilmeath was difficult to work with or for. I said, "I know you're full. I don't want to put you out."

"We do it like hotels. Save a table for unexpected, important guests."

"Who knew?" I said, smiling.

"Mr. Carlisle told me to take very good care of you."

"You would anyway," I said. "Have you heard from him?"

"Through his attorney. He called to say Mr. Carlisle would be awhile, but that he would be here for closing. Can I get you something from the bar?"

"Chardonnay, please, and, Mr. Gilmeath, I'll have an appetizer at the bar."

"You sure?"

"I had a wonderful lunch at the Polo Ground and I'm not that hungry. Maybe a shrimp cocktail."

"I'll fix just the thing for you. Come this way." He turned and led me into the bar. "A nice Pahlmeyer 2007?" he asked over his shoulder.

"Can't afford it."

"On the house, and much better than the 2006. Nicely focused, some mouthfeel and succulent lime and mellowing nutmeg."

I would say Baxter raised his son very well. "Sold."

The sommelier opened the white wine locker, and Oliver Gilmeath dropped his role as the charming maitre d' and moved away to commit to the wine ceremony, giving me time to size him up. Six feet tall, his unsmiling face featured a melancholy man with a perfect, straight nose that cut between deep blue eyes. His jaw was strong and his thick brown hair was expertly barbered. Stylish in every aspect was Oliver Gilmeath. A trick of my mind, however, saw him as a rock musician, hair down to his shoulder, disheveled, a two-day-old beard and dark chest hair exposed by an unbuttoned shirt. Very sexy.

He carried the bottle and a fragile wine glass to where I perched as elegantly as I could on the high stool, poured, and invited me to taste. It was quite sumptuous. Holding the glass, watching the legs, I smiled up at him. "Am I supposed to describe this delicious stuff?"

"Only if you can."

I sniffed and drew in a mouthful again. "So smooth, like velvet on my tongue. Buttery, but not too. I taste the citrus, no oak."

"Excellent." He pushed the bottle toward me. "It's yours."

"Do you run a taxi service for drunks?"

"I promise, you won't get intoxicated."

"Can I speak with you for a few minutes?"

He sat on an adjacent stool and angled his body toward me. "You know who I am, don't you?"

"I have a researcher."

"It's ludicrous, the charges that girl makes. Baxter has his low points and particular tastes, but pedophilia is not one of them."

It was interesting that he didn't call him father, or daddy. Neither Baxter nor his son was daddy-calling types. "Can I ask about his low points?"

"As you've said, you have a researcher."

"There are rumors," I said. He gave me a quizzical, dark look. "He travels to places . . ."

He glanced at the bartender who was busy fixing a Manhattan. "Travel is something the rich do with their money. They can only wear one suit at a time. Baxter trusts you."

"I have to deal with rumors as well as facts. Sad to say."

"Be that as it may, put some faith in him, until you learn otherwise."

"Wisely said. Do you know Damian Hansel and Cho Martine?"

"I wish I didn't." He noted my raised eyebrows, but he made no move to elaborate.

I said, "I'm getting glimpses of them. It's important to understand the personalities involved to understand why someone disappears. With Damian being an artist and . . ."

A noise came from the back of his throat. "Athens, Georgia, would like to think itself the Paris of the twenty-first century, but it's not even close. There are some good journeymen here, but Damian isn't one of them. He's a pretender and Cho Martine is a chimera."

If I recall Greek myth correctly, a chimera is a monster represented by a lion's head, goat's body, and serpent's tail. I hadn't seen her tail. "Are you an artist, Mr. Gilmeath?"

"I have no talent, but I've learned to appreciate art. My partner was born in Prague and is a sculptor."

"Uli van Uum, an interesting name."

"An interesting individual. I met him in Paris when I was a student at a place where foreign nationals hang out."

"Does he exhibit in the states?"

"In New York, yes. And he's subordinating himself to sculpt for our restaurant." The glow in his eyes showed how proud he was of his partner. "He's doing Uga, the Georgia Bulldogs' mascot. It's to hang in Power House."

Uga is a real live bulldog. On game day he wears a spiked collar and a red official game jersey. He has an air-conditioned house at the stadium because bulldogs are susceptible to heat stroke. As a specialist in gay art, I shuddered to think what Uli van Uum would do with the white bulldog. "Very pricey," I said. "The art, not the steakhouse."

He shook his head. "You might drop by Studio Two-O-One during your stay here. Uli donated a sketch of the work. Also, you might be interested in a showing of Ceramic Progressions by Julian Cross. Tonight is the closing reception at Gallery Two-O-Five. They'll still be there."

"You're being mysterious," I said, looking at my watch.

"I think you'll be interested."

"Then I'll drop by on my way to my home-away-from-home tonight."

"I hope you're comfortable." By the look on his face, I knew the comfort level couldn't be beat.

"One more thing," I said, holding up a finger. "I understand Cho Martine is a musician."

He shrugged. "I heard." He watched two men walk into the bar. "I must attend my duties, Miss Dru . . ."

"Just Dru."

He grinned. "Dru."

"Can we talk later?"

"Of course. When you need expense money, come to me."

"I'll do that."

He rose. "Enjoy the wine. Ah, here comes your shrimp. Bon appetit."

"One more question, Mr. Gilmeath . . ."

"Oliver."

"Do you think Baxter will let me see his doll collection?"

"Maybe you'd better stick with Mr. Gilmeath," he said, grinning, and his eyes gleamed.

CHAPTER NINE

Head bowed against a wind of at least twenty miles an hour, I walked through the Art School courtyard. Light shone from the square glass rectangle. On the second floor, I stopped at Gallery 205 and slipped through the open door. A man stood in the center of a circle of diverse people—artists, students, professors, and business people if you went by their clothing—engrossed in Julian Cross's speech. On tables and stands were ceramics that had been painted and glazed mostly in gold, green, or lapis lazuli. Quite handsome, I thought, for gargoyles. *Chimeras, gargoyles? What next.*

Cross noticed me. "Welcome."

"Thank you," I replied. "Quite lovely. Don't let me interrupt."

"As it is almost nine, and the wine and cheese have disappeared, I think we can call it an evening." He nodded at the group. "It's been my pleasure to present my work."

A man cleared his throat and took a step forward. "Julian, you are always welcome to our humble gallery. We look forward to your next showing and lecture here."

Julian kept looking at me—curiously and slightly annoyed. Me, the interloper—someone who interrupted his final words of ceramic wisdom. When he realized no one was talking, he swept his eyes over his admirers and said, "If you'll pardon me then, I shall leave you with a little gift." He reached down to where a chair held a gift bag, picked up the bag, and presented it to the man who had stepped forward. The man opened it and drew out a box. Inside the box was a small horse, painted and glazed red. The man gushed, "Oh my, Julian, how beautiful. It's the year of the fire horse."

"Indeed," Julian said with a sly grin that seemed meant for me.

I imagine things sometimes.

"It shall have a place of honor here," the man said.

Julian bowed from the waist. "I'm pleased by your gracious-ness, and, now, I bid adieu." He swept past me, and before I could turn to leave, he tapped me on the shoulder. "You are Miss Dru?"

Surprised—but maybe not—I nodded. He said, "Oliver Gilmeath." He tapped his shirt pocket that outlined the shape of a cell phone.

"He specifically told me to be here," I said.

He curlicued his finger. "Come with me."

I followed him from the room where already workers in white were bringing in boxes. Time to move the collection on. At the end of the hall, he opened a door. The rather large room was filled with easels. The painting studio. A man stood at an easel, hands clasped behind his back. After a few seconds, he turned toward us. Importance, I thought. Stout, but not fat, a load of gray hair combed back from a low forehead. Green-hazel eyes, wide mouth, and ample lips. He came forward, arm stretched, hand open to take mine. "I'm Henry Hansel." I shook his. "I hoped you would come this evening."

"Oliver Gilmeath suggested that I do . . . in a most mysteri-ous way."

When Damian's father shook his head, his body seemed to vibrate. "I'm happy that you obliged him, but if you hadn't, we would have met at some point."

I looked at Julian. We had become Dru and Julian on the

walk to the painting studio. "Did you know Damian?"

"You can be frank, Mr. Cross," Henry Hansel said.

"He came here last week," Julian said. "We had a conversation. He was interested in ceramics as it relates to the evolutionary idea of art. I couldn't relate to his opinions though. I am not a conceptualist."

Julian was showing signs of a man who wants to get going, so I said, "Thinking back, was this a man who would voluntarily go missing? Skip classes, take off for parts unknown?"

Julian seemed hesitant. "He was very excited about something. I don't know what. He didn't say. To him, it was something important. He spoke of his advent."

Henry Hansel listened to this with his arms across his chest, standing still and erect. He'd heard this already. He spoke. "Damian has a showing called 'The Advent' at a little gallery off Broad Street." His baritone was nice and held no signs of apprehension, just a certain humorlessness.

Julian had shrugged off Damian's exhibit, the gallery, or both.

Henry Hansel said, "I don't like my son belittled, Mr. Cross."

So much for inviting frankness.

"Nothing of the kind, Mr. Hansel. I encouraged him to lighten and broaden his scope if he wants to be a commercial artist."

"That's just it, he didn't," Hansel said. "He would never be starving."

Silence hung for a moment or two. I asked Damian's father, "When was the last time you spoke with your son?"

Julian held up his hands and said that he needed to get the collection boxed and on the road. He jutted his hand for Hansel's; then cupped it on the ball of my shoulder and wished me the best of luck in my quest, making me wonder what he thought my quest was. Then he was gone, leaving me with a stern-faced Henry Hansel.

"Like a cup of coffee?" I asked. "We need to talk."

"Not coffee," he said. "I'm in for a martini. Let's go to Carlisle's."

I had doubts about going there. Did Hansel know that Baxter had been taken to the police station? Or the latest news regarding his son's disappearance?

"This way," he said, ushering me to the door. My car was parked two slots from his. During our walk he said that yesterday he'd gone to Carlisle's to talk to Mr. Carlisle. Mr. Carlisle wasn't there but he talked to Mr. Gilmeath who assured him that Mr. Carlisle wasn't avoiding him. He told me that his son and Mr. Carlisle didn't agree on the subject of art. "My son is opinionated and speaks his mind." He shrugged. "In the end, it is Mr. Carlisle's restaurant."

That nagged me. *Why did Damian feel free to suggest changing the art scheme in the restaurant, and when thwarted, have the nerve to argue about it?*

I asked, "Have you talked to the police today?"

"Not since noon. They told me they'd let me know if anything turned up."

He didn't know about Damian's cell then. "Why don't we go to Pastiche instead," I said. "Baxter Carlisle isn't at his restaurant."

"Fine with me."

Hansel tailed my car closely. I called Lake. He said he couldn't talk, but I told him where I was going. Before I could tell him with whom, he disconnected.

Revitalization in the early 1980s had preserved some of the historic buildings in downtown Athens by the time Portia had enrolled in UGA. Athens is the typical college town with Victorian era charm. It's loaded with shops and restaurants and taverns and clubs, but not an abundance of parking. I finally found a place two streets over and lost sight of Henry's car. I got out, stepped into a wicked wind, and ran most of the way.

Inside the narrow establishment I spotted an empty table and sat. Because of the high tin ceiling, the noise hurt my ears. Watching out the glass window for Hansel's appearance, I wondered how long it was going to take for the wind to strip the striped awning from its brackets.

Henry came in, stamped his feet, looked around, and found me in the corner. It was cold here, but not as crowded as the center and back of the room. A sign requested that patrons order drinks at the bar. Henry asked my preference, and I told him the house Chardonnay.

It usually takes a healthy swallow of booze and a few sentences of small talk before the subject at hand is brought up. "Nine-thirty and Athens is jumping," Hansel said. "They roll up the streets in Tallahassee."

"Athens is always jumping," I said.

"Damian loves this town," he said, scooting his drink on his napkin just so. "UGA was his first choice."

Damian, his father said, chose Georgia because of the art school. He also said his son wasn't smart enough to get a scholarship but the art school people liked his projects and enthusiasm. He said Damian was a serious student of art, not of rocket science. He held up his glass. "Cheers."

"Cheers to you, too."

"Damian always liked to create things." He wrapped his hands around his martini glass. "It was Leonardo da Vinci's drawings that inspired him. No one's going to mistake a Hansel drawing for a da Vinci, but what he lacks in smarts is made up in wit and personality. He is a doer."

"You never know about genius," I said. He gave me a quizzical glance and drank from his glass. I reasoned, "Your son could hit on the next big thing in art. Take Andy Warhol and his soup cans. Twenty years prior, they would have called him a crackpot, no-talent."

"Perhaps," he said, and I looked at the big ring on his third finger—a ruby, class of something

"It seems Damian traveled a lot with his artist friends."

"Why not?" He shrugged. "It's not like he's going to have to work at hard labor, or even go into management. He's got money of his own from trust funds. He promised me he'd graduate, and he will one day."

"Would you describe Damian as a follower?"

" 'Neither leader nor follower, me,' Damian said of himself. He was just Damian, opinionated, like I said, and outspoken about it. He was like a savant in a way. He could see something, say, like Carlisle's interior and redo it in his head. He sometimes couldn't understand why others didn't have his vision."

A waiter came with a bowl of almonds and shelled pistachios. I sipped from my glass and asked if he'd talked to Cho Martine.

"Can't," he said. "Lawyered. A firm I don't know."

Wonder what that was about? "Had you met her before Damian's disappearance?"

"We dined at Carlisle's."

"What did you think of her?"

"Quiet. Getting her to talk was like pulling words out of her mouth."

Another aspect of the chimera. "When I met her, she was anything but quiet," I said. "She was enraged at Baxter Carlisle. She insists he stalks her."

He shook his head. "Where Mr. Carlisle fits into all of this is a mystery."

I reminded myself that he didn't know about Damian's cell phone, where it was found and where Baxter Carlisle grew up. Henry said that it was inconceivable that such an accomplished and heretofore respected businessman could be involved. He professed himself a good judge of character and Mr. Carlisle did not fit the profile of a stalker, much less a kidnapper of a young man.

Heretofore aside, he was correct. Baxter liked ingénues, not Cho Martine types, and stalking and kidnapping was much too messy for him. "Does your son hike or jog in out-of-the-way places, like the woods?"

"The police are considering an accident. His Jeep is in the parking lot, but his bicycle is missing. Damian is a runner and a biker, bicycle mostly. He owns a Harley-Davidson which is in its place in a garage he rents. The John boat is there, too, although the oars are missing."

Oars and a bicycle? He didn't go to Atlanta on his bike, I didn't think. "What kind of bike?"

"A Columbine Road."

Those frames started at three grand, then you put on the rest of the gear and you're talking five or six.

He swallowed a couple of times and picked out three almonds. What terrible thoughts came into his head that he needed time to collect himself? "Last time Marcella, that's my wife, talked to Damian he'd been for a run. He was out of breath, she said. Huffing out his words."

"When was this?"

"Sometime Thursday afternoon before he met with this girl, Cho, to study."

"You say 'this girl, Cho.' Wasn't she his girlfriend?"

"I didn't get that impression, tell the truth. They didn't look star-struck or walked hand in hand. But Damian's a little backward with girls, especially . . ."

"Especially?"

"He goes for the blond, cheerleader type. If they're not smart, all the better."

"The antithesis of Cho."

He bobbed his head, drank from his glass, and stared into his own distance.

At that moment, Lake walked through the door. I raised my hand and startled Henry from his funk. Lake weaved through the tables; Henry and I stood. I introduced the men. Lake pulled up a chair and we sat. "What's happening?" I said.

"Baxter Carlisle's been released. No charges." He turned to Henry. "The Athens police are trying to find you."

Anxiety spooled through my blood. He was going to tell Henry . . .

Henry's jaw clenched. "What is it?"

Lake took a moment to preempt the agony he was about to deliver to Henry Hansel. "Something the matter with your cell?"

"It's on the charger. I haven't checked messages. What happened?"

"Your son's cell phone was found in Atlanta."

Henry's mouth opened and closed. "In Atlanta? Where?"

His face dour, Lake tapped a finger. "In a park by a creek."

"My God."

Could that explain the missing oars?

Lake held up a hand. "Don't assume anything yet. It could have gotten there any number of ways. Left by Damian even."

Henry seemed to have trouble breathing. "It's always hooked up to his person."

"He visit Atlanta much?" Lake asked.

"He—uh—yes, he does."

I said, "Would he skip classes to go to Atlanta?"

"If he thought . . ." He paused as if something occurred to him. "Where's this creek?"

Lake said, "We need to know how often he went to Atlanta and what he did there."

Hansel nodded. "The museum. Exhibitions. He spoke of the clubs. Ballgames."

"Can you remember anywhere specific?" Lake asked. "If there's a connection here, I need to find it."

"What creek?" Henry asked.

"Peachtree Creek. He ever talk about that creek or any others?"

He frowned and shook his head. "Damian's a strong swimmer. He likes to fish but his boat and Jeep are here."

"But no oars," I said.

Lake gave me an odd glance. He said, "Atlanta's creeks are slow moving and shallow until the rains come; then they flood. Peachtree Creek is flooded now."

"I remember Atlanta's creeks very well. Damian was born there. You live in that region, you live by creeks and springs. We lived in Sandy Springs before we left Georgia." He shrugged at the past. "Who—who found the cell phone?"

Lake explained the circumstances of the find.

"Took the cops long enough," Henry said, his anger chasing away his fear.

Lake told him that the Atlanta police didn't know Damian Hansel was missing. After they received the report, the patrol cop remembered the name and retrieved the cell from lost possessions. Then they needed to locate and talk to the jogger.

"And?" Henry asked, leaning forward, eager.

Lake explained that the jogger ran the same route every morning. The day before he found the phone, the healthy maple tree was standing. Next morning the jogger noticed the tree had been sawn down and the cell lying on the stump. APD determined that the tree cutting was a deliberate act by someone unknown. The wood was taken away, perhaps for firewood. Beyond that, there was only speculation.

Henry had finished his drink. He rose and asked Lake if he wanted a drink, and when Lake and I declined, he went to the bar. I asked Lake, "Does Baxter's story check out?"

"Tiffany checks out. He was there. She's of age, but dresses like a kid. Neither APD nor Athens PD have enough to charge him—with anything."

"Just a person of interest."

"Baxter's got a savvy lawyer."

I gave Lake a quick thumbnail of what Henry said about Damian.

"A rich kid playing at being an art scholar," he said.

Henry walked back and settled in his chair. Lake said, "Where does Damian stay in Atlanta?"

"He and Arne—that's Arne Trammel, his good friend—stay with a boy who works at the High Museum. Marshall Logan. He was planning to go with them to Italy and Prague this summer." He swallowed half the cocktail, then reached into his jacket pocket and took out a card holder and a pen. He wrote on the back of a business card. "Where I'm staying here and my cell number." He gave the card to Lake and took out a wallet.

I asked, "Do you like Arne Trammel and Marshall Logan?"

"Uh, sure."

Didn't sound too sure, but I didn't want to pursue it, because I intended to talk to Trammel and didn't want my mind tainted. Lake would tackle Marshall Logan in Atlanta.

Henry drank the liquid in his glass, rose, and tossed enough green money on the table for a generous tip, even though there was no wait staff. "I'm going to the police station."

Lake rose, too. "Stick to facts and keep the faith."

"I will," he said, brushing past us.

"Where to?" Lake asked when the door closed on Hansel's hurried steps.

"Is it too late to pay Arne Trammel a visit?"

"It's never too late to pay a person of interest a visit."

"You going back to Atlanta tonight?"

"Unless I get an invitation to crash with my girlfriend."

"The way you winked at me, I thought you wanted to spend the night with me."

"I don't sleep with every girl I wink at, but I'll make an exception in your case. Where you taking me?"

"To some fancy place overlooking the river."

"I'm in. I'll bring the gin."

"Got it covered. Trunk of the Audi." I took out my car keys and the keys given by Oliver. "Lionell Place on Oconee Street."

"I'm starved," he said.

"Want to give Arne Trammel a pass and go directly to Burger Doodle?"

"Tell you what, I need to check with Athens PD, so let's tackle Arne in the morning. Artsy-fartsy types are liable to be toked by this time. Let's go directly to Power House. I could use a steak."

"I'm for it."

Walking toward my car, I noticed something odd about the radiator. The Audi has a distinctive grill, one with four interlocking circles over an egg crate chrome background. Something was stuck on the right circle. "Something's stuck in the grill," I said. "The wind probably . . ."

"Hold it," Lake said.

He squatted on his heels to study the object. He glanced up. His narrowed eyes and sly mouth—sort of pleased but worried—put me on edge. "You seemed to have gotten someone's attention," he said, standing straight and motioning me to have a look.

A rectangular black thing was stuck in the circle. I asked if he thought someone jammed it there.

"Carefully placed. Recognize it?" I shook my head that I didn't. "Magnetic money clip. It's quite noticeable under the street lights. Did you happen to notice the grill when you locked the car?"

I reeled back to that moment. "No, I was watching for Henry."

He scanned the sidewalk. The few strollers paid no attention to us. "Stand back with me and unlock the car." I prayed it wouldn't blow up and it didn't. He raised the hood, gave it a few seconds' glance, and then got down on all fours and checked the undercarriage. That done, he rose, straightened his jacket, and said, "I'll start 'er up for you. Then you can lead me to Lionell Place on Oconee Street."

"It has a garage."

"That answers for the Audi's safety," he said.

It cranked without blowing up, and I let the air out of my lungs.

"Who knows where you're staying tonight?"

"Oliver and Baxter."

Lake told me to stay put, but alert while he went for the squad car, a block over. When he came back he had his tool case out and extracted the money clip from the grill with forensic tongs and slid it in a baggie. There was no money in the clip or identifier on it except for a pricey designer logo. Lake thought it best to leave the money clip with the car and locked it in the glove compartment.

CHAPTER TEN

The courtyard condo was a two-story built on the bluff overlooking the Oconee River. The furnishings looked modern and expensive. Whoever designed the interior was a Frank Lloyd Wright fan. As that famous architect said, or something like it, pictures deface walls more than they decorate them. I'd etched that line in my memory because my parents' home was so crowded with art and photographs and myriad other hanging artifacts, I used to imagine our house without them. My little cottage displays a few select pieces that mean something, otherwise my attic is home to some sentimental and relatively valuable art.

Lake—rustic loft dweller, owner of refinished old furniture that we troll for in Little Five Points and Virgina-Highlands—scanned the rooms with total disinterest and went to the fridge. It was well-stocked with beer, white wines of considerable vintage, a bottle of pricey vodka, and mixers. In the freezer were fancy plastic containers of food prepared at Carlisle's and Power House. Dated labels named the foods and the restaurants from whence they came. As a bonus, whoever packed them rated the containers with stars. I saw mostly five stars.

"Is this for us?" Lake asked.

"Could be, I suppose, but no one knew before a couple of hours ago that we would be here." And before I got out the next sentence—that I would call Oliver and check—the phone rang.

Lake picked up the house phone. "How's it going, Bax?"

Baxter replied something short and Lake said, "Hang in there. Tomorrow we begin the good fight in earnest. Say . . ."

Lake listened while Baxter spoke, then Lake said, "Just what I wanted to know. Is the five-star the best you have?" Baxter spoke at length while Lake nodded. "I know it's all great food. Any desserts?" He got his answer and smiled. "Fine. We're set here."

During the conversation, I made gin martinis, lemon drop for me, original with two olives for Lake.

Lake said to Baxter, "We're going to talk to Athens PD first thing, then start with people who knew them both. Now, go home and get a good night's sleep."

A few minutes later, Lake hung up and breathed in deeply. "He's a pain in the ass."

"But he's our pain and his ass is paying lots."

"Do I get half?"

"For moonlighting?"

"I can't moonlight, smart aleck."

Lake had taken a swallow of his martini when his cell phone rang. "I'm not answering," he said, looking at the display. "I'm off duty."

It kept ringing that obnoxious tone that doesn't bother men. Frowning and speaking to his cell, he said, "I'm entitled to sit here and relax on my time off, so shut up."

It stopped briefly, having gone to voice mail before it started up again. He mashed a number on the cell's face. "Lake, here."

When he sat alert and put his glass on the cocktail table, I knew my night of love had gone with the wind.

"Where?" he asked. He looked at me, his mouth open in awe of something or someone. "Be there." Clicking off, he stared as though in a trance.

"Takeout?" I asked.

"I'll snatch a dessert on my way past the freezer in the

garage." He'd be as happy as if he'd ground his teeth against a two-inch medium-rare slab of beef. With one gulp, he finished off the martini. As he put his arms in the sleeves of his jacket, he said, "At the Nancy Creek Trail, security found a scarecrow tacked to the huge oak tree by where Nancy Creek runs into Blackburn Park. It was dressed in clothes labeled Damian Hansel. The straw face had a photograph of him stapled to it."

It wasn't the most bizarre thing I'd heard, but a surreal stirring in my abdomen made me whisper, "What's it mean?"

"I wish I knew. Somebody's idea of a joke, maybe?"

If so, it was one serious joke.

Lake said, "Joe's already there. I want to stay in this investigation." He came up and brushed my hair back and put his lips to my forehead. "If for no other reason than that my favorite girlfriend is involved."

"What if I wasn't your favorite?"

He put his arms around me. "I'd have to think twice."

I was getting used to Lake's references to other girlfriends. A handsome man—one who's in the headlines often, appearing on television as an expert in all things mysterious and criminal—will have a crowd of groupies. They call day and night. They think they are uniquely suited to the challenge of taking Lake away from me. Okay, I was born jealous and possessive of things that are mine. Lake is mine. I hugged him. "I could come with you."

"I'll be back in the morning."

"When are you going to sleep?"

"While I drive. It's boring anyway."

I made another lemon drop martini and settled down in front of my laptop to record the day's events. The soft leather chair at the desk in Baxter's study had me realizing how tired I was. After typing the facts of the case, I thought about the money clip. Who put it there? Could it have been jammed in by a stranger walking along who didn't like Audis or designer money clips? Cho? Baxter? He was in jail. The cops? I smiled and made a noise. Henry Hansel? He'd left the restaurant before Lake and me—but really. He didn't strike me as a prankster. Could Devus McFersen have had me followed to further harass?

I called Lake. "Where are you?"

"Halfway to Atlanta. What's up?"

"Devus McFersen probably has a money clip or two to spare."

"I thought about that," Lake said. "But, you know, those animals don't stray off their reservation. They got a territory to protect."

"Peachtree Hills isn't their territory."

"Okay, so Devus made an exception for you. Watch out for dump trucks."

"I'm getting an early start in the morning. Call me as soon as you learn more about the scarecrow."

"Go to sleep, pretty one. You're eyes get puffy if you don't get enough sleep."

"Drive safely. Love you."

"Love you, too."

Try as I might I couldn't sleep thinking about a scarecrow dressed as Damian and a money clip in the Audi's glove box and what it signified. Ideas foamed in my head, then fizzled only to bubble up again and pop. This is about Damian, but is it Damian the student, Damian the boyfriend, Damian the artist, or Damian the rich son of Henry Hansel? Look for the money trail, the money clip says. Look at Cho, the temperamental girlfriend. Love is a strong motive for murder. I hated to think of Damian dead, murdered, but the few sketchy facts could mean that he was. Damn, my head hurt. I turned on television and watched *Strangers on a Train* on the classic movie channel. I fell asleep just as two men agreed to . . .

Haydn woke me up. I shook myself and massaged my neck.

"Bad news?" I asked Lake.

"Crime lab techs found folded money in Hansel's clothes. A money clip indentation was still on the bills. No clip found."

"My God, Lake, what *is* going on?" Suddenly I had hope. *Damian wasn't dead, just playing tricks.*

"A game, like Treasure Hunt. You follow clues. One leads to another."

My mind was chattering about things I couldn't make out. "What's the treasure?"

"It's very macabre here with the scarecrow. Call Athens PD. Joe wants to go over your car and send the clip to the lab. But first we let Athens cops in. Tell them about the clip and that I extracted it without touching it and bagged it in case it was significant. We're in this deep enough they're not going to try to X Atlanta PD out."

Two Athens detectives showed up and didn't stay long. They flashed the light in the grill, opened the glove box, shut it without touching the bag, and called a wrecker. My car was going to the GBI's forensic garage in DeKalb County, a metropolitan Atlanta county. I didn't mind. I was happy to rent a car that no one knew I was driving. Unless they'd been following me. *They. Who's they? Don't think about it. You'll have nightmares.*

I didn't have nightmares because, despite another martini, I didn't sleep.

Chapter Eleven

So many people to talk to. It was a day for phoning, even at seven in the morning. Drab, misty, chilly. I snapped off the television. The media hadn't picked up the story of the scarecrow yet, and I hadn't heard from Lake. I didn't call, hoping he was getting a few hours sleep. Eventually, I would call for a cab to take me to a car rental agency. Until then I wrapped a thick terry bathrobe around myself and finished a second cup of coffee and the last crumbs from a cinnamon roll that I'd taken from Bax's freezer and nuked. After that I settled in with the phone.

I started with Webdog. "Get me all you can on Kirin Littlefield; she's a neurosurgeon who was a playmate of Baxter's when they were kids. I think she's four years younger . . ."

"She's four years and two months younger," Web said. "Lives and practices in Savannah. Degrees from Emory in Atlanta and medical degree from Duke University, interned at Mass General, settled in Savannah with her daughter . . ."

"She has a daughter?"

"She's thirty-five and is an assistant professor at the University of Georgia, where you are at present, I'm guessing."

"I'm still here. Baxter told me Kirin never married."

"Elena's last name is Littlefield."

"How'd you latch onto Kirin and her daughter?"

"Baxter's past. Tracking back to the incident when Littlefield was nine."

"Where'd you come by that?" Portia wasn't on the bench then, but she knew about the case. "Porsh wouldn't tell if you pulled every last tooth out of her mouth."

"Actually, Kirin Littlefield doesn't hide the fact she was molested as a young girl and that her daughter was born when she was fourteen years old."

"Uh-oh, Baxter's in a world of . . ."

"Don't rush to judgment."

"What are you telling me?"

"Ten years ago, Kirin Littlefield published a handbook for physicians on the sexual interaction of stepfathers and young stepdaughters. Kirin's stepfather, the now deceased Stanley Marx, got her pregnant. She wrote the book after her mother died and states she believed her mother knew all along what was happening to her. She also says in her book that an unnamed teenager had been blamed for the stepfather's misdeeds."

This was what Baxter told me I would learn. "Okay, Web, we move to Damian Hansel." I thought about the scarecrow and the money clip and wondered if this was all for naught, that we'd find the bored student sitting at the end of the Treasure Hunt with—what?

Web said, "I just got off the phone with a teacher who taught Damian Edward Hansel. She returned my call from yesterday. Hansel, age nineteen, was a sub-mediocre student in Tallahassee private schools—from the third through twelfth grades. No serious girlfriends. His interest in art appears in a paper he wrote in eleventh grade after he traveled to Italy with his father. The paper was titled: 'Me and da Vinci: What We Have in Common.' According to the essay, Hansel thought he was just like the painter, sculptor, architect, musician, scientist, mathematician, engineer, inventor, anatomist, geologist, cartographer, botanist, and writer."

"You're joking."

I heard Web laughing. He said the teacher gave Damian an A for his online research. Thereafter the student became obsessive about art as if he'd found his life's work. The teacher said Damian was well-liked, nothing exceptional about his personality, but what was exceptional was his wealth. It came from his grandfather, a Wall Street banker. The teacher said he often bragged about being able to buy everyone in the room. That aside—he was generous with money. Of course, most of the other kids were rich, too.

"Interesting," I said. "And Cho Martine?"

"She doesn't exist."

You got to give Web a high mark for suspense. "What do you mean precisely?" I got up from the easy chair and opened the blinds. The mist had turned to a steady bombardment against the windowpanes, sort of like a rattler before it strikes.

Web said, "Precisely that I can find nothing about her. Let's start with her name."

"Good place. Baxter said the family has residences in Paris and Savannah."

"I can't find any records of a globe-trotting Cho Martine. By the way, Cho is a variant of the Japanese Chou, which is pronounced with a long o. It means butterfly, but is not used often as a first name."

"I'm assuming you checked Chou as the legal spelling of her name."

"You assume right. Cho is also a popular Korean last name, but since she's said to be Japanese I'm staying with that for the time. Did you know that the Japanese people are thought to have evolved from Koreans? Of course many disavow that, favoring sun goddess roots." I grunted and Web hurried on, "Last spring Cho was accepted and in the fall enrolled at the university as Cho Martine, no middle name and no back trail."

"Where'd she graduate high school?"

"Her university transcript says she spent four years at Franklin High School. I had Pearly Sue initiate conversation with the staff yesterday. The school has a diverse population, high percentage black. We thought it odd that the daughter of a renowned maritime architect would attend a crowded public school. The principal's records show that a student named Cho Martine matriculated last year, but she did not know Miss Martine. She recommended Pearly Sue talk to Miss Weatherford, which conversation took place last evening. Cho's computer transcript shows she made an A in that English class. Thing is, Miss Weatherford says she never had a student named Cho Martine. Pearly Sue also contacted a history teacher and a physics teacher. No Cho. Her grades are all A's, by the way."

"Teachers remember their A students, no matter how crowded their classes. What do the parental records show?"

"On the application, her father is listed as Viktor P. Martine, a French national. His occupation is maritime architect. The mother is Saki Takahashi Martine, born Osaka. They are real people, according to Who's Who, but it doesn't list children. That's not unusual for high profile folks who don't want their babes snatched for millions."

"Sounds like Cho could be a foreign student."

"She's enrolled at UGA as an in-state from Savannah."

"Savannah's playing prominently in this saga," I said. "So she was born here of foreign parents. Then what?"

"All A's her first semester at UGA. No behavior marks against her. No problems until she called police on Baxter Carlisle, which is not yet noted in her files. Her advisor is Ludlow Parsons. You might want to contact him."

"You bet I might."

"As I said, she's not for real," Web said. "Somebody faked that transcript. As a math major, she'd have the knowledge and skill to put back doors on computers, but I'll find out if she did or not when I get crackin'. Maybe an agency did it for her."

It popped into my mind. *The Witness Security Program.* I crossed my fingers against being involved in a WitSec case. The Marshals Service hasn't proven itself foolproof in keeping fake identities protected. Otherwise thriller writers would have to devise other plots.

As if Web zeroed on my wavelength, he said, "You know that the Witness Security Program doesn't only shield people testifying against drug lords and mafia types, they protect people who will rat on terrorist organizations."

"Like foreigners. Cho Martine's resume is phony, but she's a real person." I thought about all her personalities. "If she didn't attend Franklin, which has bogus records of her, then where did she attend?"

"I'll find out," Web said, and I could see the steel glinting in his geeky gray eyes.

"Run down Cho Martine's parents, if they are her parents. I'll corner the advisor today."

I heard the doorbell chime *Für Elise,* by Beethoven. "Gotta go, Web. Talk later."

Baxter stood on the stoop looking like a male model holding an umbrella with one hand and an obvious bag of food in the other. It was how he carried it that made me laugh—waist high, knuckles showing. "I already raided the cinnamon rolls in the freezer," I said, standing aside for him to drip in his own foyer. "Lake is responsible for the missing chocolate cupcakes."

Smiling happily, he handed me the bag of food. He was, after all, a restaurateur and delighted in pleasing palates. He placed the wet umbrella in a stand in the corner and hooked his expensive raincoat on a hanger in the coat closet.

He followed me into the kitchen where I poured two cups of coffee and asked, "Why are you up and out so early?"

"I was never down or in last night."

I sipped from the cup and scrutinized his face. Not a puff under or around either eye, no lines, no blear covering the eyeballs. How can he be so perfect? "You make me sick. Look at me. Bloodshot and puffy."

"After closing last night, I drove by and saw the lights on."

That statement made me shiver, and I tightened both hands on the cup. This place wasn't on his way home. But it was on his way to Cho Martine's condo. Whatever; I don't like people spying on me. "What else did you see?" I asked, thinking about my car. I knew the answer before he said it.

"I saw the Athens Police Department tow away your car."

"Am I the investigator or the investigated?"

He held up a hand. "Don't be offended. I'm concerned about you."

"I can take care of myself, thank you very much."

When I refused to say why they took the car, he made a grumpy face. Then he hitched his shoulders and grinned. I got the feeling Baxter let a lot of crap roll off him without a second thought. He said, "I saw Rick leave. I went home. I got worried. When I came back by, his car was still gone and the authorities came."

"You're creeping me out."

"I'm keeping an eye on you. You're getting me out of this mess."

"I'll get dressed. I need a ride to a car rental agency."

"I'll be happy to deliver you to wherever it is you want to go."

I came from the bedroom carrying my possessions in the overnight bag. He said, "Leave that here. You can stay as long as you want."

"I stay mobile, Bax. I never know where a case takes me."

"Keep the keys and the garage opener."

He retrieved his coat and umbrella, and I slung my peacoat over my shoulders. I wished it had a hood. Bax poked around in the umbrella stand and came out with a large, heavy canvas umbrella and handed it over. The rain slanted into us as we made for his car.

We spoke of the ugly winter day until I had to ask him about the cell phone. He was not forthcoming with information, which is often suspicious, but also a sign of self-deprecating reticence. "The cell phone number belongs to a cell phone I keep in my automobile," he said, looking straight ahead. "I have no idea who used it to call Damian at nine-thirty in the evening."

We arrived at the rental agency on Oak Street. He got out and dashed inside, eschewing the umbrella. I chose an American made auto with Bluetooth technology. Outside, Bax asked, "Where would you like to go now?"

Holding the umbrella against a torrent, I told him to go home and get some sleep. He shook his head and asked where I was going. I said I was going alone to the Athens cop station. "Come by for lunch," he said. "We're not open, but I'll have Oliver prepare something delicious."

I didn't answer since I didn't know where the day would take me.

He just stood there, waiting, looking abject with soaking streams drenching his glorious hair and sheeting off his sculpted nose.

I blinked at him—thinking *fool get out of the rain,* but laughing at his romanticism. I asked, "Oliver's a cook, too?"

His eyes sparked. "New York Culinary."

"I'm impressed, but don't count on me being there." I thought about the scarecrow and the clip and where was Lake that he hadn't called me yet?

"Fair enough. When this is over, we'll prepare a banquet for you and Rick."

"Fair enough. Now get out of the rain!"

At the cop shop, the first person I saw was Felix talking to the desk guy. He averted his eyes like he wanted me to ignore him. So I did. I asked the clerk if Sergeant Perry Thomas was in. He shook his head no. I asked if Special Agent Hagan was back in Athens, letting him know that I knew Joe had gone to Atlanta.

"Haven't heard," the disinterested man said. "You want to wait for Sergeant Thomas?"

"If I may." I held up my cell phone. "Can I go someplace to make phone calls?"

At that point, Felix intervened. "I'm ready for a break." He looked at the desk officer. "Can you spare me half an hour? I'll bring you a latte." The desk man seemed wary, and Felix said, "You can put it down as a bribe."

The officer shrugged. "The grande one. Be back by eight-thirty."

Outside, Felix looked at the rental. "I heard they took your car. Nobody's saying why. It's a need-to-know thing."

I got into the passenger side of the police car, told him about the scarecrow and the money clip on the way to the internet café. I also said that I'd gone to the café with Cho yesterday.

"FYI, we don't think that's the last place Cho and Damian were together."

"Can you talk about it?"

"Nobody told me I couldn't, but it's between you and me— unless we go under oath."

I liked this cop more and more. "What's the last place?"

"The Nature Center."

"Who saw . . . ?"

My cell sent strains of Haydn echoing through the cop car's

interior. Lake. His voice sent delightful tremors through my interior. "What's up, Lieutenant?"

"No fingerprints on the cell cover. It's pebbled leather. Chainsaw cut down the tree. They're still collecting at the scarecrow. I'm on my way to Athens now. I'll need to talk to Henry again, have him identify photographs of the clothes. Damian's name was stamped on the collar and waistband. Not sewn."

"I'm with Felix now. He told me that Damian and Cho were last seen at the Sandy Creek Nature Center. We're about finished, so I'm headed there, but first I'm going to rent a bike. Can't drive on the trail."

"I'm half an hour away. I'll stop by the shop and check in with Thomas, then I'll run you down."

"Such talk."

When we walked outside the café, me fighting with the umbrella and Felix carrying a cardboard tray with three cups of coffee, Sergeant Thomas hailed us from his squad car. I said quickly into the cell, "Gotta go. Thomas just drove up. Webdog got some interesting stuff on Cho Martine. Bye-o."

Tucking the phone into my pocket, I walked to the driver-side door. "Good morning."

"You're out early," Thomas said.

"Got a lot to do. Any news on Damian, the scarecrow, and his money clip?"

"You mean you haven't talked to the Atlanta PD guy, *Lieutenant* Lake, or *Special Agent* Joe?"

Cops and their rank envy. "Just fingerprint results on the cell."

He nodded and looked like he wasn't going to say anything else, so I said, "I dropped by your shop."

"I heard." He glared at Felix.

"I wanted to clear my itinerary with you."

"What's that?"

107

"Speak to Arne Trammel, and Ludlow Parsons, Damian's advisor . . ."

He waved impatiently, and said, "You know you don't need my okay to talk to people."

I wanted to tell the jerk it was a courtesy. "I like to work with police."

"That's good to know," he said, pulling the gear shift, and looking at Felix. "Kona, you finished here?"

"Yes, sir."

Thomas cruised away, and I turned to Felix. "Hope you're not in trouble?"

"I'm not. He's that way with everyone. Actually, they call me one of his favorites."

"I'd hate to be one of his un-favorites."

Felix asked me not to go directly to the Nature Center because Thomas would know that he'd clued me. I told him that Lake planned to meet me there and if Thomas said anything, tell him I asked where I can rent a bike because Henry told me that Damian's bicycle was missing. It's not genius to put two and two together. Two clues to Damian's disappearance were found on water trails and Athens has one—the River Greenway.

"Who reported seeing Cho and Damian on the Greenway?" I asked.

"Security there knows Damian and his fancy bike. They don't know Cho, but they said it looked like her from the back."

"Riding a bike?"

He laughed. "No, the girl was on skates."

CHAPTER TWELVE

The yellow arm of a gate was open and I pedaled past the sign that said this was the Sandy Creek Nature Center. *Hadn't Henry said they'd lived in Sandy Springs? Creek. Springs. Coincidence? I'm not fond of them.*

A sign spelled out the nature of the Sandy Creek Nature Center: "Environment, Natural Science, & Appropriate Technology Center." By all means, be appropriate.

I'd rented the bike from a shop on South Milledge, along with helmet, pads, and a water bottle. Don't know why the water bottle. It was cold, and the rain promised to make a day of it.

What a pain in the butt that geek was. Even though I told him I owned a Contessa Spark, he refused to rent me one that he had. He made a concession though, and, not knowing me and my skills, as he said, would take a chance with the Contessa 50. It was a good solid bike under the seat, and sold for a thousand less than a Spark.

I pedaled along the park road, a half mile through the woods to the North Oconee River Greenway. It was slippery going and a heavy mist spread across my coat's dark material. I smelled the river, and then got intermittent glimpses of the mud-red water lapping at its banks. With the rain coming down in earnest, this path would soon flood. The path segues onto city streets, and I crossed at North Avenue and rode the smooth rolling Contessa into Dudley Park. I halted at the Murmur

Trestle, an old wooden CSX railroad overpass that was partly torn down. The reason it was only partly dismantled was because the famous ruin that spans Trail Creek was featured on a rock band's first album, titled *Murmur*. The R.E.M. band was bred, born, and nurtured in Athens, and fans raised holy hell when CSX started taking apart the trestle. The bike geek told me that they were going to extend the trail and refurb the overpass if a one-cent tax was passed at the next election.

Another R.E.M. landmark was Weaver D's, near where I stood astride the bike by the Greenway's bridge over the North Oconee River at East Broad Street. An R.E.M. tune was going to stay in my head all damn day—about the one I love.

Get the hell out of the rain!

I was hesitant to push the pedals because something significant was connected to this place besides R.E.M. Having learned that Damian's bike and oars were missing, it seemed a good plan to check out the woods, creeks, and marshes around the town. There are dauntless plenty of them, but Felix had narrowed the territory for me. The Greenway isn't much of a challenge for experienced riders and the bike Damian owned showed him to be one, so why was he tarrying along a concrete path next to a girl on roller skates? Anyway there were no oars on the banks of Trail Creek and I pushed off.

Along the three mile trail were several spots of overhanging tree branches, thick tall grasses, and brush understory. The river angled away to the east, and the kudzu and wisteria were so tangled they created green arching caves. When the invasive vines became less invasive I dismounted and led the bike into the scrub pines at the water's edge. The river was rising, and I didn't see any bikes or oars.

Rolling again, I wondered, *what is it about trails*? What did it mean that his personal possessions turned up on water trails? With the exception of his money clip, trails figured large in Damian's departure. The Treasure Hunt theory, innocent or malevolent, wasn't setting well and the chattering whisper of ghosts at the edges of my sanity rose anew. Maybe they were telling me if I got out of the fog and rain I wouldn't be so spooked.

I rode on to the Nature Center and locked the bike in a stand under the long green entryway of the ENSAT building, where technology was appropriate. Inside, the one-story building was deliciously warm. A middle-aged woman wearing a name tag with "Miss Davis" printed on it came through a door and offered to brush my coat. She returned with a toilet brush. My eyes must have said it all, because she laughed and said it was never used for its intended purpose. I had to believe her. And it did a good job of squeeging the wool of my coat.

"I saw you go on the trail," she said. "I was just arriving. I was late. We open at eight-thirty but no one comes early this time of year. In this weather, no one comes at all. You ask me, better conservation of resources to open at eleven and close at dusk when the trails close."

I couldn't disagree, but I'd learned a long time ago to hold my tongue on civic and political issues. I introduced myself and showed her my license and card.

"Child Trace, Inc.," she said, handing it back. I told her to keep the card. She looked worried. "Some little kid going missing?"

"Not little," I explained. "I'm looking for Damian Hansel."

"Ahhh . . . him," she said. "So bad for his father. I told him to hold out hope. He was here, you know."

Henry hadn't told me, but he must have made the same assumptions that I did. Miss Davis said the police had come on Monday to search the Greenway, and I asked her how well she knew Damian.

"Well as I want to," she said, then her mouth made a guilty O for speaking ill of the possibly dead. I was talking to a realist and urged her to speak plainly, saying that it might be the key to finding him. She said, "I'm not a supervisor, and I told him several times he needed to go to the top with his ideas."

"What ideas?" *As if I didn't know.*

"I don't like his art, and I don't want it here, but I didn't tell him that. Bold as brass he was, but if the powers want his sense- less twigs, that's for them to say."

Twigs. Ideas. A gap in the synapse of my brain transmitted an idea, not well-formed yet, but a hint of what Damian was up to.

I asked her, "You couldn't put up a picture or two?" She looked accusingly at me, and I said, "Damian seems to have wanted to spread his work all over Athens."

"Truth, I could have, but I didn't want to."

"Good enough."

"Him missing. I'm sure they'll find him. Those artists, they have nutty ideas. Go off half cocked. He isn't the only one. One screwball wanted to have the Murmur Trestle painted orange."

"Orange?"

"He said he wanted it to express the novel *Clockwork Orange.* That movie was a disgrace. My husband, rest his soul, we went to the movies that night. We heard it was good. Well, we walked out after ten minutes."

The door opened and Lake walked in. He had a crimson bicycle helmet under one arm. His hair was rain-sodden, and he looked so good I wanted to throw myself at him. Since I've learned self-control I primly introduced Lake. "Miss Davis. This is Atlanta Police Detective Richard Lake."

He nodded and said, "Pleasure, Miss Davis." She looked at him as if she thought he didn't look like any detective she knew, either from fiction or real life. Then seeing his rain jacket drip- ping on her floor, she scurried away, promising to return with something to wipe away the rain.

"Where'd you get the bike?" I asked.

"Same place as you. Milledge Street. Twenty minutes to rent a damn bicycle."

"What did you have to beg for?"

"You got the best available. I got a Perimeter. It's a nice enough ride for conditions."

Not nearly as nice as his own, which is a Fezzari Fore. Lake and I rode fifty miles at least twice a month when our schedules and the weather permitted. Lately in drought-ridden Atlanta, rain was not a problem.

He asked, "Did you see anything on the trail?"

"No, but plenty of places to hide bikes and oars."

"And bodies?"

"I'm not sure about bodies yet." I told him about the screwball wanting to paint the Murmur Trestle orange.

"Damian's father's putting up a good front. I went by the shop before I got the bike. Hansel was waiting for me. He recognized the clothes from my photographs. Somebody's playing us."

"It's looking like an art prank."

"Damian's father didn't say it was a prank, but possibly a concept Damian's trying to pull off."

"Did you tell him that when the concept is realized, it's going to cost him and Damian some serious money for the time spent investigating his disappearance?"

"It isn't against the law to disappear."

I heard Miss Davis's scurrying footsteps and lowered my voice. "You ready to tackle Arne Trammel?"

"Anxious to."

Lake took the large towel from Miss Davis. "Thank you, ma'am." He wiped the water from his face and neck. "This is temporary since I'm fixing to go out into the rain again."

"Put that towel around your neck and keep it warm," she said.

He smiled and said, "I think I will." And so he did.

No offer of a towel for me, though.

Outside, we unlocked the bikes. Lake said, "Fifteen bucks to rent a padlock. Can you believe?"

"Baxter's paying."

We pushed off, heading onto the North Oconee River Greenway, the silver rain pelting my face, the birds sounding like crumpling paper as they scattered over the river. Halfway to Dudley Park, Lake halted and let one of his long legs act as a kickstand. "You should have gotten yourself a towel," he said, adjusting his wet neckerchief.

Putting a foot on the ground, I flipped the collar of my peacoat at him. It was doing an all right job of keeping my neck dry. The coat is large on me because it's a man's. It had belonged to my late fiancé. He put it around my shoulders at a Braves game one cold Atlanta night. It's been mine ever since.

We discussed the placing of artifacts on the trails. Damian's other things had been in plain sight and agreed it would be natural for the missing oars to be found by a river. Lake said when the rain halted we'd rent or borrow a canoe and search the banks.

My mind fastened on the money clip. It wasn't on a trail. The prank now involved me.

Rolling again, we scouted the Greenway—me right, Lake left. The rain had let up a bit when we stopped at the bottom of the Murmur Trestle where Trail Creek was gaining momentum from runoff. "It's still in dispute," I said.

"About what," Lake said, adjusting himself and his bike alongside me and mine.

"Whether the trestle is going to stay or go."

"Looks damn near gone."

"You know the story, don't you?" He frowned as if he wondered what it had to do with our being here. "R.E.M. had a photograph of it on their first album cover, *Murmur*. It was the early eighties. Years before my time, but R.E.M. fans from all over came to see it. It's still a landmark. *Automatic for the people*."

"What are you talking about?"

"Fuddy-duddy, it's one of their album titles, too." I glanced over the trestle. "Years later, the railroad company started to tear down the trestle and R.E.M. fans put up such a cry, they stopped. Then the city bought the land to build a rail trail, like in Atlanta, but the trestle was deemed too unstable. . . ."

"*¡Ay, caramba!*"

His terse shout startled me. "What?"

"Look up there."

"Where?"

"Let's get closer."

We wobbled our way to the edge of the creek that flows under the trestle. "Look up," Lake said.

"My eyelids do not have wipers," I said, squinting up, blinking into the rain. Then I saw it—them.

Someone had threaded two oars into trestle's upper timbers.

"I'll be a son-of-a-bitch." He took out his cell phone. He spoke briefly then looked at me. "Was this a plot?"

"Plot?"

"You were here earlier. Did you lead me here so I could *discover* the oars?"

"I'm not that generous. I had the strangest feeling when I was here, but I couldn't connect to it."

"Wooooooo."

"Hush. I couldn't explore thoroughly, because I had to get back to meet you. So there."

"She doth protest too much."

We walked around the trestle—the timbers of which were sunk into concrete foundations—checking for marks in the mud or things on the ground. Lake said, "Forensics is going to have fun finding evidence."

"I need to catch you up on what Web's come up with," I said.

"Don't tell me how he got the info."

Grinning, I tossed my head and told him about Kirin Littlefield, her stepfather and father of her daughter, Damian Hansel's school and travel resume, and, as I was about to lay the bomb about Martine on him, I heard a car door and looked up to see Felix get out of his squad car. He'd driven on the trail. I guess if foul deeds are done, driving a car on the trail was allowed.

Lake pointed toward the oars. "Son of a gun," Felix said.

Sergeant Thomas came next. "Well, I'll be damned."

Joe was a minute behind Thomas. "Well, fuck me."

The five of us stared into the timbers. Thomas said, "This is the craziest damn thing . . . Everybody knows that trestle is dangerous. A boy fell off it couple years ago."

Joe walked around and under the trestle. "Wait until I get hold of the morons who did this. Goddamn waste of resources. I'll get the lab." He trekked back to his squad car.

Joe was a proponent of the harmless Treasure Hunt theory by art students turned morons.

Lake said, "Sergeant, unless you need us, we'll mosey on and talk with some folks. Have you talked to Arne Trammel?"

Thomas said, "On Saturday, when he was bitching about Damian being missing. He had no clue where he could have gone, except he accused Martine of making him disappear."

"He say how?"

"Nah, he was upset because they were working on some mumbo-jumbo art crap."

Lake studied the oars. "Could Trammel be doing this?"

He chewed his lower lip as he considered. "He's from Gaines-ville, Georgia. Probably knows Atlanta pretty good, too."

"What about Martine?"

He shrugged. "We got the complaint ready for her to sign, but so far she's a no-show. Fine with me. You showing up on the Greenway, you probably know she was seen with the Hansel kid that day. Maybe they put the oars there. I got to send my people up to get them, and that puts them in danger."

I probably should tell him about Web's research on Cho, but I'd discuss it with Lake first. And I wanted to give Web time to dig deeper and find the Martine couple. They were not fictions, but I very much doubted they were the parents of our Cho Martine.

Thomas was saying, "I'm not liking Baxter Carlisle for all this crap even if he don't have a solid alibi for putting stuff on trails."

"Strange case," Lake said.

"And promises to get stranger," I said.

Thomas shrugged again. "It's these artists. You mix students and art—same with music—and you got a bunch of maggot fuckers."

I couldn't even imagine . . .

Lake asked, "You got my cell number, right?"

"Yep," Thomas said, brightening at our leaving. When his radio crackled out a call, we walked our bikes back to the trail. I said, "Can we get warm? I got some news from Web."

"I thought you'd never ask." He patted his tummy and looked at his watch. "Past one. No wonder I'm starved."

"What'd you have for breakfast?"

"Sausage-egg-cheese biscuits and pancakes."

"Baxter said Oliver would fix us a delicious lunch."

"I got a better idea. Let's go to the condo. I need to shower and dry out. They got food there."

Perry Thomas's squad car eased past us and turned onto North Avenue. He hit the lights and siren. Lake stopped and so did I. Lake said, "Wonder where he's going in such a hurry? Want to follow?"

I laughed. "Let's tackle Arne Trammel." When Lake hesitated. I said, "If he's a real artist, he'll think nothing of a cop and a PI showing up on his doorstep on bikes, soaking wet."

"If you say so."

No matter if we rode north, south, east, or west, the rain slanted straight into my face. Maybe it has something to do with travel dynamics. We pedaled by the Jackson Street Cemetery and turned onto South Lumpkin. We glided past UGA buildings when Lake pulled up short and I almost bumped him.

"Tire going flat," he said. We pushed on to the bike shop. While the bike geek changed the tire, Lake talked to Atlanta PD.

"Anything new?" I asked.

"Not with the Hansel case, but there was a homicide at the Rave Club on Simpson in the Bluff. During questioning, the shooter wanted to bargain info. Said a large drug buy was going down in Big DD's territory over the weekend. By the way, your driveway has new white gravel, your yard new grass, and your busted window is paned again."

We were back out in the mist, pushing off. I said, "DD's power is growing. He beat a rap. He's *the man.*"

"Narco's hearing he'll skip, maybe Miami. Be an even bigger kingpin."

We wheeled around the corner onto Milledge. Damian's apartment building had official visitors. Two squad cars were parked on the street, their blue lights flashing. Lake sped ahead and turned onto the cracked walkway. The door to Damian's apartment was open. So was the one two doors away.

Perry Thomas walked out of the one two doors away. He spoke into a cell phone. Lake leaned his bike against a tree. So did I.

I heard someone call my name and Felix came from behind, on the run.

"What's up?" I asked.

He breathed out. "Arne Trammel's dead."

No.

"When?" Lake asked.

"Awhile."

"How awhile?" I asked.

"Days. Monday, maybe. Hung himself in a closet."

"Son-of-a-bitch," Lake said, and hurried to where Thomas stood on the sidewalk, the phone plugged into the side of his head. Thomas held the phone away and said to Lake, "Get covers, Lieutenant. Go on in. M.E.'s on the way."

Lake handed me the towel from around his neck and I wrung it out, having unconsciously realized that the rain had stopped. I looked up. From the looks of the black-bottomed silver streaks overhead, it was a momentary reprieve.

I followed Lake. No one shouted for me to halt. Felix lifted the lid to Thomas's car trunk and ripped three pairs of forensic booties from a box. I hung the towel over my shoulder and followed Lake and Felix up the three steps to Trammel's door. Under the overhang, I pulled on the latex covers and followed them into a living room filled with tables and easels. I smelled him, but the decomp wasn't enough to gag me yet. Drawings were scattered on tables; oil and watercolor paintings were pinned to frames on the easels. Leaving that room, Lake tugged at the towel on my shoulder and pinched his nose, a signal to use the towel. I'm sensitive to odors.

Felix and Lake put on hand covers. Wrapping the towel around my lower face, I put my uncovered hands in my peacoat pockets. I heard someone behind me and turned. Sergeant Thomas pushed ahead and turned into the open doorway at hall's end. He spread his covered hands, looking ready to lecture. "You know the drill. You know what this is going to look like." He stared at me. "Being law enforcement, you seen it before, haven't you?"

I nodded.

"No puking, okay?"

"I never do," I said behind the mouth muffler.

He actually grinned, a little.

The door to the closet was open. The anticipation, preceded by the odor, is usually worse than the sight, and I steeled myself. I stopped behind Lake and heard him give a slight groan. I'm almost as tall as Lake and could look over his shoulder.

I never puke, but my eyes water when I see young flesh reviled. By anybody's hand. By one's own hand is especially appalling.

My first thought was the impossibility of the act, that the closet was narrow and the ceiling low, that a grasping hand could stop the struggle.

No doubt glaringly dead, I didn't need to let my eyes linger on that fat tongue and engorged face. It shone like plastic. From his shoulders, he hung like a long sack of cotton. I noticed how rumpled his clothes were and that was what made me think cotton. His neck was elongated. I closed my eyes, feeling my marrow liquefying, oozing through bone. Lake's hand went to my shoulder in a buck-up gesture. He knew that death had a terrible effect on me. I pressed my lips and nodded my head. My glance went to Trammel's feet. So did Lake's. Naked, they were less than a foot off the floor. Oddly, one of his large toes touched a shoe on the floor. He could have saved himself if he'd had a second's change of mind. A folding chair lay collapsed against the back wall where he'd presumably kicked it away.

Sergeant Thomas said, "These short drop hangings are brutal. No clean, quick execution by long drop. You'll find he died from slow suffocation." He tossed a hand toward the dead man's head. "Rope's pretty new and with a horseman's knot. If you're going to hang yourself, get acquainted with a hangman's knot."

Lake said, "I see no evidence of autoeroticism."

"Me, neither," Thomas said. "Those playing the choking game have their knots in the back of their necks—and it's a proper hangman's knot."

Thomas's offense at the knot had me studying it. It was on the left side of his neck and the release end looked to be about two inches long, as if the knot-maker didn't want to waste rope. Then I was struck by the gauge of the red and white rope. No more than a child's jump rope without the handles.

"And," Lake said, "autoerotics are usually naked, except for duct tape and straps around their bodies."

Thomas shook his head. "You wonder about these things." He sighed, "People."

I kept looking at the knot. I held the towel away from my mouth and asked, "Was he right handed or left?"

Lake nodded. "Good girl. Suicides hang themselves from their handed side."

"Nothing more we can do here for now," Thomas said. "Felix you go on and find out the particulars about kin from the university."

Felix saluted and left.

"Who found him?" Lake asked.

"Anonymous phone tip to the station." He had an odd look on his face. "You two got here sooner than I expected."

"Anything on where the call came from?" Lake asked.

He'd been so forthright, his eyes going wily told me it was about Baxter. "Power House."

In my memory of ten years ago, I saw the row of phones

along a back wall in Power House. A printed sign above them said local calls were free. The words had been obscured by the scribbles of patrons. I also remembered Power House's hours and checked my watch. "Power House wouldn't be open. It's just four-thirty now. They used to open at five."

"Still do," Thomas said. "I called Baxter to meet us there."

CHAPTER THIRTEEN

At the bike rental shop, Lake asked the owner to store the bikes for us. We still had some time on the day rate. I got in Lake's squad car and heard the clunk of the windshield wipers. We had two inches of rain and it still streaked into the fog, glistening like strips of metal.

We braked to see Baxter key open Power House's doors—first the heavy doubles, then the old-fashioned swinging barroom type. Inside, he released the alarms.

Inside, physically the place hadn't changed in years. Like walking into a time capsule, it still had the same dark wood and brick walls, a long walnut bar with an old-fashioned wall mirror reflecting rows of liquor bottles and taps. The mirror distortion hadn't changed, either. Way back then, I watched myself get snockered in the fun house. The stale boozy smell assembled by forty years of quaffing hundreds of varieties of beers was signature Power House. Cigarette smoke of yore had embedded itself in the brick and wood. But overriding all this was an obscene odor—one of meanness and evil. Of dirty jeans and filthy skin and oily hair. An odor new to Power House since my days here.

I walked to the side door and looked into the second room. Still here was the pool table, video game machines, dart boards (how I loved to beat Portia at darts), and shuffleboards. The marks of a jumping game on the floor were nearly invisible now. Playing drunk usually resulted in skinned knees.

I came back to where Lake stood. Baxter came toward us looking like a huffy movie star. For some reason, he'd turned the multitude of televisions on. On football Saturdays, the walls flashed red because all channels were tuned to the University of Georgia game. UGA had cracked down (seriously) on taking booze inside the stadium, so, for we hardcore drinkers, this was the perfect laid-back bar after a morning of tailgating.

Baxter threw car keys on the bar. "What is this about?"

Lake smoothed his wet hair. "Were you here earlier, say two o'clock?"

"No," Baxter said. "I don't open Power House. My bartenders do. At five o'clock." His eyes roamed over Lake and me. His bright smile flashed for an instant. "Look at you. You've been playing in the rain." When I told him we'd been riding bikes in the rain he looked solemn. "Not the best day, to my way of thinking. Sergeant Thomas called to meet me here. Now you're here, too. So I must ask: what is this all about?"

"He's going to ask you if you made any phone calls from here this afternoon."

"At two o'clock, you mean?"

Lake nodded.

"Then I shall tell him that I did not."

I asked Baxter, "You still got the old wall phones back by the restrooms?"

"Only one now. For broadband and Wi-Fi." He brushed straying strands from his forehead. "Who am I supposed to have called?"

"Someone called Athens PD from here and gave an anonymous tip."

"That someone was not me."

"Where have you been this afternoon?" I asked.

His eyes damn near glared. "You *are* working *for* me, right?"

"I'm looking for Damian Hansel and for facts surrounding

Cho Martine's accusations against you. And, yes, you are paying me to find both."

"Fair enough." His eyes shifted to Lake.

Through the plate glass, I saw the police car stop behind Lake's.

Baxter crossed his arms. "Early this morning I went to Lionell Place to check on Dru." He canted his head toward me. "She can confirm that. I knew about her car being towed away in the night. Then, I went back home and had a bite to eat, updated the menu on my website, ordered wine over the net, which I do myself, and finally reviewed spreadsheets until Thomas called me to come here. I believe computers have timelines and you're welcome to check mine."

Thomas walked in the door. Baxter offered his hand. Thomas seemed a split second reluctant to take it, but in the next instant grabbed onto it. Two short chops, and the greeting ended.

"Lieutenant Lake told me about the anonymous call," Baxter said. "I know nothing about it. I've worked on my PC nearly all day at my home on Prince Avenue. You may check it."

Sergeant Thomas nodded like he would certainly be doing that. He said, "The call came from a landline number at this location."

Baxter turned toward the rear of the tavern. "Let's see what's going on back there."

"No," Thomas called. Halting, Baxter looked over his shoulder. Thomas said that the lab folks would be here shortly to go over the place. In the meantime Bax recited his whereabouts today and ended by saying that he couldn't remember the last time he'd used the landline here.

I spoke up. "Spoofing."

Thomas said, "What?"

"Telephone spoofing. There's an app for it. On Caller ID, the caller plugs in a different number than the real telephone number from which he's calling."

"That's illegal."

Lake almost rolled his eyes. "Next to murder, a mere foible."

Thomas wasn't amused. I said, "Actually it isn't illegal. It might be if the House ever gets around to passing a bill. I hope they don't."

"Why not?"

"We use it. Most PIs do to protect their real phone numbers from Caller ID. It undoubtedly happened with Bax's cell phone the night Damian disappeared."

The shrewd expression in Thomas's eyes told me he'd considered that possibility. "Most of that spoofing, as you call it, is students. We can find out the real number."

"Sometimes you can't," I said. "Depending on how smart the spoofer is. Also, spoofing apps have voice-changing ability."

"It's something we'll be looking into," he said, eyeing Baxter like he was a spoofer, a voice-changer as well as a murderer.

A man dressed as an old-fashioned bartender entered. Baxter gave a nod to his surprised face. The man acknowledged with a finger wave and walked past to the back room.

Baxter said, "For your information, Sergeant, I'm going to sell this place."

That transition seemed to perplex Thomas. "You losing money here?"

"Quite the contrary, but this place has never been my favorite bar, and you know what's been happening here lately. I can't get anyone to help me clear out or control the rednecks."

"Watch who you're calling a redneck, Mr. Carlisle."

"You know I'm not talking about honest-to-God farmers, Sergeant. I'm talking about the trailer trash from up the road. I've asked you, and your predecessors, to help me get this place back to a fun bar for students, but no one hears me."

"There's a lot of bars in Athens, Mr. Carlisle. Rednecks have to go somewhere to buy their beer. Maybe if you didn't offer a hundred brands of beer—some pretty cheap especially at Happy Hour—then maybe they'd stay home in their trailers."

Baxter flicked his eyebrows. "Be that as it may be. And since we've cleared up the telephone mystery . . ."

"I don't know that we have," Thomas said.

"I need to go to Carlisle's," Baxter said.

"If you travel much farther, let me know."

"I'm not traveling," Baxter said. He scooped his keys off the bar, turned to me and said, "Come for dinner, at any time." He hurried off before I could answer.

Crossing his arms, Thomas surveyed us. "Isn't it funny, he didn't ask what the anonymous tip was about?"

"Maybe he doesn't want to know," Lake said.

"Isn't it great," I said to Lake when we were seated inside the squad car. "You don't have to dole out duties to men under you. You don't have to take orders from your commander. We can just go and find Damian Hansel and who killed Arne Trammel all on our own."

"What a cheerful girl you are, and what an ideal prospect," he said, reaching over and shaking my knee. "But first, let's get to the condo where I can get dry, have a drink, and phone home." Home to Lake was the cop house.

Lake stopped at the bike shop, and I got into the midsize rental car. As I was pulling out, with Lake on my bumper, two male students passed on the sidewalk. I got the weirdest feeling and thought about Damian and Arne, buddies, traveling companions, two young men I'd never seen alive. Could there be any doubt that Damian was dead? Did Arne kill him and then himself? Was this all over Cho? I tried to keep the only image I had of Arne from my head, but I couldn't. He hung there like a horror-house ghoul, only he'd been real.

A short mildly impatient toot came from behind. Lake, telling me to get a move on.

Before my cell could play Haydn, the Bluetooth voice told me Baxter Carlisle wanted to speak. My elderly cars don't have Bluetooth, and the hands-free system takes getting used to.

"Where are you?" Bax asked.

"Driving to Lionell Place. Lake needs to change . . ."

"I need to know what's going on. It's like I'm in a nightmare. Oliver tells me you should keep me better informed."

I told him to come to the condo with takeout, lots of it because Lake missed lunch and the dinner hour was nigh. "We can eat and talk. I don't know how much Lake will want to confide. This is a police matter. You know how secretive they can be."

"My God, you think I'm liable to broadcast this crap to everyone I know?"

In the condo kitchen, I told Lake, "Bax is coming here."

"Fabulous," Lake said, looking not so fabulous at the prospect.

"Funny, at Power House he was annoyed at being inconvenienced, then he calls and all of a sudden wants to know what's going on."

"Sounds like the flake I've always known," Lake said. "Everything's outward appearance with Bax. You never knew what went on in that head of his. Linda used to worry about him."

"In what way?"

"She thought he was a sociopath," he said, going for the fridge.

"I wouldn't think she'd know what a sociopath was."

"Buckhead has its share, and living with Bax, she heard the word, I'm sure."

"Do you think he is?"

"Hmmm," he said, searching the shelves.

"I asked a question."

He glanced over his shoulder. "Baxter isn't a deep person, but he cares. Sociopaths don't care about things and people."

"Not exactly correct, Lieutenant. They can *act* like they care."

"I care about food right now."

"Baxter's bringing food."

"See, Baxter cares."

"He's a restaurateur."

"What's he bringing?"

"His most caring takeout specialty."

"You don't know, do you?"

"Uh-uh. Listen to this. When he called, he said *Oliver* told him he needed to know what was going on."

"It's Oliver who wants to know, is that what you're saying?"

"I see Oliver as his father's protector."

The lines in his face looked etched in wood. "I see Oliver as a possible suspect."

"Why?"

"He had access to Power House."

"You suspect everyone."

He straightened. "You winnow too early. Who's your best guess?"

"I don't guess. What we *know* is that somebody knows Arne is dead. Somebody called Athens PD from one of Baxter's businesses or spoofed the call to Power House when it was closed. All this to implicate Bax. Don't forget the spoofed call from his cell phone."

"Spoofing is as yet an explanation, not proof."

The doorbell symphony blared. Opening the door, I greeted Baxter. Behind him Oliver stood, hands holding big white metal boxes of delicious aromas. I looked over my shoulder at Lake, at the black scowl on his face. He didn't like it that Oliver had come uninvited, even though it was Baxter's condominium and Oliver had given us the keys, and Oliver now carried food, commodities precious to Lake's heart.

We'll get through this, I thought.

Oliver took the boxes into the kitchen, and like a perfect waiter, began to disassemble them. First, the setup: tablecloth, napkins, rings, china, silver, glassware.

Baxter said, "We begin with a fennel and almond soup."

I didn't look at Lake. Liquid licorice and nuts? Oh boy.

Lake went to the refrigerator. "You know me, Bax, I'm happy to graze standing with the fridge door open."

Baxter said, "Oliver will lay the table and prepare the meal for us while we speak in the study."

"Fine," Lake said, holding a wedge of cheddar. "You got any crackers?"

Baxter took the cheese and control of the refrigerator door. "Go into the study. I'll be right there with the Boursin and toast points. After the soup, we'll have boeuf tenderloin with caramelized onions and horseradish."

Lake beamed. "Be damned, Baxter. You remembered. Linda's specialty. My weakness."

"Asparagus topped with wilted spinach."

"Another favorite," Lake said.

"And for dessert, cherry cheesecake with rum whipped cream."

Lake had a hungry grin on his face when we entered the study. I leaned against a credenza and studied the oriental rug, a beauty with a white background and blue birds-of-paradise. Lake and Baxter sat on white leather chairs. Without ceremony, Lake told Baxter about the scarecrow and the money clip in the Audi. Baxter said that the money clip sounded like one he'd seen Damian carry. "And," he said, "that leaves me out. I was in jail at the time. I certainly wasn't at Nancy Creek Trail with Damian and his money clip."

"I'd bet the clip never left Athens," I said. Baxter looked like I'd betrayed him.

"This stuff's good," Lake said, biting into a toast point.

"What was that anonymous tip about?" Baxter asked.

Lake stood. The look on his face said he didn't want to spoil the meal by telling Baxter about Arne Trammel's death. "We'll get to that, I'm starved."

Baxter stood and glanced at me. "Rick and his food. And look at him, a thirty-inch waist and a body mass index of an underwear model."

I laughed. I once told Lake he could be an underwear model, not that I would encourage that. I had enough competition as it was without fighting off gay men, too.

Turns out, Lake slurped the fennel and almond soup like it was a hearty Brunswick stew. I ate the soup but passed on the steak. Arne Trammel's hanging in the closet like a side of beef didn't do anything for meat-eating. The spinach-topped asparagus was divine. The wines were fine, too.

The cherry cheesecake turned me flat off. Reminded me of Arne's face. Lake ate three large wedges. Meal over, Oliver wrapped the leftovers and refrigerated them. He began the cleanup, which was putting all the dirty things into the white boxes to be returned to the restaurant and its hyper-hot dishwasher.

I followed Lake and Baxter into the study. Lake faced Baxter and said abruptly, "Arne Trammel is dead."

Baxter's face went whiter than the walls. If Baxter knew about Arne's death, he's a candidate for an Oscar. Trying to speak, his mouth reminded me of a goldfish's.

Lake said, "Appears it happened a couple days ago."

Baxter staggered to a white chair. "Happened?" he breathed

out. "Happened?"

Something about his reaction mystified. *Happened.* That's all he could say? Most people would say *what happened,* or asked how.

Lake waited while Baxter stared at the floor like he was counting the feathers on a bird-of-paradise.

"*Paradisaea rudolphi,*" Baxter said. "From Papua, New Guinea, exclusively. Hunted for its plumes. On the world's Vulnerable List." He looked at Lake. "Related to crows and jays; family *Corvidae.*"

Lake ran his foot over the carpet. "You inherited this rug from your and Linda's mother, I remember. She knew all about birds-of-paradise."

"She went there, you know?" Baxter said. "Had to see them in the wild. The males, when they're mating, they hang upside down from a branch and fan their violet plumes." He folded his hands and hung them between his knees. His thumbs worked a steady rhythm. He looked up at Lake. "Would you do that for Dru?"

Lake grinned. "It wouldn't be as impressive a sight, but if she wanted me to, I would."

Baxter straightened and sat back. "This is about the anonymous call to the police from Power House, isn't it?" Lake nodded. Baxter fingered his collar. "I didn't really know him. I really didn't like him. But I didn't kill him."

"Nobody says . . ."

Bax raised his hand. "They will. I was there, at his place, you see."

Lake's eyes narrowed. "You saw him dead?"

"No, Sunday he was very much alive and wagging his fat tongue at me."

Oh my God—the fat tongue. Was this an inadvertent misspeak on his part? I glanced at Lake. Did he catch it? I couldn't tell.

"Why would you go to Arne Trammel's place on Sunday?" Lake asked.

A ticking quiet lengthened. Impatiently, Bax broke in. "Day before, Arne came to the restaurant and accused me of doing something to Damian because Damian didn't show for a party Friday night, and didn't meet him that morning like they'd planned. Then, he warned me against stalking Cho. I told him I wasn't stalking her. It got nastier from there. I stopped by his place on Sunday to apologize for my part in the argument and ask if Damian had returned." He rolled his shoulders as if to ease muscle tension. "Arne was so angry he literally spit at me."

Was he trying to cover a slip of his tongue?

"That the last time you saw Trammel?" Lake reminds me of Dick Tracy when his face looks so unyielding.

"Swear to God."

"Yet, you told us that you hadn't seen Arne since the beer incident in Carlisle's."

"I lied."

"That was dumb. Had you told us sooner, we would have gone to Arne's place sooner and he would have told us about talking to you on Saturday and Sunday. You see how this looks?"

It looked like we should have gone to question Arne sooner than we did, but it wasn't as if we were diddling around. Sometimes you don't grasp your priorities until they're past being priorities.

Baxter said, "I'm a dumb liar, but *I am not* a killer."

"I never said he was murdered."

"Rick, please. Don't play games with me. He was, wasn't he?"

"Maybe. Do you want to know how he died?"

"Not particularly, but you're going to tell me, aren't you?"

"By hanging, slowly choking to death, his fat tongue sticking from his mouth."

Holding a slender glass of Grand Marnier at ten o'clock that evening after Baxter left the condo so badly shaken Oliver had to steady him out the door, I said to Lake, "With all that's happened, I haven't had a chance to tell you that Cho Martine doesn't exist."

"I know," he said.

"You talk to Webdog?"

"Thomas told me they can't find her. A neighbor said she saw her leave about noon. Neighbor said it looked like she had suitcases in the back of her car."

My heart beat bumped up.

Lake went on, "Thomas was waiting for her to come in and sign another complaint."

Sometimes you don't grasp your priorities until they're past being priorities—or they flee.

Lake said, "They want to question her about Arne Trammel, as well as Damian Hansel. Seems Arne was her alibi for being in Athens over the weekend when Arne and she were supposed to have been together looking for Damian."

"Arne's death calls that into question," I said. "One or both could have gone to Atlanta and put the cell phone on the trail, but only Cho could have put the scarecrow on the trail and the money clip in my car's grill, because Arne was dead, and that's *if* she's involved in the disappearance of Damian and the death of Arne."

Lake breathed out, looking dour. "Two college kids kill their friend, string clues from Atlanta to Athens, then one of them kills himself and the other flees?"

"Damian may not be dead and I wouldn't bet Arne Trammel killed himself."

134

"What we *know* is that Trammel's dead, Damian might be dead or not, and Cho Martine is nowhere to be found."

I took a deep breath like I was pushing off for the hundred-meter backstroke. "You weren't listening carefully when I said Cho Martine doesn't exist."

Lake raised his chin and pushed hair from his forehead. Troubled as I was, the gesture still made my heart bounce. He said, "What are you saying?"

I told him what Webdog had reported this morning, and, before I'd finished, he was judging me harshly. "Son-of-a-bitch."

I couldn't breathe for the adrenaline flowing. "I wasn't holding out."

"Yes you were," he said, dead serious. "You wanted to find out her identity by yourself."

"I wanted to find who she was, yes, but . . ."

"Dru, you can't hold back stuff like that. It's clear now, she skipped, and they could have had her before she ran."

Heat rose from the base of my spine. "It was my employee who discovered the information. Thomas and his crowd could have found out if they had investigated Cho's stalking claims against Baxter. They took her word against his, even when her boyfriend went missing. Joe Hagan and Atlanta PD could have found that she was an imposter. All you had to do was a backgrounder, starting with the school."

"Dru, look . . ." He blew slowly from his lungs. "I don't have time to argue with you."

"There's nothing to argue about. When I came into the case, not much had been done by the Athens police. They took Cho Martine's word over that of a longtime citizen of this city. Not until Damian's father came to town demanding answers did they get off their duffs."

"We better brief Thomas and Joe Hagan."

"You might suggest to them that they contact the Martines."

135

He pressed his lips. "Let's go."

"Have they tried yet, or do they *like* to stay behind the curve?"

"Let's go."

"I'm not going anywhere," I said, standing, "except to bathe and get under the covers. I'm exhausted. I've a lot to do tomorrow."

"If Athens PD lets you."

"They damn well better. You got Henry's card." I held out my hand. "Tomorrow I get hold of Henry and check out Damian's apartment."

Lake continued to stare, keeping his mouth tight. When Lake's inflexible it puts my back up. I wriggled my fingers. "Give."

He got up and adjusted the hardware at his belt and under his arm in the official way cops do when they have an objective. "He's staying at the Classic City. Room 268."

"Thanks," I said, to his back when he walked out of the study.

Lake got back to the condo at midnight. "You're awake," he said.

"Observant."

"Let's not argue."

"What did Sergeant Thomas say?"

"We'll discuss it in the morning."

"Now."

"In the morning."

"Did you talk to Webdog?"

"Yes. He confirmed what you told me. He's hasn't been successful locating the Martines."

"And?"

"We'll discuss it in the morning."

I rolled over. "Good night. Close the door on your way out."

CHAPTER FOURTEEN

Located at the Classic Center, the Classic City Hotel is a hop-skip away from Carlisle's. Henry answered his cell promptly. I told him I was in the lobby and that I wanted to see Damian's apartment. While I waited I watched the rain come down, flooding my heart and soul.

Henry Hansel held out his hand to shake without saying hello. Instead, he asked, "Any news about my son?" I shook my head as we walked side-by-side toward the turnstile. "Does that mean something's turned up you can't talk about?"

"Perceptive, Mr. Hansel."

"It's still Henry." At the revolving door, he motioned me to go first. "My car's being brought up from valet."

When he emerged from the stile, I said, "Something has happened. I shouldn't be the one to tell you."

"You want to see my son's place?"

A Mercedes appeared from the underground ramp and stopped. "My car's in the visitor's lot," I said.

He said, "Ride with me and tell me about it."

I'm not fond of brusque orders, but I understood. He pulled from the canopy into the rain, and I said, "It will be on the news soon anyway." I took a deep breath, not to heighten drama but because I don't like to impart bad news. "Arne Trammel is dead."

His foot hit the brake. Tires squealed on the wet pavement. It's a good thing he was approaching the street from the hotel's ramp and not driving in traffic. "No," he said, and hit the steering wheel with a fist. "No."

I watched him closely. His skin had paled; he looked shiny like the cooling dead. "Sorry," I said.

I told him the how of Arne's death, but couldn't come up with the why. I said that the medical examiner would tell us soon enough about the when. Speechless, he reached inside his coat jacket to press his fist against his chest. *Please, don't have a heart attack.*

Both hands on the wheel now, his stiff arms methodically steered the car into the street.

I said, "There are several ways a murderer can make it look like suicide, but there are several ways a medical examiner can see through the attempts."

It took time but he finally found his voice and said that he'd last spoken to Arne Monday morning, that they had gone to Damian's place.

I asked, "What was Arne's mood?"

"Now I think about it, he was distracted. I sensed he wanted to get out of there. He wanted to get away from me."

"Did Arne say anything?"

"He said something about class and left. I locked up and went to see if Cho knew anything."

"Did you talk to her?"

"Monday afternoon, after class. She was upset and vague. All I got out of her was that she and Arne searched possible places over the weekend."

We'd reached Damian's apartment. One squad car and a crime scene van were parked in front of Arne's.

I folded the umbrella and hooked it over the rail while Henry inserted the key. "My boy may be gone, too," he said, and unlatched the door. "I have to get used to that idea."

"You don't know, and, until you do, keep hoping," I said, feeling that Damian was indeed gone.

He pushed the door, and I followed him in. Stale sweat and turpentine had my nose twitching. The oil of the turps, like the idea of death, slid icily beneath my skin.

Walking through stacks of watercolors and drawings on easels, Henry said that Damian had never been neat. "Once he took up art, it was like he'd found a reason to be totally disorganized. His mother gave up nagging him about cleaning his apartment."

I checked out chairs loaded with clothes, lamps without shades, computer lights winking, cigarette butts in ashtrays. "Damian smoked," I said, inspecting a waste basket. Waste baskets contain good information sometimes.

Henry turned to stare at me. "Wherever Damian is, he'll still be smoking."

"Sorry about the past tense. Didn't mean to."

He took a deep breath. "You're a reasonable person. A reasonable person would think Damian's dead, especially now with his best friend dead."

I said that yes it was possible that Arne killed Damian, then himself, but I didn't think that's what happened. There were too many blanks to be filled in.

The computer seat was the only tidy chair in the place. I sat and pressed a key. The monitor lit, asking for a password. "Damian password-protected his computer," I said.

"We do at the office. It's stupid not to."

"We'll try something."

"Try what?" he said.

This wasn't going to be easy, but I opened Start>Run, and typed "cmd" and hit Enter. Then I typed in "net user" and hit Enter. The list of accounts showed that only Damian had a user account. I typed "net user Damian" and hit Enter. The computer asked for the new password, and I typed in Damian.

Could be that was his old password, but it didn't matter. I went back to the password prompt and typed Damian into the bar and, voila, the desktop appeared.

"You're a hacker," Henry said.

A hacker wouldn't call what I did hacking. "Baby stuff. I find myself at computers other than mine. A good friend taught me that elementary lesson. Good, too, if you forget your own password. Might as well just use Admin."

He looked unamused. "There's got to be a way to protect against this type of an invasion."

"There is. The software costs, but in your office, it's probably worth it."

I concentrated on the desktop wallpaper. It was horrid. "What in hell?"

"Goya's Black Paintings period," Henry said.

I studied the grim figures floating above black treetops and a silvery rendition of a meadow or river. *What kind of person would have this as desktop wallpaper?*

Henry stood beside me. "The Fates," he said.

"They look like witches."

"See the scissors there," he pointed to a gargoyle's hand that held a small scissors. "The Fates cut a man's life at its end, or something like that. Goya painted the original on the walls of his house near the end of his life."

I didn't like this symbolism at all as it pertained to Damian.

"I recall now," I said, "Goya's the painter who did the thing with God eating one of his children."

"More precisely, Saturn eating one of his many sons, all of whom he devoured because an oracle foretold that one of them would overthrow him. Except that Zeus's mother hid him on an island, and Zeus did conquer his father, Saturn—known also as the Greek Cronos."

"Makes you wonder about a mind that illustrates such horror," I said.

"Francis Bacon observed that left to himself, man is a cannibal devouring himself."

"I prefer Renoir—the optimist." I said.

He said, " 'The pain passes but the beauty remains.' "

I clicked the icon for Word and opened Damian's document files.

"Wait," Henry said. "I've always respected my son's privacy."

My hands hovered over the keyboard. "Turn your back," I said.

"He would be furious." It was Henry who was furious.

I looked up at him. "Damian's been missing for six days. Searching for him are state cops, Atlanta PD, Athens PD, and me, hired by a man who is paying a bunch to find Damian and clear his own name. If Damian shows up in the next half hour, he'll be the one who takes the rap for the invasion of his privacy and wasting law enforcement's time."

Henry swallowed. "I see."

I heard Henry's footsteps walking away. "Blog essays," I said. "Art sites and more art sites." On the Internet I found Damian's web blog. "Damian's blog is called *Art's Outer Limits.*"

From across the room, Henry said, "Thanks for that information."

There was an avatar—I assume of Damian—a drawing of an open-mouthed, wide-eyed artist, a cross between Saturn's eyes and *The Scream.* I scrolled through titles and first lines. Without exception, the entries contained illustrations that looked like unfinished drawings, some obscene and others grotesque: a stick tree with a stick man holding something at his groin as if peeing against the tree; a bird pecking at a squiggle, a worm I presume; a cat disemboweling a small creature. I'm lost in this type of art. I moved on to the next entries, and the next. A blog post that was dated last month caught my eye. "Outwitting the Rules." I looked at the art. A stick man and a woman walking, a man following, his nose outsized. Could he be Baxter following Damian and Cho?

Moving down, I came to a post called, "Art or Destruction of Public Property?" I turned my head to see Henry looking out the window. His rigid stature said outrage. But I spoke anyway. "Listen to this Henry."

He turned and nodded, meaning, *if I must.*

"I quote the post: 'The dissolving boundaries between art and life, yeah, even death, are broadening art's scope.' Damian writes that though some call it subversion, it is a legitimate form."

"Intervention Art," Henry said. "It's all the rage in Europe."

"He goes on to say that if properly performed, it is not vandalism. He speaks of an intervention with the work of Goya. What's the White Cube?"

Henry weaved around an easel, drawing closer. "London gallery. Young artists. Off the chart avant-garde."

"Damian writes about two artists who painted faces on Goya's etchings, *The Disaster of War.* He says this intervention in the original work is an expansion and not mutilation. One of the interventionists said, and I quote: 'Sometimes it is difficult to make the original Goya etchings any nastier; in one I found a witch sexually molesting a baby.' " I looked at Henry. "I can agree with that last quote."

"How far back have you gone into Damian's files?"

"Into last month."

"Then there's nothing that tells us what happened to him a week ago. Please, quit."

I shut the website. "Now for his emails."

"That's going too far."

"Let me try something."

"I draw the line."

Ignoring him, I said, "He uses Bellsouth."

"You won't get in."

"I need to try. Time's wasting."

Henry was clearly torn between invasion of his son's privacy and needing to know if his computer held a hint of what happened to him.

I clicked the email icon. The email page came up, asking for an address and password. "What's his address?" I asked.

Henry breathed out acquiescence. "DHanselArtist."

"Let's go with Goya here," I said, and typed it in the password bar. "Nope." I looked up at him. Even if he knew, he wasn't going to tell me, but I asked anyway. "You know it?"

"I do not. Damian wouldn't even tell his mother."

"What's her maiden name?"

"Damian would not use his mother's sacred name."

Wow. "Okay," I said, and logged out.

Another job for the Webdog.

I hadn't yet risen from the chair when the doorbell chimed. That would be Lake. I stood.

And Joe. And Sergeant Thomas. Lagging behind was my friend Felix.

This was not going to be fun.

Lake came up. "Dru."

"Lake," I said, meeting his stare.

Joe moved to stand by Lake and said, "Your researcher was correct. I talked with the super of the school. They confirm Cho Martine was never a student, and they don't know how she pulled off getting a transcript from them to the university."

Sergeant Thomas, who'd joined us, gave me a hard stare, which I was getting used to. "It surely would have been nice if we had that information yesterday when you received it. Cho Martine has cleaned out her apartment."

143

"Did you look in the dumpster behind her place?"

Thomas turned to Felix and nodded. Felix seemed happy to depart. Thomas looked at me. "We could have stopped her leaving."

"I was busy searching for oars." That sounded weak and even stupid.

"They'd have been there after we stopped her leaving." He motioned to follow him outside. I looked at Lake, who nodded, but didn't follow. Joe followed, and as we left, I saw Lake moving around the easels.

Since the rain slanted against the small porch, I opened the umbrella. Sergeant Thomas and Special Agent Joe Hagan huddled as near me as possible. When Sergeant Thomas twisted his mouth, I was so close to him, I hoped he wasn't a spitter when he talked.

He was more of a croaker when he was angry. "We lost a valuable witness, thanks to you."

"Or a suspect."

"She'll be out of the state by now."

I raised my chin, not fearful of his verbal assault. "That doesn't mean she can't be found."

"Look Miss Smart—Miss Dru. I cannot tell you how bad this is."

"You mean how mad you are."

"That, too."

"I meant to talk to Cho again, not mentioning what I'd learned," I said. "See if she'd give me an insight to her life and why she might hack her way into this university."

"Why didn't you tell your buddy, Lieutenant Lake?"

I told Thomas that other developments intervened, that since Damian's expensive bike was missing, and that since articles belonging to Damian had been showing up on bike trails—with the exception of his money clip—that the Greenway was a place to check out. Besides, it was too early to start knocking on Cho Martine's door.

Joe spoke up. "Why the Greenway? Damian's stuff was turning up in Atlanta, not here. Better to run with some information you just got on Cho Martine."

"It didn't enter my mind that Cho would bolt. At that point she had no reason to suspect she'd been found out." I said this thinking that she probably did suspect someone had found the back door where she had created her identity.

"Something spooked her," Thomas said.

"Web's working on finding the Martines."

"When did you plan on letting us in on this info?"

"I came to your office. You were not there."

"One of my officers was," Thomas said. "Why didn't you tell him? He's an old buddy." He'd made it sound silly. "I'll tell you why you didn't tell anyone about Cho. You're a glory hound and you wheedle out information. You got Felix to tell you that we knew Hansel was seen on the Greenway with Martine. That sent you off on a Greenway expedition, when you should have been telling us what you found out about a very important person in this case."

"That expedition as you call it resulted in finding evidence, and then Arne's death was reported by an anonymous caller. I'm sorry my timeline doesn't fit yours."

He drew in a deep breath like he was about to sing an aria. "I'd like you to stay away from this investigation from now on."

"Is that a polite request or demand?"

"It's as polite as I can make it."

"I have a client. I have his interest to protect. I'm allowed to do that under this state's PI regulations."

"You go babysit Baxter. That's all he needs. Don't mess me up any more than you have." He turned and looked at Joe. "You got anything else to say, Joe?"

"I say we continue to cooperate." He shrugged at Thomas. "It *was* her guy that got the info."

That's right, my body language said, *it was my guy that got the info.*

"We weren't far behind," Thomas said and stalked inside.

I wasn't going back inside, I knew that.

"It will be okay, Dru," Joe said. "Just share what you and your web guru dig up, and you'll be back in our good graces."

Before he went in, I said, "Are you looking for the Martines?"

He patted me on the shoulder. "Bet your boots." He looked down at mine. "You need some dry ones." I sort of grinned and he stuck his thumb up, turned, and disappeared through the door.

Lake came out and stood by me. "You got me, babe."

"You're still pissed."

"That aside, this case has started to roll for you. I trust your instincts. Always have."

"Anything in Damian's trash?"

"He was pretty savvy. He nuked a lot of CDs. They're still in the microwave."

That was about the only way you could destroy information on a CD-ROM. "The art stunt went wrong."

"What did you and Henry find in there?"

I rushed through what I'd found on Damian's computer.

"Intervention Art," Lake said. "Sounds like those artists downstairs from me."

Avant-garde artists and musicians leased the ground floor storefronts of Lake's loft. I said, "Depends if you view sticking up posters and painting on city buildings as art or graffiti."

"They get permission," Lake said. *They* are four young men and a woman named Trinity. Lake approves of them now that they've soundproofed their studios, and he can't hear the flute and drums in the middle of the night.

"I like some of their stuff," I said. "The less weird."

"Trinity told me they use wheat-pasting for the posters."

I felt a smeary smile cross my lower face. "That answers for waving wheat when it's not in the frying pan."

"Mixing your metaphors again? It's better than glue for the buildings."

"Environmentalists. That's good."

"You plan to locate Elena Littlefield?"

Nodding, I asked, "You seeing a thread to this case?"

"Too many," he said, groaning with the words. "Web say anything else you're keeping to yourself?"

Pieces of me spun into the mist and I brushed past him.

"Dru?"

I stopped and didn't turn back. "What?"

"You'll redeem yourself."

Ass.

I got to my car and found Henry Hansel standing beside his Mercedes, a few cars up. "Giving you a bad time?" he called kindly.

I walked up to him. The umbrella was doing a bad job of keeping my head dry. "Things are starting to roll."

"It's you making them roll," he said, canting his head toward Damian's apartment. "They didn't take Damian's disappearance seriously. They're like everybody else in this place on weekends. It's football, football, and football. They didn't start to deal with it until their hangovers cleared on Monday."

"To be fair," I said, "Damian is nineteen and free to come and go."

"When someone doesn't show up for an arranged event, something's wrong."

"I can't disagree."

"Did you tell the police about what was in Damian's computer?"

"I don't have to. They'll take it and find out for themselves. They'll crack his emails, which reminds me . . ." I almost said too much.

"Easy as that?"

"They got the computer, and experts; that's all they need."

"Doesn't it bother you, breaking the law?"

"Look counselor, when we find Damian if you want to open an investigation into our techniques, go ahead, but I don't think you will." His eyes were unblinking marbles aimed at my face. "You want to bet I don't find Damian?"

He just stared.

"Here's the deal. I find him and you forget about any computer breaking and entering."

A loud thump came from Damian's apartment. He said, "They're tearing the place apart."

"That's what they do when they get serious about someone being missing."

He waved and got into his car. I got into mine.

CHAPTER FIFTEEN

Web said, "So far I've not hooked into a bank account or credit card info for Cho Martine. But—ta-da!—I got into UGA's and the high school's operating systems."

I said, "Piece a cake, right?"

"UGA's system shows that our girl genius created her own transcripts. She got the high school's templates and gave herself all A's."

"Who else would do it?"

"Oh you can find hackers for hire, but they leave traces. She'd know better than to trust anyone, and she'd want to keep the back door open to feed the hidden documents into whatever she needed to."

"I seeeeeee."

"There's a neat back door on the high school's OS that's got the system administrators fooled. Back doors can be spotted if the school ever got a real software guy in there, but they cost too much."

"Surely they'd have virus alerts?"

"Back Orifice, aka BO2K, isn't a virus. Used for sinister purposes, it's malware. It has legitimate uses for remote system administrators. They can control computers from remote locations. BO2K usually is blocked as malware by firewalls, but when these admin people—clueless about little more than script kiddies—get a malware alert that BO2K is running, they ignore it, because they're the ones running it. Since BO2K operates silently, it will not warn the legit logged-on user that a secret user is having fun, or, in this case, creating a personal identity."

"Don't you use Linux systems?"

"I use several OSes and BO2K works very well with Linux, thank you very much. You might be interested to know that it was developed by a hacker group called The Cult of the Dead Cow. The code was written by Dildog."

"Who's that other hero of yours?"

"Ah, Sir Dystic."

Webdog also works with an ad-hoc group of hackers (not crackers, who are thieves) in conjunction with a branch of the U.S. government to develop stronger encryptions.

I thought about the Hansels' obsession with passwords and asked, "Wouldn't she need a system password?"

"A good back door like BO2K stays live on the *system*. Our secret user has managed to log in to the high school system without being logged in because she sneaked in a rootkit, possibly in the kernel, and that's where she's hiding the files she created. I see where she moved data around with the mouse and keyboard, but I can't see the data. It's there, just not visible to anyone without her *personal* pass code."

"Can't you break her code?"

"I can try a few tools, but they may be ineffectual and unsafe if the rootkit code is well-written and adaptable. A virtual memory dump could be performed, exposing the rootkit because it can't hide itself, but that takes hardware interference. The best way is to reboot the OS to clean it and fetch the data for a forensic study."

My brain seized up. "Fascinating. So the documents Cho created can be found."

"Yes, although I don't know that anyone can prove she created them."

"Why not?"

"She's either using a proxy or masking her IP."

I'm not even going to ask.

He said, "The high school admins need to get UGA involved." I perceived his hesitation. "Will the authorities be calling me?"

"Worried about illegalities?"

"Not with Lieutenant Lake. The state guy—he was curt."

"Joe's fine. The Athens PD guy wants to tear out my tongue and feed it to me. Let me ask you something before we ring off."

"Shoot."

"What do you know about Art Intervention?"

"Large subject."

"Narrow it, Web, just for this pea brain."

"Gee, where to begin. Briefly, it's art acting upon existing art or space."

"Space, huh?"

"Give you an example I saw this summer. You know that the city's trying to build a running-walking-biking path along the old railroad right of way, don't you?"

That perked my ears. "Ah-ha."

"This particular artist excavated a cavity amongst the roots of an old oak on Copenhill, which is part of an old railroad right of way by Freedom Parkway. He embedded his nude body in the tree as an offering to the success of the project and stayed there all night."

"He picked the right time. Summer."

"He wins awards."

"What's the point?"

"Give you a better example. A woman named Tracey Emin, who does Confessional Art, presented a work called *My Bed*. Two men jumped into it wearing only underwear. They renamed it, *Two Naked Men Jump into Tracey's Bed*. They said they were improving Tracey's work."

"I get it, I guess."

"Performance Art and Intervention Art are separate, but sometimes it's hard to separate the two. You call yourself an artist and call nine-eleven a work of art and congratulate *the artists* who created it—those douches that flew into the towers." Web sounded really pissed.

"Changing the subject before you blow a gasket, here's something else to keep you busy."

"When you find this Cho girl, send her here. I could use an assistant."

I told Web that we weren't going to find Cho. I was dead sure of it. "I want you to get into Damian's email."

"You got his ISP?"

I told him, and said, "The cops are taking control of the computer. Get on it."

"Will do."

"Hey, hey, before you pull a Portia and hang up on me, thanks for the info."

"Yea!"

I met *Doctor* (I had been corrected) Ludlow Parsons on the fifth floor of Aderhold Hall, a big square brick building that houses the education department. A tall, thin man with butch hair going gray, he had an exacting way of bobbing his head. After he bobbed me toward a wooden chair, no padding on the seat, he sat behind a desk with just his name holder on it. He folded his hands precisely on the desk top. "I have talked to the police," he said. "As I told you on the telephone, I don't know that I can be as forthright with you, but as I agreed to speak with you about the missing student, Cho Martine, I'm at your disposal."

My, my. "I appreciate it, Dr. Parsons."

He bobbed and glanced at his watch.

"How often did you see and advise Miss Martine?"

"I saw her countless times on campus, the halls, etcetera. I acted as her advisor twice."

You'd expect a math professor to know an exact number. "What is your impression of her?"

"Quirky but brilliant."

"With computers, too?"

He gave a short jerk of his head. "She had an accomplished grasp of computer languages and programming with ASP, PHP, JavaScript. She showed proficiency in web design and developing a database with MySQL and SQL Servers."

Web had viewed her work. "You said quirky. How quirky?"

"I'm not a psychologist, Miss Dru."

"Moody quirky? Funny quirky?"

"Both."

He had heard about her stalking charges against Baxter and had last seen her in the hall on Monday, but they did not speak. He said she seemed preoccupied, unlike her assertive self. He did not know either Damian Hansel or Arne Trammel, but was acquainted with Baxter.

"You said that the police have advised you that Miss Martine is an academic imposter. Did you have an inkling. . . ."

He raised his chin. "I told you on the telephone that I can't answer that as I am not part of the admissions process."

"I don't understand why not." His hands stayed rock solid on the desk top; the muscles in his face were just as rigid. "You were her academic advisor, the logical person in the university system that could or should have known her academic qualifications. I'll ask this then. Is it the duty of advisors to review and investigate academic qualifications?"

"It is the duty of admissions. I was not her initial advisor for registration. After that, she made an appointment with me. Our sessions were brief. Miss Martine did not ask questions. She was quite self-assured."

"Did she seem mature for a freshman?"

"I formed no opinion."

"Does it surprise you that she is an imposter?"

"Arrogant people pull off quite a bit, or try to."

People like himself? Advisor and murderer? My mind goes astray occasionally. "A student is dead, Dr. Parsons, one who knew Miss Martine. Now she and another student are missing."

"I have been informed and have cooperated with the police."

"Did you meet with Miss Martine's parents during orientation?"

He cricked his neck. "Parents of freshmen are not encouraged to accompany students to orientation. There is a separate parent orientation that deals with their part of the process."

"Which is?"

"Set up of a student account, certification of immunization and medical history, that type of thing."

"Why are student accounts required?" My community college didn't require one.

"UGAMyID is created for incidental billing such as placement tests, should they be necessary."

"Is it silly of me to ask if Cho Martine took placement tests?"

"Her high school transcript and SAT scores exempted her from placement tests."

"Except that they were forged."

"That is not my problem."

"Yet in math, one solves problems." He didn't think that clever at all. "Did Martine's parents attend the parent orientation?"

"They were out of the country, I understand."

According to Joe Hagan, the university deferred parent orientation until the Martines returned to the country.

I said, "It appears, Dr. Parsons, that Miss Martine created some very large cracks to slip through."

He blinked, I think for the second time since our talk began. And that was about it for Dr. Parsons.

I'd had my phone on mute while I talked to Parsons. Walking down the sidewalk, I was up against a headwind so fierce it almost hurled me into the street. So I ducked into a lobby and checked my missed calls. Lake. Portia. Baxter.

Lake first. "Dru, where are you?"

"Just left Parsons's office."

"Get anything useful?"

"He doesn't like her, probably because she out-pompoused him. Web couldn't find any financials on Martine."

"Joe and Thomas have another meeting with university types this afternoon. I'm leaving Athens. You are, too."

"Not yet. I want to . . ."

"You should have gotten the call from Portia by now. There was a banger shootout on DD's turf over a drug operation. Johndro Phillips has disappeared."

"Johndro's disappeared?" He was the twelve-year-old in the Devus Dontel McFersen drug trial. One who didn't testify, thus ruining the case. "I'll call Portia. What else can you tell me?"

"His aunt reported him missing. Child Protective Services came this morning to get him. His room was empty."

"Slow down, Lake. What's he got to do with the banger shoot-out?"

"Though he denies it, Johndro was acting as a spotter and became a witness to a murder that involved Devus McFersen's thugs. It's connected to the Rave Club murder."

"I thought the buy was on for the weekend."

"Who knows why it was changed. Johndro already talked to detectives."

"With a lawyer?"

"With and without. You need to get back there, Dru, and find

155

this kid. Let the Athens cops and the GBI find the college kids. You belong in Atlanta."

He was probably right, but I don't give up before I find what I'm looking for, and I didn't like the tone in his voice.

After a small silence, he said, "Let's hit the road, Dru. We're done here."

"I'm not."

"Baxter's looking good to the authorities here. That's what he needed when he hired you. Job well done."

"I'm not leaving until I talk to Porsh."

"Suit yourself. You need a ride, though."

"I'll take the rental and charge Bax for the drop-off fee."

"See you in Atlanta."

CHAPTER SIXTEEN

The steady rain was my friend on the way to Atlanta. No cops were out clocking my ninety-mile-an-hour haste. I had an appointment with Porsh while she was between cases and an hour to get there.

She didn't say anything about my being ten minutes late, and I listened to her summation of the case. "Police say it looks like a kidnapping." She hesitated a moment. "Although I wonder. Johndro's no dummy."

Portia melded into the elegance of the room, an elegance that was fine-lined rather than plush. Portia's grace is born of her lithe frame, one that can wear a burlap sack with style. I've known her since first grade at Christ the King parochial school, and from that day to this, I admire the way she swans her dark head on a long neck and the way she sways her slender, delicate hands when speaking. Portia is not delicate, however. One look at her hawk-like nose and large brown eyes tells you that. Those two features also tell you she's in possession of a brilliant mind.

"CPS fucked up," she continued. "Because of the murder, Johndro was no longer safe with his aunt and was supposed to be moved immediately after his statements to police—from the police station to a house unknown to family and friends until the matter was resolved." She moved forward in the chair and placed folded hands on the desk top. "By order of *my* court."

"I'd hate to disobey that order."

"Because of cutbacks, no family was available. So the idiots take him to the Eggers until they can find a place." Portia fingered her cigarette holder. She doesn't smoke any more (that I know of) but having the holder at hand reminded her of fonder days, those days in her grandmother's Bentley when we sat in the back seat and sucked our lungs dry. The same Bentley now behind a security fence across from Lake's loft.

"There's a lot to be said for institutions," Portia went on. "Safe homes for children, run by the state, but I've lost faith in the present foster care system. CPS and police took him home last night, left him unguarded, and this morning he was gone. He'd left his cell phone on his nightstand. What kid leaves home without his cell phone?"

So true. If you can't find a missing woman, but find her purse, it's a good chance she didn't leave it behind voluntarily. I said, "I'm off to see Mrs. Eggers, if she'll speak to me."

"Damn well better, if she wants to remain guardian of Johndro once this is over. I'll send someone to pick her up." She tapped her index finger on the cigarette holder as if it held a cigarette in need of de-ashing. I stood and told her I was off to the Eggers home. She said, "Lake and his minions can handle the neighborhood. Trashing your yard was one thing, trashing your head, I don't want on mine."

"You got my butt here to find Johndro. That means I'm going into that neighborhood." I'd mounted my high horse mostly because of Lake's intransigence, but Portia could be just as mulish. And if you don't stand your ground, she'll run you over.

She held the cigarette holder between an index and third finger and rubbed her forehead. "Wish I still smoked."

"Coughing is not an elegant thing." I strapped my wet backpack onto my shoulder. "I'll call you when I know something."

"You call me whether you know something or not—every half hour. I don't think for one minute Devus McFersen's in

Miami. Too much competition there to give up his street rights here."

"He may have Johndro with him."

"Maybe you can get more from Mrs. Eggers. Don't believe anything Gibb Eggers says. He's not related to the boy and would just as soon hand him over to Devus McFersen to get rid of him." She gave me a copy of the police report which I'd read.

"Family ties," I said.

"Watch yourself. Do it for me."

I drove through Martin Luther King's old neighborhood, Vine City, on the west side of downtown—Atlanta Police Patrol Zone One. Known locally as the Bluff, the territory lies roughly along Northside Drive just beyond the Georgia Dome and the Georgia World Congress Center, barely a mile from downtown. Ninety-eight percent of the population is African American. Entering the Bluff from Northside Drive, I saw that nothing had changed despite the mayor's lofty vow. Abandoned buildings and homes shared attempts at revitalization. I locked my doors and turned on Simpson Street. When I passed the Simpson Street Church of Christ, I turned right onto Joseph E. Lowery Blvd.

At a stop sign I said a silent prayer for the soul of the late Kathryn Johnston. At Calender Street I turned and thought about the ninety-two year-old woman who was shot to death by APD narcotics officers when they stormed her home looking for a boatload of drugs. There were no drugs in her home. The narco cowboys blamed an informant for bad info, but four cops went to prison for civil rights violations. Confidential sources and no-knock warrants will get a cop killed or jailed. Kathryn Johnston had been ready with a shotgun and got off a shot before the hail of cop bullets tore her body apart.

The Eggers house was a tan craftsman bungalow in respectable shape with a painted picket fence. I wasn't looking forward to questioning her since she blamed me for getting the kids involved in the Big DD court case—even though she waged a war with police to save her nephew from the drug kingpin who came to town and set up shop in territory once possessed by a deceased banger.

Portia was down on Gibb Eggers, Lolonda Eggers's husband, but I liked him. He didn't wear rosy glasses like Lolonda. I can excuse an aunt's sentimentality, but she seemed unable to take a firm hand with Johndro after his mother died of an overdose three years ago. The last time I talked to her—before Big DD's trial—her expression was fearful. I could never figure out who she was afraid of, Johndro or Big DD. Johndro was a big boy for his age. Gibb and Lolonda Eggers were small people. When Johndro became a runner of smack and crack for Big DD, along with his eleven-year-old girl cousin, LaRisha, he came to Portia's attention through CIs—confidential informants.

Lolonda opened the wooden door but not the screen. I'd come prepared for hostility.

"Hello, Mrs. Eggers," I said. "May I come in?"

"Johndro's not here."

"If Johndro Phillips were in there, I wouldn't be here," I said. Curt begets curt.

"He goes by Eggers now."

"That's legal."

"That's what his lawyer said, Miss Dru. It was legal to go by what name you want."

"Do you have any idea where Johndro might be?"

"I'd go get him if I did."

"Judge Devon assigned me to find Johndro, and I'm starting with you."

Hitching her thin shoulders, she said, "With me's the place

to start," and unhooked the screen door.

I know Lolonda Eggers to be in her fifties, but her taut skin and the freckles across her nose and cheeks make her look in her thirties.

She waved me into the front parlor. "Would you like a cold drink?" Said as if even the devil deserved hospitality.

"If you're having one, I will, too," I said.

"Orange okay?"

"Orange sounds fine." I hadn't had an orange soda since I was ten.

I'd settled into a small sofa chair by a window, and Mrs. Eggers (we used to be on a first name basis, but she had called me Miss Dru) sat in her platform rocker. I've been in this house three times, and know that's her pride of place. Gibb Eggers's big recliner sat opposite. A sixty-inch hi-def television had been mounted on a wall. There wasn't an article in the room that was dirty or out of place.

"When did you last see Johndro?" I asked.

"Last night when he came home from the police with the CPS people."

She said that he ate a sandwich, they talked briefly, and he went to bed. "I told him to lock up tight."

"Were you afraid for him?"

"We told the CPS he would be safe until they came and got him in the morning—to take him to school and then to a secret place."

"What was his mood?"

"Johndro always with a smile. He gives a big hug to me and waves to Gibb." She looked at Gibb's recliner as if to rebuke the man. "Gibb don't like Johndro. He'd like him to go." She thrust her legs straight out. "Johndro be thirteen come February. My sister's boy was a Groundhog baby. Lord the fuss. He's smart, Miss Dru. Very smart." She let her legs relax but her feet never touched the floor.

"I know he is." That was one thing in his favor. He went to school and he made middling grades, enough to get him into a community or technical college. His future was up to him.

Lolonda said she and Gibb did not hear anything unusual in the night; in this neighborhood, the unusual is usual. I said, "Tell me about this morning."

She folded her arms. "I went to wake him, but his bed wasn't slept in. Johndro don't make his bed, I do, so I know he didn't sleep in it. This house isn't big so there wasn't no looking up and down."

I asked if his window was open and she said it wasn't, but also that it was not locked. She said that his cell phone was on the bedside table. "It's an old trunk by his bed. His neck chains, his money clip, his watch, and his ring laid on it, too. He don't sleep in his jewelry."

I recalled Johndro's chains and a big fake diamond ring, one like the real thing Big DD wore in court. "If someone took him by force, which would mean a gun, any idea who?"

She looked at me like I'd just landed on the planet. "Them drug pushers for what he seen. I ask the police to rid us of them, but they don't. And Johndro don't have no choice if he wants to get along and stay alive."

I nodded then offered a different idea. "Johndro may be hiding himself and left his cell and jewelry to make people think he'd been kidnapped. It's an old trick, Mrs. Eggers." She didn't say anything but looked as though the thought had entered her head. "I wish we could have gotten Big DD locked up with a conviction."

"The lawyers said Johndro and LaRisha would have to go into Protection if they testified."

Witness Security. A short time ago something I'd associated with Cho Martine. "If Johndro went into Protection, you'd have to go with him," I said. "Parents or guardians must."

"That's why I testified so Johndro and LaRisha wouldn't have to."

Maybe she didn't remember that a court judge handed down a self-incrimination ruling regarding their testifying, and that her testimony turned out to be worthless hearsay.

I asked if she'd talked to LaRisha's foster parents. "I did," she said. "LaRisha slept in her bed last night and don't know nothing about Johndro."

I tried a different tactic and I asked her how much money Johndro had. Her eyes shifted before she answered. "He has some."

"He still getting tips?"

"I told you, he doesn't do that no more. And he don't smoke neither."

Her defenses were up. Johndro and LaRisha were tested and found drug free on several occasions before Big DD's trial. Johndro might not smoke, shoot, or snort smack or coke, but he had, in the past, advanced money to addicts. He told that to Portia in my presence. As go-betweens for Devus McFersen, both kids delivered the drugs, but if an addict was unable to get around, Johndro made the buy and got reimbursed and a fifteen percent tip.

I asked her, "Where does he get money?"

Her skin seemed to sag, especially around her mouth and eyes. "He gets the checks now."

"The checks?"

"The social services checks."

"You give him an allowance from them?"

"Used to, but now he takes all the money."

"That money is for you to give him a home—shelter, hot water, electricity, food."

The per diem of twelve dollars a day did not include other allowances like clothing, medicines, food, transportation. Lolonda and Gibb probably got around seven hundred a month for fostering her nephew. I said, "Even rich people don't give their twelve-year-olds hundreds of dollars a month to spend as they wish. He even gets free breakfasts and lunches at school."

She shook her head. "We got a recession and Johndro don't like school food. He goes to the store on the corner. Jiffy Eats."

And pays six dollars for a drink and a honey biscuit. I'd passed the store several times and shuddered. Roach races, rat round-ups.

She went on, "He buys special clothes and takes them to the cleaners."

Gangbanger clothes sport expensive labels.

"What happened last night? The shootings?" I asked.

She shook her head. "Johndro didn't tell us."

I reminded her, "I need your help to find him."

"I don't want Johndro taken from me, and Johndro don't want to go from this place where he was born just up the street with his mama."

She was probably seeing the foster money drying up, too. Gibb Eggers had a job at the tire store, but the money meant she didn't have to ask him to pay for Johndro's upkeep. "I need to know what Johndro told you about the shootings."

"I don' know why I trust you, but I do. Johndro don't, but Mr. Eggers, he does, too."

"Johndro doesn't trust me because he's under Devus McFersen's influence. Devus has a hold on your nephew. We need to find Johndro, and get him away from that influence. As you are aware, Mrs. Eggers, the life of a drug king is not a long one. I predict Big DD will either be dead, jailed, or have moved on within the year. If your nephew stays with him, the same thing applies."

Lolonda shook her head. "Johndro says Big DD's going to

Miami. This place is too cheap."

"Tell me what Johndro told you," I urged her.

"Johndro didn't name names to the police," she said, "but he named Devus McFersen to Gibb and me. I don't want you telling the police what Johndro told to me."

That's always a toughie, so I skirted it. "If Devus is involved, the cops already know it. There was a shooting the other night at the Rave Club, and the suspect wanted a deal and told police about a big drug buy in this neighborhood—the one that got a man killed last night."

"Johndro said the police weren't there until the shooting started."

"A man was killed last night," I said, hoping to open her up.

She had a habit of looking at Gibb's recliner when she didn't want to answer. "Johndro said this driver was sitting in his van, with it running, smoking a cigarette."

According to the police report, the van's driver said he was waiting for his girlfriend to come out of her house.

Lolonda said, "At the same time, Johndro is waiting under a tree for a friend."

Spotting. I asked if she knew Johndro's friend's name.

"Don't know most names of his friends." She glanced at the ceiling as if asking the Lord to forgive her fib. "The van driver looks behind him like he hears footprints walking up. Johndro says he hears them, too, and he sees this man stop by the back of the van. The driver tosses his cigarette outside the window, and the man walking comes to the driver's window. Johndro hears the driver say, 'Go away, beggar,' or something like that."

According to the police report, the van driver says he thinks the walker is a homeless guy—a panhandler, come begging.

Lolonda lowered her chin and said, "The man walking reached into his waistband."

The van driver told police he thought the walker was going

for a gun and picked his gun off the seat, flashed his arm across his body, and shot the walker in the face. Defending himself, he said. But there was no gun; the walker was no panhandler. The walker was reaching for a handkerchief. Lake said the handkerchief was a sign to the driver that he was a legit buyer, and not a narc or a plant. The police found five thousand dollars in his pocket, presumably to make the buy.

Lolonda continued, "Johndro hears the shot and he knows nothing good's coming, so he lights out. Running up the street, he sees DD's car. And then he sees a car coming from the other end of the street. They get the cars face to face, the van in the middle, parked on the curb. Johndro hides himself in some bushes. Three men get out of DD's car and go to the body on the street. Then gunfire comes from the other car. One of DD's men gets hit. The van driver starts shooting at the other car. Somebody called police and said they saw Johndro there, too. That made him a witness."

According to what Johndro told police, he said that gunfire came from all three cars, that when he heard the police sirens, the cars took off leaving behind a dead man and a wounded banger. The van had been hit and wouldn't go, so the driver got out and ran, but his bolt hole was closed up. Police caught him at the fence.

"The drug buyer was from Decatur," I told Mrs. Eggers. "His friends shot one of Big DD's men. Could be his friends might be looking for the witness."

"Uh-uh." She rocked back. "Big DD looking for him cause he knows Johndro was there and seen the shooting."

"Either way, we got to find Johndro."

"Johndro wasn't involved."

"He saw Big DD's car, and his man get shot."

"Johndro only knows a bum got killed. Shot's not killed."

"The man wasn't a bum," I reminded her. "Five thousand in

his pocket."

"Johndro didn't know that."

"Mrs. Eggers, your nephew knows this neighborhood like the veins in his arms. He knows the driver smoking in his van was one of DD's men and was waiting for the buyer. Johndro knows that the man who walked up with the handkerchief wasn't a bum. He knows who was in the other two cars—one he admits was DD's car. I'm betting he knows the bangers in the third car and that he was witnessing rival dealers protecting their buyer and their money from Devus's robbers. They never intended to sell heroin to the man, just kill him and take his money."

"Johndro don't know the man that was killed. Johndro says the fool should have been *wearing* the hanky. Not have it in his waist."

"Who might know where Johndro would hide out?"

She shook her head. "Trouble," she moaned at the recliner. "Trouble, trouble, trouble."

CHAPTER SEVENTEEN

After I reported to Portia, I called Lake and gave him a summary. "Was a CI in the third car?" I asked.

When he didn't answer readily, I knew he knew, but cops are rightly closed-mouth when it comes to confidential informants. He said, "The snitch said the buy was going down over the weekend but wasn't more specific."

Neither was Lake going to be more specific. "Maybe they rushed the buy, suspecting that the Rave shooter would make a deal."

"Good thinking, but it would depend on how handy the product is."

"Any other street people interviewed besides Johndro?"

"The shakes didn't reveal anything. People hear, they know what's going on, but they're not talking."

Shakedowns in neighborhoods like the Bluff don't yield anything because of reprisals. "There must have been at least three guns blazing," I said. "Anything on the casings?"

"Two nine-mils and a three-eight. That was from the seller in the van."

"He say anything more?"

"Claims self-defense."

"No drugs in the van?"

"Nope. It was either to be an off-scene purchase, or they never intended to sell, only to kill him and take his money. A Decatur CI said the dead guy was purchasing for his territory.

The van guy has a rap sheet, but unless a witness comes forth, murder's a hard case to make. Look, you want to get some dinner?"

"What I want is to go home and see how the place looks in daylight, which is fading fast."

"Meet you there. Stay in your car until I get there."

"Which reminds me, I've got to get the Bentley from your parking lot."

"The Bentley's safer where it is. Keep the rental until you get the Audi back. Charge the rental to Bax."

"Bet your slim a-double-s."

The driveway and yard looked like nothing had happened, except maybe the white fence was whiter and the replaced pane of glass clearer.

Lake had stopped at a fresh food market for costly steaks and salad: spinach and arugula. Bet he'll have a carton of the mashed potatoes and some gooey dessert. Why peel and mash when grocers will do it for you—for twice the price?

Waiting for Lake in my car wasn't going to happen, so, going to the freestanding garage at the back of my property, I turned the dial on a locked steel cabinet and retrieved a Smith and Wesson that I bought when I was with the APD. It was my bug—my backup gun. I unlocked the door and went inside the house. It took no more than thirty seconds to see that no one hid in the nineteen-hundred-square-foot cottage. I admit exhaling relief. The place smelled like fresh lemon oil polish. Lake had called the quarterly cleaning lady, and, no kidding, had an officer check the place and drive by while she cleaned.

When he came in, carrying the groceries, he saw the satin hardwood floor, groaned, and trod gingerly to the kitchen island. In the past, he'd slipped a couple of times. He swore he told her not to oil the wood on the floors, but since she ignores me, why should she do what he tells her to?

While I tossed salad and put the potatoes in the microwave, Lake grilled the steaks, his a twelve-ounce rib eye, mine a small filet mignon. Both rare. When meat is fresh and tartare quality, it's a waste of good money to overcook it.

I lit candles; he decanted two bottles of cabernet sauvignon, not of Baxter Carlisle's vintage, but my favorite—tasting of currants, a hint of cloves, and having long legs.

We raised our glasses and sipped. Lake looked at the salad. "Is this rabbit food really going to make me live ten years longer than my genes say I will?"

"Promise. If I'm going to live a long time, you have to, too. I need company." My voice trembled on the last word. My mama's face had come into my head. I didn't look at Lake.

"Wouldn't any old company do?" he chided.

I stuck my fork into the greens. "I'm used to you. I don't want to break in a new body."

His hand touched my arm. "And I don't want you to."

After an unsettling interlude, he took away the salad plates and served the steak and potatoes. I piled a gob on my fork. Hey, I'm Irish, I love potatoes. It's twined in our DNA strands. Inseparable. We've been known to die without potatoes.

While Lake cut into his rib eye, I asked, "What's on for the weekend?"

Chewing, he said, "Uh, I'm off, unless something comes up with the Devus slugs. The usual."

"I have to see Mama." *Why did I tell him that now?*

"I know," he said. "A duty you hate." He looked abashed. Clearly, he hadn't meant to trot that out.

I glanced at his plate. "How do you know that?"

His fork stopped its progress from plate to mouth. "I know you."

"That's scary."

"Oh, I don't know everything," he said, chewing meat in slow motion. "I'll never know everything. You're good at protecting your secrets."

"What secrets?"

He grinned, splitting my heart at its seams. "If I knew, they wouldn't be secrets."

"Richard Lake, how did you know I loathe going to that place?"

He set his fork on his plate and reached for my hand. "I know because I see the anguish in your face when you're reminded of an upcoming visit."

"She's all by herself."

"In a high-priced nursing facility. I also saw the ads in the paper for a round-the-clock-nurse in the Peachtree Hills neighborhood."

"When . . . ?"

He picked up his wine stem. "Ah-ha, I ferreted out a secret, didn't I?"

"I was going to tell you."

"But you didn't."

I sipped wine to gather my words into sentences he would understand. "You and I, our arrangement—we go back and forth—your place and mine . . ." I took another sip. "I want Mama home where I don't have to go to that place to see her. But . . ."

"You think I'll take it to mean you don't want me staying here anymore?"

"Maybe. But not. No. I'm exploring how it could work. It wouldn't always be round-the-clock. When I'm here, at nights, and then when I'm away . . ." I was losing focus. "With only two bedrooms and one bath, my place is too small for round-the-clock help and . . ."

"Me."

"No. You weren't listening." I'd lost my appetite and laid the fork down and picked up my wine glass. "I was exploring the cost, that's all."

He had the expression he gets when he's pissed or waiting for more information. It's the kind of look he gives suspects—attentive, anticipating, ready to pounce on a wrong answer. And it makes me mad. "If I told you I wanted to explore the idea before I put the ad in the paper, you'd have acted the same way."

"What way?" he said, dark eyes blinking.

"Like you are."

"How am I?"

I pushed back my plate. "I'm going to scream in a minute."

He reached for my hand. "No, you're not."

Despite willing them not to, tears brimmed. "Mama . . ."

He squeezed my hand.

"I'm losing it," I said. "I want you in my life, all the time, every day, with me in my cases. Everything."

"I know that."

"But Mama." A tsunami of tears burst through my eyelids. "I can't stand it."

"I'll go with you to see her as often as we can."

Dabbing a napkin at my eyes, I said, "I can't ask you to do that."

"I can't bear to see you so guilt-ridden."

"I miss her."

"She's a fine lady. I miss her, too."

"Lake, I can't expect you to go with me."

"When I can, I will."

"It's depressing."

"So, we'll both be depressed."

I was able to smile, but sadly. "Sorry I didn't tell you about the ad." Then a question occurred. "How did you happen to see it?"

"We check the ads all the time. Certain words mean certain things for buyers and sellers of anything illegal."

"I know that, but a lieutenant in major crimes doesn't do that."

"I run through the ads, usually with my coffee. It's an old habit."

I didn't believe him, and he knew by my expression I didn't.

"Truth," he said, reaching to brush hair from my forehead. "Now you know what's really depressing? Our food is getting cold."

I got up and went into the bathroom to cry.

When I came back into the dining room, Lake had cleaned up. He gave me a side hug and said, "I'm a klutz." He coaxed me into facing him, and, with a gentle motion he touched my eyelids, my nose, my mouth, and a warm prickle began to flow under my skin. He lifted my chin and kissed my lips, pressing gently, a kiss not meant to invite. The pressure on my mouth eased, and he backed away. "I got a call while you were away. I'm needed on watch until midnight. Two shootings, two rapes, and a stabbing. You think you'll be all right here."

"Of course; it's my castle."

"Let the dragons loose in the moat tonight."

"You're my dragon."

"Then I'll be here after watch."

It wasn't too late to call Baxter, so I did. I heard the din of diners in the background. "Where are you?" I asked. "Doesn't sound like Carlisle's."

"I'm at Power House. The freaking police won't let me alone. I had to talk into a machine to give them a voice print. Now they're questioning the staff."

I was confident Lake was right and that Baxter was not a prime suspect in Arne's murder. It just didn't fit, but he could have gone to Arne's and saw him hanging there. "They have to investigate," I said, weary of the case. It had stalled. Getting taken off made it worse. "How's Henry Hansel doing?"

"He came into Carlisle's for dinner. He wants me to have lunch with him tomorrow before he goes home. A waste. Food should be enjoyed or why bother."

"There's always cocktails and wine."

"One cannot live on spirits alone. It's all so depressing."

Everyone was depressed.

My call to Henry extracted no more information and I bathed, poured a glass of pinot noir, and settled in to wait for Lake.

He got to my house at three. I had fallen asleep on the sofa in my small study. I awoke when he picked me up to carry me upstairs. I'm almost as tall as he is, but he has sixty pounds of solid muscle on me. He didn't struggle and laid me in the bed so gently I felt like a baby. "You're too good," I said softly.

His tenderness transported us into a night of soft love and caring words.

CHAPTER EIGHTEEN

Jiffy Eats. The black letters were painted on a white board over the front door. All three—black letters, white board, front door—could have used a paint job. I folded the umbrella and went inside.

Like most small sidewalk stores, the place stank of bug spray and rodent decay. This place also smelled of oil. The retailer next door sold used auto parts, so maybe that accounted for the oil aroma. Lolonda Eggers had said that the original owner, a Korean man, had died and his son now ran the shop. Lolonda at first accused the Korean son of being the go-between for the skag trade until faced with the truth that her Johndro was the tip-and-fee entrepreneur.

When I entered, the bell mounted on the door jingled. Groups of what my mama called hooligans were hanging out around a few game machines. I thought about the visit this weekend and my discussion with Lake last night. It had left a raw conflicted feeling in my soul. He understands. I know he does. He loves me. I know he does. But Mama needs to be with me. He's right. I can't get over the guilt of stashing her in a high-priced home and thinking periodic visits sufficed. They didn't.

While I'd drifted off into introspection, the young black men meandered from the store. I looked at the plastic shield that protected the shopkeeper and saw eyes in a round face staring my way. I smiled, held up the identification badge, and walked up to the lip-high hole in the shield. "My name's Moriah Dru," I said. "When you get a minute, I'd like to talk to you."

He grinned, turned, and walked through a door that hooked up to the guard shield.

Late thirties, short, thin, and strong, with black hair cut short on the sides, leaving the top to fall from a middle part halfway to his ears. He rounded the coffee and hot chocolate bar saying, "Mal-Chin Choi at your service. Call me M.C."

"Reminds me of K.J. Choi, the golfer."

"Ah, yes. Kyung-Ju Choi. He is a hero in our country, although America is now my country. I have become a citizen." I congratulated him, and he continued, "K.J. Choi and I are not related, although one might say everyone is related. Choi is a name like Smith." He zeroed in on the ID badge hanging from my neck. "You are Miss Dru, as you say. You work for Child Trace, Inc. I remember seeing you in the neighborhood, and now I'm pleased to meet you."

"Same here. Child Trace is my company."

"Like me, here, I am my own employee." He roamed his arm over the small store, which was jam-packed with high-priced, high-caloric edibles and drinkables. Among nonfoods were firewood, trashy magazines with masked covers, dog collars, gaudy jewelry, and racks of video games for rent.

Motioning my head in the direction of the game machines, I said, "They keep the kids coming in."

"Seventy-five percent of my customers are under the age of sixteen," he said. "Like the young men you saw when you came in."

"Nice kids?" I asked.

"Yes, very nice," he said, his eyes not meeting mine.

"I'm trying to find Johndro Phillips," I said. *How could a face go blank so fast?* "He disappeared from his home last night."

176

"I had wondered. He did not come into the store this morning."

"Has there been any talk about last night?"

His brow wrinkled like a worried man's would. "I do not evaluate my customers, Miss Dru." I started to say I wasn't asking for an evaluation, but he held up a hand and said, "I find that listening is good, but speaking is not so good."

I told him I had been hired by juvenile justice to find Johndro. M.C.'s unyielding eyes stared at me. I explained that Johndro was not in trouble with the law as far as I knew, but he had witnessed a shooting that took place the next street over and his disappearance could mean he's in trouble.

He interrupted, "You want to know if I will help a kid who's probably in trouble?" He looked at the back wall as if seeing kids playing games. "Most of the kids in this neighborhood are in trouble of one sort or another." He stood erect and stretched his short frame. "I have two sons. We live in Roswell now. Before I married, I lived in this neighborhood. I inherited the store from my father, who was very strict with the customers. When my father died, I decided to help the young people, do outreach, especially the young boys turning into men. They think they are men before their ages are double digits. It didn't take long before I learned a lesson. I tried to help a young boy—ten he was—who was a truant. I trusted his desire to get an education. His mother was a doper who didn't take care of him. I spoke to her and she ran me off; I spoke to the school officials. They sent the authorities. One day, I turned my back and this ten-year-old kid stabs me. I am lucky he missed my liver."

I heard the pain in his voice. "They know not what they do sometimes," I said, reaching into my card case.

"They know," he said, his voice hard and hoarse. "I thought about selling this store, but I decided to be a shopkeeper and not a social worker. When I married, I moved. As things stand

177

here, the kids trust me not to interfere in their lives. It's unspoken, but if I leave them alone, they won't rob my store and beat me up."

I handed him my business card. "I get the message, M.C. If you hear from him or see him, will you call me?"

He didn't answer.

It was a short ride to Christ's Mercy Church on Chestnut Street. And who to my wondering eyes should appear—I knew in a moment it must be Lieutenant Lake—the detective without peer.

He didn't need an umbrella, what with the new blue fedora rakishly angled on his head.

I was ten minutes early for our eleven o'clock appointment with the Eggers's pastor—the eloquent Dr. Thurmond Jennings who appears every Sunday morning at seven o'clock raving and finger-shaking out sermons to his television congregation. We have awakened to his shouts of eternal damnation when we've not reprogrammed the television for the weekend.

I found a parking place, got out of the car, raised the umbrella, and crossed the street. In the mist Lake's face lost its definition. I suddenly felt vulnerable and tense. I thought about last night. We would get through this. Seeing Mama. Making decisions.

Sometimes Lake's expression tells me his world is complete with my arrival. He said, "How's Hippolyta this morning?"

Like a magic spell, his words eased my anxiety. "Shakespeare before noon?" I said and stretched my neck and raised my chin. *"Four days will quickly steep themselves in night; Four nights will quickly dream away the time; And then the moon, like to a silver bow, New bent in heaven, shall behold the night of our solemnities."*

His eyes shimmered, brightening the day. About a year after we met, I persuaded him to come with me to see Shakespeare's

Midsummer Night's Dream. Since then, when the situation calls for it, he calls me Hippolyta, Queen of the Amazon warriors. As Hippolyta says in the bard's comedy, *"This is the silliest stuff I ever heard."*

Lake said, "Don the magical girdle, warrior queen, methinks we're going to have a hell of a fight before this is o'er."

The murmur of voices intruded, and I looked over my shoulder to see a line of people at the side of one of the church's ancillary buildings. Young and old turned wary eyes to the cop. Lake, wearing the trademark chapeau of APD homicide detectives, looked exactly like what he was.

We walked up the broad steps. Mercy Church looked more like a cathedral than most Protestant churches in this city. A plaque at the double doors claimed the church was established in 1836. It had, however, been expanded on all sides but the front. The original sanctuary soared like Notre Dame. Despite the mist, I looked up to see the steeple puncture low glistening clouds.

Lake removed his hat, and we waited in silence in the vestibule for the church secretary. An organ played, probably someone practicing for services that were held morning and evening, seven days a week. The church doors were open from dawn to dusk; meetings were held all day and into the night. It was a church of specialty groups, catering to its city and neighbors, embracing young, old, poor, and poorer, welcoming gangbangers and drug dealers, rapists and murderers alike as sinners needing salvation. Those standing in the line outside waited for the cafeteria to open. The ladies of the church served lunch to anyone who was hungry, who didn't have a dime. Pastor Jennings called his television ministry one that worked for the Lord, feeding hungry people and lifting up their sorry souls.

While thinking all this, I watched a pretty young woman walk from a side office and close the door quietly. She approached and smiled. "Welcome to Christ's Mercy. Are you waiting for an audience with Pastor Thurmond Jennings?"

"We are," Lake said, half-rotating his hat in his long, slender hands. These little things he does cause a pleasant tightness in my chest. He introduced us. "I'm Detective Lieutenant Richard Lake and this," he nodded at me, "is Moriah Dru, of Child Trace."

"Yes, Child Trace," she said, broadening her smile. "You saved those two little girls."

"I had a lot of help," I said, looking at Lake.

"I love the story of those dogs."

After their heroics in what I've dubbed the end game case, Buddy and Jed were featured in our city's newspaper. The piece got picked up by the wire services and appeared in newspapers across the country, prompting a dog specialty magazine to write another feature, which circulated across the country, too. They were famous, but were still working. Which gave me an idea. I said to the woman, "Search and rescue dogs love finding people. Their reward is here on Earth in the form of food and toys."

She revealed nice dimples when she said, "Dogs go to Heaven, too. Come this way." She beckoned. Her glance at Lake lasted a fraction of a second longer than necessary. He'd made another woman's eyes gleam. Church person that she was, she should know the Tenth Commandment. *Thou shalt not covet they neighbor's wife or servant, ox or donkey.* Coveting somebody's lover is tops on my cardinal sin list, too.

She led us into the nave, walking smartly down the aisles and around the chancel to a door, where she tapped three times. A strong male voice bid us enter. Inside the office, I was reminded of the oriental rugs on Baxter's floors. This office was spacious and these rugs must have employed half of India. Pastor Jennings rose from his meticulously cluttered rosewood desk, came forward, and shook our hands. "Happy to meet you," he said. Vocal chords made the orator and had since the bards of ancient history and the emergence of tent revivalists.

Greetings over, we sat in two soft black leather chairs parked in front of his desk. He seated himself in a stunning, cardinal-red chair and shuffled some files before he folded his hands atop the desk. "Johndro Phillips is on the cusp of going two ways. To Christ or to the devil."

Lake said, "He's proven himself headstrong. I don't have high hopes, unless . . ."

"Unless," the pastor finished, "he gets scared shitless."

Lake and I smiled, for obvious reasons. Lake said, "Do you know where he is right now, or where he might be?"

His headshake was more avuncular than a no. "I've tried with Johndro, short of taking the strap to him, of which you," he looked at me, "would soundly disapprove."

I raised my shoulders, indicating *not necessarily.* "Beatings make brutes," I said. "Light spankings get their attention and curtail their arrogance. All children are arrogant. It's the *me* thing."

He turned brown, brooding eyes to a photograph on the wall. "The woodshed put the fear of the Lord in me. I can tell you that I went three times with Daddy. That was all it took to drive the devil out of my soul."

Lake said, "I've felt the power of the strap, but you strap a child today and you're in jail and they're in foster care."

"Ever since that devil Devus McFersen moved in, Johndro's changed. Now the boy is growing up so he's naturally going to change, but he was heading in the right direction with Mr. and Mrs. Eggers—pillars in the work of the Lord. We need more like them."

"But they couldn't stop Johndro hanging with the wrong crowd."

"The wrong crowd is mostly what's around here," the pastor said, "but we try. We believe in nurture by love. Love of God and love of each other."

Wasn't he just talking about taking a strap to Johndro?

Lake asked, "And you have no idea where Johndro Phillips would go?" He'd grown impatient. He wanted evidence, facts, not a sermon.

The pastor puffed his lips and made a humming noise.

"Would he come to you for help?" Lake asked.

He sighed. "In the past he has. Find Devus McFersen. It is my understanding Johndro witnessed a shootout with the McFersen gang and has disappeared. If that devil is involved, I fear for the boy. I talked with Mrs. Lolonda Eggers after services last night. She told me you came by, Miss Dru. We all need to pray for her." He looked at me like I had something to answer for. "The poor woman is distraught."

She hadn't seemed so yesterday. Something was amiss with Thurmond Jennings, too. I felt Lake's eyes on my profile. I believe he and I were on the same wavelength.

"And," Lake stood. "You have not seen Johndro since the shooting?"

"I have not. Tell the truth and shame the devil."

We ate lunch at a little meat-and-three-veg place down the street from the newspaper. Southern fried places are getting as rare as eight track tapes. We are an international city now. Blink your eyes and downtown changes along with food choices. Asian fusion, German brats and sauerkrauts (not yummy), Indian served by belly dancing waitresses. But there are some Southern cheap-eats places and we have a favorite.

A line ranged out the door, but we, servants of the city, were waved in by the owner, who yelled, "Let's get these cops back out fighting crime!" I'm no longer a cop, but that doesn't count with her, and most of her patrons were regulars and knew the drill.

When my plate was loaded with mashed potatoes (the owner always gives me extra), green beans cooked for several hours in fatback (I'm a genuine southerner after all), butter beans, and fried chicken breast, I found a table we could squeeze into by the window. Lake came along balancing two plates, one piled with pork chops, collards, butter beans, and rice with gravy; the second held five cornbread muffins and ten pats of butter. We were going to have a food fight over the fifth muffin and two pats. He set his plate down and went to get the iced teas. Sweetened. I figured I would have twenty-five hundred calories to work off before dinner. But I was feeling much better. Lake had made my day by calling me a warrior—something I am for kids.

After slathering butter on cornbread, I said, "Buddy and Jed."

Lake stopped his fork halfway to his mouth. "You reading my mind again?"

"At least we got something from the preacher. Is it a greater sin for a man of God to lie than it is for me?" Lake frowned as if wondering where that came from. "I'm convinced he knows more than he's telling us."

"They never tell us everything. Even men of God," Lake said, around a mouthful of collards.

When we'd finished, Lake got into a verbal fight with the owner. She wouldn't take his money.

"I got a raise, Celia," he said.

"You're money's still no good in here, Detective Lake."

"What about a tip?"

"A tip will be okay."

So he gave her three twenties, enough to cover the meal and a generous tip.

On the sidewalk I raised the umbrella and he adjusted his fedora. "Come to the shop," he said. "I'm going to call and see if Buddy and Jed are free. The air's heavy with moisture and the ground is soft, but maybe they can get something, if Johndro's holed up in the neighborhood."

"Betcha."

"I never bet against you, my love." Crossing the street to the parking garage, he said, "I do love you, you know."

I bobbed my head. "I know. I love you."

"So. No problem."

"No, no problem." I gave him a quick push forward. "You go on, Lake. I want to question LaRisha Brown."

He shook his head. "She'll be in school."

"I'll call her CPS worker, get her out of class. Portia will aid in that."

Our eyes met. I made a kissing moue that he returned, then got into the unmarked cruiser and drove away.

Five minutes later, Portia told me that LaRisha Brown was missing. She'd left for school but didn't make it to class.

"God damn me."

"It's not your fault foster parents are morons. I warned them to keep LaRisha in their sight until we find Johndro," Portia said.

"Priorities," I said. I'd let Cho Martine slip away and now LaRisha Brown.

"If you insist on wearing a verbal hair shirt, at least explain."

"I stopped to talk to the Korean grocer where Johndro hangs out. He couldn't help. I talked to a pastor who I believed lied, then I had lunch with Lake. My whole damned day was squandered."

"Don't self-flagellate just yet. The police are looking for La-Risha."

"She knows where Johndro would go. She'll be with him, if

she's not now."

"These street kids get around. MARTA."

That's the Metropolitan Atlanta Rapid Transit Authority. MARTA subway trains travel north, south, east and west, and feeder buses run on every major street. I said, "She'll be in the Bluffs by now."

"So go back there." Click.

My head began to pulse with the mother of all headaches. My cell phone played Haydn. *Another case heard from.* "Baxter, how are you?"

"I'm fine. And are you, my personal private detective?"

"I don't know when I'll be back on the case, but there are enough LEOs on it now, if anything happens . . ."

"That's only partially why I called. I am inviting you to dinner at my house in Augusta."

The doll collection, oh boy. "A big affair?"

"Nothing like that. A quiet dinner. With a special guest." His exuberance was infectious.

"Having to do with the case, right?"

He laughed and told me he'd learned something significant. Something that I could appreciate, and that after I learned what his guest had to tell me, we could go from there to break the case *wide open.*

"Tell me now, Bax."

"All I can say is that it will be of great interest to you."

He remained mysterious even after I asked if he'd found and tamed the fiery Cho. He said he'd invited me because I was good at analyzing information. Then he said he ran into Felix accidently on purpose. Felix told him to relay—if I didn't already know—that Special Agent Hagan and Sergeant Thomas hadn't talked to the Martines, but they knew they were in Iceland and were incommunicado.

"Why incommunicado?"

"Felix didn't know or I believe he would have told me. He knows damn well I don't talk to his sergeant."

"When is this mysterious soiree?"

"Tomorrow night. At Ammezzato, a name given to the house, but not by me. The gates are always open because they're old and creaky."

Saturday. My day with Mama. An excuse. *You are a cruel girl.* I dry-swallowed guilt. "I'll damn well try. I'll keep in touch. How is Henry?"

"He's gone home. The police won't tell him anything, either."

"That's probably because there's nothing to tell."

I apologized again for not having time to personally devote to his case and assured him my staff was working on it.

"The newspapers are a-glee with speculation," he grumbled.

Maybe some enterprising reporter would dig up evidence. Also Bax's giving serious thought was a good sign. "One more chance to tell me what I can expect at this enigmatic dinner."

He said, "I'm not certain when I'll get away so if you arrive before me, you will find a spare key in the carriage house under the floor mat of an old Model T Ford. The alarm may or may not be set, depending on my caretaker's memory. He's old and lives in an apartment above the carriage house. You know my alarm number. Same as the condo, my birth date."

"All your properties the same?"

"I'm of the opinion, if a burglar wants in, he's going to get in."

"I certainly could," I said in a joking way, but I wasn't joking.

I put in a quick call to Web to tell him about the Martines. As usual he already had the answer. "Paul Ardai emailed. Martine's in shipping negotiations with the Swedish government."

"I heard Iceland."

"A ruse for secrecy. Also, the French National Police haven't been helpful. Thank God we've got Paul."

Yes, thank God. Monsieur Ardai was most helpful in solving the deadly Scuppernong affair. Web said that Ardai had a man keeping tabs on Martine and would approach him when he surfaced. Ardai also told Web that Mrs. Martine was ailing and that there was only a caretaker at their Paris house.

"Keep me posted."

"As if I wouldn't."

CHAPTER NINETEEN

I anticipated the arrival of Buddy and Jed with supreme happiness. Growing up, I didn't have a dog because my father, that dysfunctional hypochondriac, said they stopped up his nose. It's hard to separate fact from fiction with a man who enjoys ill-health. Southern Comfort, he maintained, was a cure for all ills but pet dander.

I'd spent the afternoon talking to LaRisha's teacher and her social worker. The only additional information I got was that LaRisha was a regular churchgoer, was quiet, got good grades, and had a happy future if she stayed away from the Bluffs and her cousin.

By dusk, a light breeze had swept the mist and fog out of Atlanta. I stood outside the Eggers home and watched the three squad cars pull to the curb. From the first car, the handler came out and opened the back door. Out jumped the handsome German shepherd named Buddy. Given the go-ahead from his handler, he moved toward me with determination and grace. We have a thing going on.

Lake got out of his cruiser and said that Jed was working another case.

Mrs. Eggers opened the screen door, shot Buddy a wary glance, and gave his handler two of Johndro's knit caps. She continued to look nervously at the dog—perhaps because a well-fed dog in this neighborhood was most likely a drug dog. Buddy is a search and rescue dog, not a drug sniffer. He and

188

his partner, Jed, once followed vomit for three miles along a city street to find a shoe belonging to a little girl. Another story.

Mrs. Eggers said, "I surely hope this dog can find Johndro and LaRisha."

"Has Johndro gotten in touch with you?" Lake asked.

She looked at him the way black mamas look at cops on the trail of their sons. "I would have told you straightaway."

After a whiff, Buddy got interested in Johndro's scent. We figured LaRisha was with Johndro so one scent to follow was sufficient. Buddy's upturned nose quivered against the cool, moist air, then he looked at his handler as if to say, "We off now?"

Lake said, "Let's go."

It's a wonder how dogs pick out an individual scent among millions, but they can be trained for urban searches where you have a lot of overlaying scents. They track—and back-track—to where it's the strongest and alert. Buddy is an awesome sight when he's working the air—his ears perk, his eyes brighten, his tail becomes an eager flag. The handler said, "Once the scent falls from the air, the ground tracker in him picks it up." The handler also said Buddy can pick up a scent from as far away as a quarter of a mile, even in bad weather.

At one time I'd thought about transferring to the APD's canine division, so I read up on how dogs detect a scent we mortals can't. They detect individual odors against countless other smells because they have more olfactory DNA than humans. Then, the scent we throw off is made up of gases we emit through pores and dead skin cells we shed. Such scent is as individual as fingerprints.

Buddy loped toward Jiffy Eats, his nose raised and working zealously. When he got to the store, he dropped his head to the sidewalk, pawed, and whined. "The boy's scent is strongest here," the handler said.

M.C. Choi opened the door. "Excuse me?"

Lake flashed his badge and M.C. looked at the APD badges on Buddy's yellow nylon coat. "If you find drugs in my store, I don't know anything about them."

I said, "The dog's looking for Johndro."

M.C. grinned. "Good. You haven't given up."

Lake said, "Buddy here thinks Johndro's inside. You know LaRisha's missing, too?"

He nodded. "He's not here; neither is she. You can come in and look through the place."

"We'll do that," Lake said. "Thank you."

Buddy pranced inside with Lake and the handler.

I stood outside with M.C. "If that dog finds narcotics, it's because dopers hide all kinds of crap in stores."

"If a doper wants a six-pack, what do you do?"

"I told you I don't like being hurt."

"Johndro's about the age to start using."

He shook his head and said if Johndro was going to do drugs, he'd have started a couple of years ago. "He doesn't even smoke grass," M.C. said. He also told me something I already knew. Johndro liked money, and there was money in running for a dealer. He said he had no idea where Johndro and LaRisha might have hidden if they were on the run. I thought his answer dodgy, but he might simply have been weary of answering questions.

The dog party came outside. Lake looked at M.C. "Johndro was in the back room."

"Many times," M.C. said. "I trusted him to fetch things for me when it was busy up front."

Lake's eyes flickered. "Make it easy on us. We're going to find Johndro and LaRisha, and we better be in time. If we're not, Jiffy Eats will not be your store any longer."

M.C. sagged like Lake had deflated him.

I said, "If you know, you're not helping those kids. They're in danger."

He shook his head.

"Let's go," Lake said, with a hard glance at M.C.

We tracked along cracked sidewalks and mucky yards until Buddy reached the church. He sniffed up the steps, stopped, whined, and looked at his handler. His paw hit the door. We couldn't legally take a dog inside to conduct a search. Rubbing Buddy's head, the handler said, "Atta boy."

Lake said, "We'll contact the preacher and get a warrant. Thanks, boys."

"Job well done," Buddy's handler said, reaching inside his jacket for a small Frisbee. He sailed it to the sidewalk. Buddy fled down the steps, jumped in the air, and caught it before it landed.

Portia was on standby and signed the warrant. Half an hour later, we parked the car so that it blocked a cart path leading to the back of the church and tried the sanctuary doors. Locked. Uncommon. Lake had called the pastor to tell him he had a warrant, but Mrs. Jennings said the Reverend Jennings was at a neighborhood planning meeting. Lake promised not to knock down the front doors, and we headed for the back of the building.

A gibbous moon hung low. I hadn't seen moonlight for almost a week. "Good karma," I said.

"You're better off to rely on your Glock."

Lake's idea of karma was doubly mine. I had the 26—another bug I own—riding snugly in its ankle holster. It was the gun I carried concealed on routine cases now that I was not police. The 17 rested in a leather holster in the small of my back. I've tried about all the guns they make and have settled on the Glock 17 when I might need added fire power. Karma or not, tonight was one of those nights. The 17 has seventeen rounds in the magazine and a long enough barrel to be accurate. When not on a job, I'm at the firing range at least two days to keep myself tuned and my guns oiled. Lake wins shooting awards, and next to him I'm passable—although he assures me I'm developing a keener eye and, most important, a strong steady hand.

Christ's Mercy sanctuary was one component of a large compound that took in six blocks. I followed Lake to the cart path at the side of the church where an arm gate restricted automobile access to the interior courtyard in back of the massive building. The courtyard is like a small city park. Beautiful crape myrtles that bloom all summer had lost their leaves, but showed off their speckled white skeletons. Evergreen magnolias threaded among benches, picnic tables, and playground equipment. Azaleas lined the paths. At the back of the courtyard, a ten-foot brick wall kept the grounds from being a cut-through. A couple of long, one-story flat-roofed buildings had been erected in front of the wall. On a couple of occasions I'd been in them. They served the church's Sunday school/Bible school/summer school programs. At the end of one building, three golf carts were lined up. Between the buildings there was a barred gate in the wall. An asphalt driveway led from the gate. It wasn't evident from the mechanism if the gate was locked, but surely, if the church was locked, it was, too. My face tightened with atavistic apprehension.

Lake said softly, "Did you hear that?"

Before I said no, I heard the sharp sounds of fear and fury. We turned from the path to see a small man blazing across bricks toward an ornamental fountain, his terrified arms and legs pumping. Involuntarily, my lips parted to call to him.

Lake hissed, "Shhh."

Two seconds, not more, three large shadows ran behind him, clearly after him. By the cold light of the moon, the weapons they carried glistened. I caught myself before I cried out. It was M.C. A short guy, he didn't stand a chance. I pulled the Glock from my back at the same time Lake drew the Sig from his belt. M.C. made a tactical error by looking over his shoulder, slowing his momentum. The fastest of the thugs was upon him. Guns out, we moved swiftly. The hulk jerked M.C. from behind, pulling his jacket, and, while he was still standing, punched him savagely in the abdomen, then sideswiped his face with the butt of a gun. Bone-crack echoed in the courtyard. M.C.'s hand struck out. The hulk's gun flew from his hand, landing at the base of the fountain. My head pulsing with outrage, I shot off two rounds to keep him from going for his gun.

"Police," Lake called. "Freeze."

The hulk beating M.C. renewed the frenzy with his fists. The other two charged us.

"Freeze," Lake shouted again. "Police!"

I kept my gun pointed straight out, arms tight against the sides of my breasts, but not locked at the elbow. The muzzle didn't waver; my trigger finger wasn't tense. Lake fired at them, although we were too far away. The .40 caliber bullet hit the bricks near the scumbags. Halting, they appeared indecisive, with reason. They aimed their weapons. Two pops. Both missed; one knocked bark off a pine tree twenty yards ahead and to the side of me.

"Thirty-eights, two inch," Lake said, meaning snub nose revolvers, a favorite of bangers because they leave no casings. Our firepower was heavier, but neither the shooters nor we were in effective range. With drag factor and air resistance, their bullets would lose momentum and drop like rocks. Knowing this, they weren't coming closer. Lake's .40 caliber and my 9-mil were effective at seventy-five yards with less than a one-inch drop. More than seventy-five yards and our bullets would become falling stones, too.

For a brief moment, we faced in pairs, four guns aiming. A standoff. They couldn't break for cover because we'd run forward, rapid-firing at them. We advanced a step; the two bangers backed a step. I thought of Devus's men standing behind him at the elevator in the courthouse—muscular, big braids, mean.

I heard a noise, the grunt of fresh pain, and looked at M.C. on the ground, slick hands covering his head while the hulk raised his fist.

Lake called out, "Freeze. You. On the ground. Stop."

Another blow smashed M.C.'s chest. "He's killing him," I said, afraid if I ran forward and shot I could hit M.C.

Lake whispered urgently, "Circle. Take cover. Get in range."

Edgy as hell, I looked for cover. A magnolia. I sideswiped toward it. Lake moved sideways for the jungle gym. Not much cover there. The bangers seemed uncertain. Still on the bricks with no cover, they backed up again.

Lake came around the jungle gym dashing forward, shooting, then taking cover behind a tall pine. With leathery magnolia leaves for cover, I shot three times. The rounds dropped in the grass. Their pops did not reach us either. Lake dashed forward, getting off three rounds and kicking concrete dust close to a banger's feet. The other shooter scrambled toward the fountain. I shot and hit concrete. He turned to run. Another couple yards was all I needed.

The hulk stood over Choi's body and raised a foot to stomp. "Nooooo," I shouted, getting off a shot that could have grazed his ear. He dropped and crouch-walked toward his gun. I shot and missed. He rolled away, jumped up, and fled, gunless.

I did some quick calculations. M.C. had run from the building on the right. If the bangers decided to take on Lake, he would be at an advantage because of his greater stopping power.

He didn't have as many bullets in his magazine, but I'd have his back.

At that moment, Lake was in the shadows of a row of leafless crape myrtle trees, twenty yards right of me.

The three thugs stood behind the fountain like they were deciding what to do. I'd dashed three trees to the left, to come around from that side, thus getting in adequate range. All of a sudden a barrage blew from the Sig. The bangers must have decided to hightail it because they wheeled as if in concert and clamored for the delivery path between the two buildings. Lake tore after them, firing. A man fell. The others reached the back path, their footsteps pounding pavement. I ran toward the school building on the left and flattened against the corner. Lake's body touched the wall of the building on the right. While changing out magazines, Lake gave a head nod. That done, we assumed the shooter's position and looked around the corner. The thugs had gotten the gate open but were not outside yet.

"Freeze," Lake shouted. "Hands at your sides."

Hands lowered. We were in close range.

"Drop your weapons," Lake ordered. Their guns clattered to the pavement. "Hands behind your head." I held my gun on one's chest, and Lake reached for his radio, gun aimed at the other's chest.

The radio crackled just as a short burst of semiautomatic rifle fire came from the backside of the left building. A couple of heavy caliber semiautomatic handguns shot off their message—one to their thug buddies, who had called for backup, and one to us. They were prepared for war.

I dashed for the safety of the right building, praying the door was unlocked. Had M.C. locked this building? Didn't think so since he was escaping his pursuers. Lake reached the door first, flung it open, and I flew inside. He turned the lock.

Semiautomatic fire slammed the building for a couple of

seconds—the signature sound of an AR-15. We were in the center aisle of the long building, classrooms on each side. "I'll go right," I said and turned.

"No," he said, "We stay together."

I wasn't about to panic, but it was there, beneath the surface. *Don't think. Act.* We sped down the hall, trying metal doors that were locked. We had no time to bust them down. If the kids were in there, I hoped they were hunkered good.

Lake called for SWAT. "Back gate breached. Arm gate on east side of church. Over. At least five—one assault."

The AR rattled off maybe five rounds, windows burst. Lake said into the radio, "Rooms locked. No basement, one floor, no attic. No kids yet. Must move. Out."

Terror stabbed the base of my brain. Where were the kids? Did M.C. tell before . . . ?

I said, "M.C.'s dead."

When Lake gets into combat, his face changes. The lines that make him handsome become callous and cruel. We reached the end room. The door was ajar. A janitorial closet. I saw a single bed and a cot. Food wrappers from Jiffy Eats.

"M.C. brought food," Lake said. "The assholes followed him." *Where were Johndro and LaRisha now?*

AR fire burst against bricks. There was a pause. It was about time the shooter switched magazines. ARs fire fast and run out fast.

Lake's radio crackled. The voice said, "SWAT's on the way, Lieutenant."

They had superior fire power, and we had a janitor's closet to bead down on an AR-15.

"Better get here fast," Lake said into the radio, at the same time the door from outside blasted open. "We've got to get out. The kids were here. Not now. Two casualties, one friendly, one banger." He grabbed my arm. "This way," he said, pulling me.

"Out of the shooting gallery."

We fled through the emergency exit as the bangers reached the center aisle. A row of magnolias shielded us as we sprinted through. Having reached the exit, the bangers fired handguns. The AR shooter didn't fire into the magnolias lest he empty his rifle in seconds—on the off-chance he'd shoot someone he couldn't see. He was a maggot, but he knew his stuff.

The line of golf carts lay ahead. The first two took bullets. Backing toward the third, we fired back. My heart raced as I jumped onto the cart. Behind came a staccato ack. Lake flipped the key and pressed the gas. The batteries had a charge. Lake raced toward the gate, crashing through trees and bushes and finally through the aluminum bars.

He flipped the cruiser's trunk open with the remote. Stopping the cart, he jumped out, pulled the shotgun from its hanger, and shoved it at me. He picked up the carbine and magazine.

A young thug who guarded the gate from a stand of crape myrtles reached the mangled gate and broke for us. Dumb. I was proved right when he stumbled and his gun fired into the sidewalk. While he righted himself, I leapt forward and raised the shotgun to knock the gun from his hand. If it went off that was too bad for him. The shotgun butt bashed his arm with a crack. He winced and dropped the gun, his face flooding with murder. It was me or him. My foot smashed into his groin. Bending, he reached to grab at me. I kicked his face and he folded, splayed on the sidewalk. It was tempting to shoot the scum, but I touched my fingers to his carotids, pressed, and felt his body go slack. He'd be out for a while.

I swung away and ran for the other side of the car where Lake had pressed the rifle magazine home. Four bangers approached the gate, the AR rattling bullets close enough to strafe the reinforced doors of the squad car. Handguns went off as I racked a shell in the shotgun.

"He's emptying. Go for it," Lake called.

Not taking cover first, the AR shooter paused to reload. Idiot. He flicked the mag out and reached into his pouch for another, He was fast, just seconds more and he'd be racking. I squeezed the trigger and felt no recoil. Adrenaline padded my shoulder. The AR gunman went down. Another banger picked up the rifle and the mag bag as I fired at a third thug and caught him in the shoulder. The second AR shooter jumped behind a row of azaleas.

I had the shotgun pointed at the gut of the fourth shooter. Lake yelled, "Drop the weapon." The guy threw down his gun and turned to run. Lake could have shot him, but he'd never shoot a retreating human being. I could see his big bad head scurrying through the crape myrtles.

"One to go," Lake said and put his eye to the scope and eased the focus. Palming the barrel, he put a round in the breech. "Drop your weapon," he called. "Come out."

The AR ack-acked from the shrubs, hitting the street.

The screams of sirens reached my ears. Gunfire halted.

Lake took a deep breath. "He moves, he's in the crosshairs."

This AR shooter was no expert like the late AR shooter, and I felt the warm rush of relief that surely he would . . .

Then the sorry bastard jumped out and fired. He evidently didn't know the short-burst theory of semiautomatic shooting. His first rounds hit the concrete in front of the squad car. Then the AR rose due to recoil and put a couple of slugs in the roof. Successive rounds flew higher and higher and to my right as he sought to control the rifle. Bullets zinged everywhere but at us.

"Son-of-a-bitch won't quit," Lake said. "I'm not waiting for him to get lucky." He hesitated a second, waiting to feel his heart's back surge, then squeezed the trigger.

What had been a black mop of hair and whites-of-eyes

exploded. Shards of skull erupted through a gush of red spray. I watched in horror as it steamed down to the concrete path.

"Here comes the cavalry," Lake said when the cop cars screeched to a halt behind us.

As always, chaos took over.

Too late for SWAT, they still swarmed the place. When they returned without quarry, I saw the disappointment in their bearing.

Ambulances arrived.

"Here comes the preacher," I said from inside the yellow cop tape, leaning against Lake's shot-up cruiser, watching Jennings alight from his Lincoln across the street. We ducked under the tape and Lake waved the warrant.

The evangelist hurried up. "When my wife called me, I figured I better get here."

"Where are the kids?" I asked.

"In the sanctuary." His speech was breathless and hurried. "The night he skipped, Johndro went to M.C., but M.C. told him it wasn't safe in his store. M.C. gave him a spare key to the school building He does janitor work for extra money. When LaRisha showed up, I brought them both into rooms off my office." He looked at me. "They promised that tomorrow they would talk to you."

"The bangers followed M.C. here tonight."

"Is he—is he . . ."

Lake said. "He was beaten, but I don't know . . ."

The sound of a rolling gurney caused us three to turn toward the cart path. As paramedics approached, joy sprang into my breast. M.C.'s head wasn't covered. He wasn't dead. Jennings ran to penetrate the perimeter of cops, but they pushed him back. "How is he?" Jennings called.

"Bad, but alive," one paramedic said over his shoulder. "Move on."

I heard a shout and looked past cops guarding the scene. "Lieutenant!"

I nudged Lake and said, "Here comes the judge."

"Goddamn," Portia said, rushing up. "Was this necessary? Where are the children? I gave you a warrant."

"A warrant doesn't mean the bad guys won't show up, too," Lake said.

"Where are the children?"

Jennings said, "Inside the church, ma'am."

"Let me see them. Now."

She forged ahead of him and up the steps. She can fly on those high heels she wears. The preacher took the steps two at a time to follow. He unlocked the door and they disappeared inside.

"I'm not going in," I said. "It's Portia's scene now."

We spent four hours recreating our moves, with SWAT officers imitating the banger moves—again and again—then we went over the same ground for two hours at the cop shop.

Commander Haskell had left the sanctity of his leather and chrome study in Buckhead to come downtown and see that his favorite cop, and ex-cop, were not intimidated by Internal Affairs. The duty watch commander told me that I wasn't going to be charged, pending a more thorough investigation. I think that decision came from on high.

Then I waited forty-five minutes while Haskell and Lake talked behind closed doors. It was three o'clock in the morning when Lake came through the door, looking harassed but still handsome. "Let's go," he said.

Outside, I said, "Well?"

"I'm on paid admin leave, and I have to report at seven for watch."

Some leave.

"We're not out of the woods yet," he said softly as we walked to the elevators. "At least, I'm not. A little thing about waiting for SWAT."

In the elevator, which everyone believes is wired, I said, "We were looking for the kids, not bangers. The sanctuary door was locked. We went around back. You had a no-knock warrant that you had a right to execute. The gangbangers were determined to make M.C. talk. Poor man, hated getting hurt, but he helped those kids. The bangers followed him, but M.C., he didn't know that Jennings moved the kids from the school building. Damn them both. They should have told us."

"It's not their fault."

"Yes it is." I'd once become very angry at the funeral of a friend who was killed riding a motorcycle after drinking. Like him, M.C. didn't look ahead at the consequences. Good heart, bad moves.

Lake sighed loud enough for the mini-mikes. "It'll work out."

We'd reached the underground parking lot. The elevator doors opened and we got out.

"The real question is," Lake said, "you were armed to the teeth. Haskell thinks there could be a problem with IA getting around that. Could mean we expected trouble."

"I expected good karma. It's a church. Besides that, I'm always armed."

"With two guns?"

"In that neighborhood, sure."

"Is that what you told your interrogators?"

"My interrogators were black. They didn't like what I said."

"You should have reminded them the kids you saved were the same color as them."

"I never found those retorts particularly helpful."

CHAPTER TWENTY

Times are few when we sleep in the same bed but don't make love. Despite what movies and novels assert, I don't feel a rush of lust after the kill. Apparently, Lake doesn't either, or he senses my sensitivity to having killed human beings, even during war, albeit urban war. I persuade myself with justifications, but I'll pay with violent emotional swings. I never know when they'll come, just that they will.

Plus, we were dog tired with only a few hours to sleep.

The light coming in the window, and the small noises Lake made while he dressed, woke me. Propping on an elbow, I asked, "Did I tell you that Baxter wants me to come to Augusta tonight for dinner and conversation with a mystery guest? His house is named Ammezzato. Did you know that?"

"Can't remember." Lake was unaccountably fresh looking for having slept three hours.

I considered for a moment, then said, "It's another in the string of A's. Atlanta, Athens, Augusta, Ammezzato, Artists. . ." Lake looked thoughtful. Then he shrugged. "Since this is Baxter's soiree, you'd better go to Saks. What's this dinner thing about, anyway?"

"Fabulously mysterious. I think he just wants out of Athens for a few nights. He has Oliver to run the show." *I wish I believed he just wanted out of Athens.*

"It's Baxter we're talking about all right."

"He's invited someone who might, as he so dramatically put

it, give information that could bust the case wide open."

He was tying his shoes when his head snapped up and he spoke quickly. "Any hints?"

"No," I said, getting out of bed. "First thing is to call Webdog and see if he's gotten a line on the Martines. Martine's in negotiations with the Swedes over shipping; the missus is apparently ill and in hiding."

Lake was frowning. "I'm not wild about you going to Augusta by yourself."

I studied the lines in his face. They seem to suck at his skull. "Lake, darling. As you said, it's Baxter. He wants his little mystery . . ."

"Bax is very literal. I don't like this lure."

"Oh bosh," I said. "Don't be so overprotective." *After all, I thought but wouldn't say, I was victorious in a shootout with the baddest sub-humans in Atlanta.* His expression went to thoughtful. "Today's Saturday."

I walked to a high industrial window and looked down at the sidewalk. "I'll drop in on Mama before I head for Augusta."

"Why don't we go see her tomorrow?"

I turned to look at him. "Sunday?"

Adjusting his shoulder holster, he said, "I don't have Susanna, so let's go visit our other dependent."

I shook my head. "You forget. Sunday is a special day for them. Guests are invited to dinner. I don't think . . ."

He put on his jacket. "We'll do dinner with your mama then."

"It's not dinner at the Ritz." How could I explain? It's a fancy place, but meals with the inmates were often unpleasant.

"Let me decide for myself. Book it."

I went to him, circled my arms around his chest, and looked into his dark, serious eyes. "You're a dear man, my love, and you don't know what you're in for."

"Then I'll find out," he said, kissing my nose.

"How long will they keep you today?" I asked.

He broke away. "Watch is over at three. Why?"

Something had infected his speech and made me wary. "Just wondering where you'll be when I'm in Athens and Augusta."

He leaned into me and chucked me under the chin, then kissed my forehead. "Give Thomas some grief for me. I need to talk to Bax. I'll tell him to feed you well."

"You'll also grill the poor man, won't you?"

"As you said, I'm overprotective."

"I feel like another of your dependents."

He laughed on his way out. Half an hour later, I was on my way to my cottage to meet with two officers from Zone Two. Lake insisted I not return to my cottage alone until Big DD and all his minions were dead or locked up. I acquiesced without argument because I needed fresh clothes, to restock my overnight case, to feed Mr. Brown, and to water my indoor plants.

Lake called to say that the dead bangers with heads had been identified, but the headless one hadn't been yet. It was certain, though, that it wasn't Devus. Damn devil, didn't even do his own dirty work.

When the self-righteous justification that I'd killed a completely useless piece of garbage masquerading as a human wore off, I'd start thinking about his shitty childhood and bad genes and feel the kind of remorse that keeps me awake nights. But right now I had other things on my mind.

I love cops in uniform and I love to feed them—especially the officers who escorted me through my forlorn cottage. Even if I didn't know them from my cop days, I'd still have stopped at a Jewish deli and bought four sandwiches—two corned beef and two turkey—plus chips and Cokes. They didn't expect my offerings, but were most appreciative.

Chores finished, I locked up and took Mr. Brown's favorite kibble to the birdbath where he hangs out. The reclusive Mr. Brown must have intuited my distress. He jumped onto the dry concrete structure and bowed his head, letting me scratch behind his ears. The kibble would save a chipmunk or two until I returned.

I was back on Peachtree Street with two cops tailing me to Lenox Square. They segued away at the mall where I bought a black evening dress and shoes that cost three hundred dollars more than I wanted to spend, but hey, this is Bax and my basic black was starting to fade and my shoes had a cracked heel from the last time Lake and I went dancing. I ate salad at the food court, got into the rental car, dropped off my soiled laundry, called the nursing home and made reservations for Lake and I to have Sunday dinner with Mama, stopped at a gun store on Memorial Drive to buy ammo and a thigh holster, then headed for Athens. On this home game Saturday, traffic was enough to get my blood up. Half the drivers behind those black windows were already drunk. My cop training taught me how to spot drunks trying to drive like they weren't. Trust me; your favorite neighborhood cop knows you're impaired, even if you're staying between the lines.

Game day. I walked to Power House. People came and went to their various tailgate encampments and Power House was ripping.

I didn't expect to see Baxter, and I didn't. I moved through the crowd to the back hall where a bank of telephones used to be, and where now a lone old-fashioned phone hung on the wall. A sign read, "Local calls free. No long distance available."

From the wall phone, I dialed Bax's cell. "Where are you now?"

"On I-Twenty, halfway to Augusta. I got held up at the Apple Store."

"Speaking of which, did your display show the number that I'm calling from?"

"No," he answered.

"Is something wrong with your phone?"

"Not any longer. I hear noise. Are you in a bar?"

"I'm at Power House, and I wondered if this number showed up on your display."

"The cops did the same test. Those rotary phones have gone the way of the dodo."

"Then the police couldn't have identified the anonymous call as coming from here."

"Perry Thomas said it was spoofed from a computer. No way to trace. You can put in any number you want the ID display to read. Problem is, they think that is exactly what I did. I have VoIP."

"He might want you to believe he thinks you did that, but he knows better. He's keeping you on edge. Anything new?"

"Not that anyone's telling me. I've done some internet research of my own though."

"You learning about spoofing?"

"And other things."

"Talk to Webdog. He's the expert on information technology. Did you talk to Lake?"

"Er, no. Should I have?"

"Er, no." *Pants on fire.*

Bax gave me his home address and directions, and then told me to plan on staying the night. I demurred, saying I didn't want to put him out. He told me Ammezzato was large enough that we'd never see each other if we didn't want to.

I know Augusta pretty well, especially the Summerville community. Years ago, a couple of times a year, Daddy drove Mama and me to visit his rich cousins. That was until Daddy pleaded ill health in favor of living like a hermit.

Turning onto Kings Way, I started seeing the Summerville Sesquicentennial signs. And Tour of Homes signs. *These historic communities and their tours of homes.* Yeah it brings revenue for charities, but you've seen one Federalist mansion, you've seen them all. Having been raised in one, I'm immune to their drafty charms. What tourists learn on their walk through the past is that Summerville came into being because the city of Augusta is partly tidal marsh. The summer heat, bugs, and a malarial outbreak drove rich people up "the Hill" to build summer homes—thus Summerville.

The community boasts some pretty exclusive favorite sons like a couple of signers of the Declaration of Independence. President Woodrow Wilson and James Brown, the Godfather of Soul, lived here, and George Washington did indeed sleep in a home here.

Ammezzato's double gates stood open as Bax said. Small signs with its name were engraved in concrete bas reliefs on the massive limestone gate posts. The drive was fairly steep and I pulled alongside Bax's car. It was parked by a two-story carriage house larger than many of the newer homes. Baxter's mansion—just a short drive from where my second cousins live in a Greek antebellum—is an Italianate antebellum, not my favorite style. Ammezzato is surrounded by formal gardens. In the front it is nearly concealed by large live oaks and crape myrtles at the bottom of the hill. From the driveway, it appeared the back gardens ended at a thick forest. The grounds had to comprise at least fifteen acres. Over the centuries many landowners had sold off parcels to newcomers, but apparently Bax's family had not.

Ammezzato's limestone had been painted white and the corbel cornices the lightest of blues. I've never cared for flat roofs or iron-work balconies, and the tower topping the three floors made the whole structure look like a tiered wedding cake. Was "Ammezzato" Italian for wedding cake?

Walking along the garden path leading to the front door, I saw that roses and lavender had bowed to winter's arrival as had cherry trees and lovely red maples. At the two-step-up entryway, four columns supported a projecting overhang. Pressing the bell button, I heard the sentient gong signaling a visitor's arrival. I waited and appreciated the intricately carved dark wooden door. I pressed the bell button and heard the bass tone of the gong. It was one of those apparently meant to resound throughout the tall house. I looked at my watch. Baxter would have been here over an hour if he'd come straight to his home after I talked to him. I pressed and listened to the gong again. Thinking maybe he took a run to the store, and smiling as I did so, reached for the door knob. Without conscious thought, I turned the brass knob and found that it gave easily. Well, I thought, Bax did tell me to go on in, and I didn't even have to introduce myself to the careless caretaker or the Model T or recall an alarm code. With a thought to the elderly caretaker of careless safety habits, I pushed the bell button again for good measure. With the door widening, the gong was loud enough to wake the dead.

What was Bax up to? I should have made him tell me who was coming to this bash, explain the mystery guest. Pushing the door in, I entered a wide foyer. Straight back, an ornate vaulted mezzanine overlooked it. An awesome crystal chandelier hung from the frescoed ceiling. Bax certainly went for grandeur here at Ammezzato. Maybe it meant mezzanine.

Dead silence is rare in a house and when I hear it, I shiver. I took out my cell phone and called Bax. Seven, eight, nine, ten rings. I expected to hear Baxter's cell phone ringing in the house, but nope. I thought about calling Lake, or the local police. What would I say?

"Baxter?" I called. Oddly, my voice didn't echo. Surely Baxter didn't invite me here to play games. I called louder, "Baxter!"

What the hell was I supposed to do?

I crept to my left, to the wide French doors of a library. Would anyone be so entranced by a book—from the floor to ceiling shelves while sitting in an overstuffed chair on the enormously expensive oriental rug by the red marble fireplace— that they hadn't heard the gong?

I lifted my nose, somewhat like Buddy the SAR dog, to detect cooking aromas. None. My olfactories picked up a raw odor, though, indefinable but not particularly noisome.

"Baxter!"

Conscious of the gun on my thigh, I looked into the room across from the library. The billiard room looked like a game in progress had been interrupted. A cue lay on the green felt, another against the side of the table. Half the balls were in pockets. Looked like someone had spilled a drink on one end.

I raised my black silk dress and drew the Glock from its holster. I looked at steps that ran straight up to the mezzanine and a pair that wound from each side of the balcony to the upper floors. Halls led to the back of the house.

I don't think so.

With my heart beating a rumba I backed from the foyer and closed the door. Maybe Bax was in the garden picking rosemary for his soon-to-be-epicurean delight. I walked alongside the carriage house and thought about the caretaker. The formal garden was obviously tended by a gardener who knew the seasons and the reasons, but otherwise there was nobody walking its paths that I could see. I called Baxter's name.

A forest framed the back of the garden, but I wasn't dressed for a trek. I wasn't going into an unknown forest alone even if I wore safari clothes. I thought of Lake's words in front of the church. *Don the magical girdle, warrior queen, methinks we're going to have a hell of a fight before this is o'er.* I'm hoping, like Hippolyta, that, "this is the silliest stuff I ever heard."

Looking up at the house, I wondered. Then I called Lake.

"You've arrived," he said. *Was he expecting that I wouldn't have? And, am I paranoid?*

"Something's wrong," I said.

"At Bax's?"

"Yes, there's no one here. At least in the foyer and two front rooms."

"Check the garden, Bax is a flower freak."

I told him that I had. "The house is creepy inside. No food aromas."

"How'd you get in?"

"The door was unlocked." Lake started to interrupt. "Listen, Bax told me about the spare key and alarm code. I didn't need it. He's not here or he's not hearing me yell or his cell phone ringing. The gong could wake the dead."

"Where are you?"

"In the driveway, in my car. Of course he may be at the store, having found himself out of truffle oil."

"You wait there. I'll be there in twenty."

Twenty? "You flying out?"

"Driving. Like you said, I talked to Bax this morning. He invited me after Watch, which I got out of early."

"Bax lied when I asked."

"I wanted to surprise you."

"If Bax is planning a surprise, I'm gong to be plenty pissed."

"If things get hairy, call the authorities. I know Joe's in Savannah. He was at the school where Cho did her fraudulent thing. Might be a good thing to give him a heads-up. I can't, I'm off the case, but you can."

"What about you being in Augusta? Bax is still part of the case."

"As a free-born male citizen, I can visit the home of my ex-in-law."

I gave thought to calling Joe. What could I tell him? Bax's house frightened me? I said to Lake, "Hurry and we'll check out the house first. Did Baxter tell you who the mystery guest is to be?"

"Nope. Bax was full of himself as usual. Carried on about finding a genie."

"A genie?"

"He's like you. Using highbrow metaphors for regular stuff."

"Hmmmm. Could be a simile, which is different from a metaphor in that a simile likens two unrelated things to one another while a metaphor compares similar things. An analogy is a cross between the two."

He hung up on me.

Five minutes later, his car skidded from the street into the driveway.

After going through the downstairs and finding nothing but a spotless house—with the exception of the billiard room—full of antiques and no signs of a meal in progress, I took a deep breath. If anything was amiss it was upstairs. Dread crawled through my chest and I felt wobbly on my heels. I took another deep breath. *Steady, girl.*

Guns drawn, walking cautiously up the ornate staircase, upwards of the balcony—another word for mezzanine—we found five doors standing open. Together we checked them out. One had a conference room setup, two were bedrooms, another a ballroom that ran across the back and overlooked the garden. Inside the last door was a large bathroom, I assumed for guests. Across from it, a gated elevator was stuck in a recess. I followed

Lake in; he pushed the gold button for three. The top floor had four doors. Three were locked. The fourth, Lake opened. It was the staircase to the tower. In the murk of a dreary late afternoon, bulb light flowed downward.

I got the friggin' creeps again, but chased them by firming my finger on the trigger.

Following Lake upward, I sang out, "Hey, Bax. We are not amused."

No sound at all—except for my breathing and footfalls.

Holding the gun in both hands, pointing it toward the stairs, I climbed the narrow staircase sideways, a step behind Lake. Lake called, "Baxter, are you up there?"

Lake reached the top and stopped. My shoulder touched his back. He moved aside to let me put my foot on the last step. It took a few seconds for my brain to process what I was seeing, and reflectively I suppressed the urge to throw up.

He was dead.

The object of our search reclined on a chaise. I could only see his face—God Almighty—amid the faces of innumerable dolls. He was surrounded and covered in them. Artfully arranged in dolls. All those eyes looking at me. His, too.

It was like something pulled my plug. *I must get out of here. Sick. Going to be sick.* My presence of mind said: *Not at a crime scene.*

Lake moved toward the chaise and Bax, and I turned and ran down, missing steps, bolting staircases and out through the foyer. On the path, I stopped. Speed had quelled the need to throw up. I holstered my gun and felt my knees begging to sag. "I've lost it," I said aloud. "Candy ass!"

I pushed back hair, rubbed my midsection, and paced like a crazy.

Who would do this insane thing? Those artists, my God, had they lost their minds?

I didn't think—ever anticipate anything would happen to Bax. Not Bax.

By the time Lake came outside and asked if I was all right, I had worked my wits so hard my head hurt.

"Sorry about the wussy act," I answered, looking at the sky, perhaps seeking a kind of solace I didn't deserve.

He put his arm around me. "The shock." He jiggled my body gently. "You liked him."

Unable to keep the tears from falling, I nodded.

Damn it all, Bax.

Raising my head, I asked, "Did I get him killed?"

"Of course not."

He brushed away the streams on both cheeks, and I looked into his eyes. They veered to the corners and his eyelids lowered.

"Tell me what you think," I said, my vocal rhythm near manic.

He stroked my hair. "Take several deep breaths and let courage return to thy fair face."

I flicked his collarbone and pushed back from him. "I should rip your tongue out for such pity."

He laughed.

Then, like a spring releasing tension, I laughed—despite sorrow, and guilt.

"I'll get the ball rolling with the authorities here," Lake said softly so as not to sound back-to-business. "I checked Bax's pulse. His body temp is cooling. It's been more than an hour."

His first call was to Hagan to give the Bureau a heads-up. "Maybe get some more points," he joked. "Did I tell you Joe called me today and congratulated us on ridding Atlanta of a couple of dirtbags? He wants to buy us dinner next time we're in . . ."

He didn't finish the thought because that dinner would have been at Carlisle's. It took all my will to not start with the tears again. To be talking instead of bawling, I said, "Athens to Atlanta to Augusta. The Damian Hansel case is spreading across the state."

When Lake finished making the emergency calls, I said, "The caretaker. He lives over the carriage house."

"You stay here," he said, body in motion and drawing his gun.

I drew mine. "No way."

He turned, and over his shoulder gave me a hard look.

"I'll keep my emotions in check," I said.

As we walked across the broad drive to the carriage house, I continued, "I'll never live this down. Going berserk like that."

"Actually," Lake said, trying the door. It wasn't locked. "Worrying about you saved me from going over the edge. I loved that guy."

Lake found a light switch. He looked around and pointed toward a rear corner. "There's the stairs." Winding through the antique autos, Lake said, "I admired Bax's bearing, his savoir faire—if I'm saying it right. Fact, I imitated him without being obvious. That would never do with Linda's family, unless I was derisive about it."

I thought about Bax's bonding with Lake. Two very different peas in a mutual admiration pod. I could see Bax's urbanity overlaid on Lake's mannerisms and felt like crying some more.

The door to the steps was unlocked. Lake turned the knob and drew it back. It was as if opening the door deserved a groan from above. I wondered if we'd interrupted something we shouldn't have. Another groan, this time of distress. We swept the guns into firing position and Lake climbed quickly. "Police, we're coming up."

A solidly built elderly black man lay on the floor next to an iron bedstead. His leg moved. Bending, Lake felt for his neck pulse. "Weak." Lake turned the man's head carefully. "Head wound. Call for an ambulance." The man's arms moved. "Hey, buddy," Lake said. "Stay still. Help's on the way."

I ran outside to get a better signal and called the emergency number. Clicking off, I heard sirens wailing through the old money neighborhood.

Too late for Bax.

Unstrapping my thigh holster, I put the Glock inside the trunk of the rental. I didn't want the Augusta cops wondering why I was carrying a gun. In my trunk was one thing, on my thigh at a death and assault scene quite another. The first sheriff's car pulled into the drive as I wondered if I should call Oliver. But no, that bad news could wing its way through official channels.

I sat in Baxter's library and watched Lake, the special agents and detectives from the local bureau of the GBI, and the Augusta-Richmond County Sheriff's Department track in and out of the house. Joe Hagan arrived, gave me a wave, and sprung upstairs to join his cohorts. Twenty minutes later he came into the library and took a chair opposite. Waiting for his opening salvo, I could read his attitude: somewhere between curious and pissed. I'd seen it in cops before. They recognized my rights. In this instance, Baxter was my client. Until he knew otherwise, Joe had to believe me when I said Baxter invited me, and I had a right to come into the home of a client. I didn't have the right to kill the client, and I didn't think Joe considered that I had. Still, he wasn't pleased.

I waited.

"Funny thing, you know," he said and paused. "I didn't share Perry Thomas's idea that Baxter was connected to the disappearance of Hansel or had anything to do with the death of Trammel." I nodded to agree. "So I can't for the life of me understand why someone put a knife in the man's back and posed him with those dolls."

Was I supposed to furnish the answer? "It's a statement," I said.

"I can agree with that," he said with a grunt. "Let me in on your thinking."

"I never anticipated this." *I wondered if I wasn't kidding myself, although I would never admit that to Joe Hagan. Isn't a mystery summons something to cause anticipation, either negatively or positively? My nagging guilt was wrapped in that obvious interpretation. My damaged ego said my conduct was unprofessional.*

As he watched me, his mind seemed stuck on something. Then he sighed. "The county medical examiner has been held up, which is fine. It will give my forensics team a chance to get here." He sighed again. "Have you figured out where Baxter was killed?"

"I didn't see blood, but the billiard table was wet at one end." He kind of smirked. I went on, "So I'd guess he was killed in the billiard room with the knife, but I haven't a clue by whom."

He sat back and grinned. "You are an amusing woman, Dru. In the face of all you've been through in the last two days, you can laugh at death."

"You'd prefer I cry?"

"Lord no. That's not you. But don't bottle stuff up by resorting to quips." I could have dropped a few more quips on him, but I said nothing. He took a deep breath. "Why did you go into the house, given the obvious suspicious circumstances?"

And so began another round of questions. I reiterated being invited, told where the key was, and found the door unlocked. I posited that Baxter could have been in the bathroom at that time, or gathering herbs in the back garden and didn't hear the gong. In answer to his next question, I said that right away my sixth sense told me that the house was freakishly empty. I did this woman's intuition thing on purpose. Joe, the old campaigner, ignored it. He said, "I have to admit that scene in the tower is freakish. The table isn't set for dinner. You couldn't tell by the kitchen that Carlisle was preparing for a dinner party." He paused briefly, and then flashed a stern expression at me. "You have no idea who Baxter invited here besides yourself?"

"Lake eventually."

He huffed. "Besides you two."

"I pressed Bax, but he wanted to keep up the mystery."

"If it's someone in Augusta who might know of or about Cho Martine, how would you go about finding that person?"

"Since he wanted me here, I'd start with his confidants here, his inner circle, and see where it leads."

"Baxter's inner circle is in Athens. He seldom comes here, only during the Masters. Three people keep up this place, the black gentleman who you found knocked out, name's Caspar, the gardener, and a daytime housekeeper."

"Baxter is not especially snobbish, but I can't see him playing pool with the caretaker and the gardener."

"You are wrong there. Baxter Carlisle is especially snobbish, but that aside, why didn't you include the housekeeper?"

"Stereotyping," I said, shrugging. "What do you know about the housekeeper?"

"Inger Petersen is young, twenty-two, pretty, and single."

"Ah-ha." An invisible finger pressed a few brain cells but nothing significant popped into conscious thought.

He said, "You know his reputation for liking young flesh, don't you?"

I stifled my distaste. *Flesh* was not a word I wanted to hear. "It's come up. Anyone in touch with Inger Petersen?"

Joe said that Inger lived in an apartment off Kings Way. Oliver informed Joe of that fact when Joe told him about Baxter's death. Oliver claimed he'd never met Inger and certainly didn't know if she was *more* than a housekeeper. "He's pretty shook up," Joe said. Oliver also told Joe that Inger graduated from a small art school in New York. She studied Nordic art, whatever that was, and worked part-time at a gallery on Broad.

I said, "Art again. Interesting."

I heard the flap of feet on the travertine floor. Lake rounded the doorway. Joe stood. I stood. Lake drilled me with his eyes. "I'd like you to take a look."

My abdominals tightened. I could do without the grim doll visual again. Dolls with their vacant stares. Bax with his vacant eyes—eyes that compelled duty. Even dead, he was my client. I'd taken his money, and, although I'd worked for it, I owed him more than time. I owed him, and me, an explanation for his shocking murder. *Did he know why he was being stabbed to death?*

While we mounted the steps, Joe said to Lake, "You have a family connection to Baxter."

"Ex-marriage. Linda's half-brother."

"Does Linda know?"

"Yes, Linda's in north Georgia. Commander Haskell asked the local sheriff there to inform her. I didn't want to tell her on the phone."

At the tower door, we waited until two Augusta detectives walked down the steps. I'd already been questioned by them. Typical of male cops, they couldn't get their arms around a PI involved in a multi-jurisdictional murder case. We are thought of as third world—a world in which we're only capable of taking photos of cheating husbands and insurance fraudsters.

On seeing Baxter's slack, waxy face again, I took a deep breath. *This is business. You must see the crime scene for what it is.* Obvious to anyone with half sense, it was a set piece. Staged. Artful. *Art.* I listened while Lake and Joe went over the details. Baxter had been moved so the techs could examine the leather and gold-handled dagger buried to the hilt in his back. The hilt looked like the wings of a bird "The heart for sure," Joe said.

"Strong son-of-a-bitch to cut through those muscles."

Lake rubbed an index finger across his upper lip. "If Bax was making a pool shot, leaning across the table, a downward thrust could do it."

"I don't see a girl doing it."

"Cho, you mean?" Lake asked.

Joe grunted. "Wherever the hell she is." He drew in a deep breath. "Or the housekeeper, Inger Petersen."

I asked if Inger was a U.S. citizen and Joe said he didn't know. I said, "Another job for the Webdog."

The sheriff sniffed. "These damn multinationals."

Lake asked me if Webdog had gotten anything new on the Martine couple, and I told him that Viktor Martine was still closeted in meetings, and that Web's Interpol pal said he'd be the first to know when Viktor surfaced.

"This Interpol pal have a name?" Joe asked.

"No doubt," I said. "But he's Web's CI."

Joe looked like he didn't believe a web geek would have an international cop as a confidential informant. I could have told Joe his name, I just didn't want to.

Joe said, "Be sure you keep me informed. Understand?" Lake cleared his throat. I didn't say anything. Joe got the message. "Sorry to sound abrupt." He rubbed his forehead. "This case is bizarre."

I nodded, and Lake looked around the room. "It's like a damn carnival house in here. I never knew Baxter collected dolls."

You never knew a lot of things about Baxter, I thought, and Lake glanced at me. I said, "Consider this. Damian and Cho are together, alive, and have dreamed up an art scheme: Murder as Art, or Art as Murder. The ultimate in Performance Art, also called Action Art or Manoeuvre Art."

The sheriff made a scoffing sound. Lake was nodding; he'd

gone down the same road as I, but Joe seemed nonplussed. "You mean Damian murdered Baxter?"

"Or Cho did," Lake said. "She's a strong girl. A two-handed stab to the back would do it. The double-edge blade has a distinctive central spine for thrust."

"More likely Cho," I said. "Baxter would have been wary of Damian."

Lake nodded. "It's a ceremonial dagger; you can tell by the distinctive handle design."

I added, "Using an iconic dagger makes Bax's murder symbolic."

Lake said, "In the American Bladesmith Society, to be a mastersmith a candidate has to design and make an Art Knife, which is a European type dagger, usually with carving on the blade or some kind of inlaid metal like gold. Look at the ornate hilt."

We all focused on the hilt.

"Eagle wings," Joe said. "I know there are people who pay a lot of money for fancy daggers, but they don't usually leave them in people's backs. A nice kitchen butcher knife would do, like Carlisle has in his kitchen."

"It's art," I said.

The sheriff scoffed again. "They brought him up here and posed him like this? What's it supposed to mean?"

"This scene looks like Baxter was as much of a doll as his collection," I said. "His eyes are wide and staring like his dolls. Whatever blood he spit up, they wiped off. His lips seem artificially fixed in place. The M.E. will tell us."

"Rigor's begun," Joe said. "Where the hell is the M.E.?"

"At another scene," the sheriff said.

Lake faced me. "What time did you say you last spoke to Baxter?"

"One, thereabouts. He said he was halfway here." *Enough*

time to be killed and rigor to set in—enough to set a muscle in place.

Joe shook his head. A tall sheriff's deputy came in and spoke quietly to his boss. The sheriff's body stiffened. When the deputy paused, the sheriff turned to us. "A young woman's body was found on the Canal Towpath."

Lake and I glanced at each other. Joe asked, "Where exactly?"

"Past the textile mills, down from the pumping station."

Lake frowned, but I knew the towpath. It dates back before the War Between the States when draft horses and mules pulled cargo boats upstream to the locks of the Savannah River.

The deputy said, "Off the dirt road, in the trees. Found by two teens. It's called lover's lane there."

"ID'd?" Joe asked.

"Thought to be Inger Petersen."

I held back a moan of pity for a young woman I didn't know and traipsed behind Joe and Lake down the stairs and outside. I rode with Lake. He followed the sheriff's taillights up Broad Street to Goodrich, where the textile mills are located, and took Goodrich Street to the pumping station. Several squad cars were parked willy-nilly. On the lighted clay path, we walked maybe fifty yards to where authorities stood in the harsh forensic lamps and watched the medical examiner's team get ready to bag the body.

The sheriff piped up, "Wait a minute, Louis. We need to take a look first."

The medical examiner exhaled like a very put-upon man, and said, "Make it quick. Plenty of photos. No open wounds."

Lake glanced at me. We'd come into one of those tiresome sheriff-M.E. feuds.

The M.E. held up a pill bottle with a latexed hand. "Here's the cause." He placed it in a baggie and handed it to a deputy. He said, "I marked it for the chain." He let out another tired sigh. "I hear I got to go over to the Carlisle castle where the king's gotten himself killed."

A real humanitarian.

No one tried to keep me away from the scene. Lake and Joe stood a few feet apart so I got a glimpse of her in the harsh light. She wore a thick black sweater over blue jeans and hiking boots. Her blond hair was plaited, her eyes were closed, and she was curled in a fetal position like she'd lain on a pine bough for a nap. Except that for a pale-skinned Scandinavian, her face was very pink. *Cyanide or carbon monoxide.*

The sheriff motioned for his photographer to snap a few before he said, "Take her away. Suicide by cyanide. Easier ways to go."

"Sure's I'm the medic around here," the M.E. said.

When the body was taken away, the forensic team from the GBI got to work with tweezers and magnifiers. We rode back to Baxter's to listen to more Billy-goat gruff from the medical examiner. I asked Lake, "Who got it first?"

"Most likely Inger," he said, weary notes in his voice. "I'm starved. Any late-night places to eat in this town?"

"There's an all-night Barney's on Washington Road."

"There's always a Barney's. They got good cardboard pies. We'll get the body on the road to the morgue and then we'll eat."

"You'll eat."

"Come to think, bet Bax has something in the fridge." When I gulped he said, "You going to get the spooks staying in the manse?"

"I'm not sleeping in the tower."

Turns out sleep was not the order of the night. After luminoling the place for blood and finding it in the billiard room—the murderer had used soap and water to swab the surprisingly small amount of blood from the billiard table and floor—the cops bivouacked in the kitchen where I'd made coffee.

Notebooks and forensic cases were scattered on a dining table big enough to seat sixteen guests. Happy to get a reprieve from the atmosphere, I went out into the cold Augusta fog for hamburgers and drinks.

At one o'clock in the morning Oliver came in the front door. He had the strangest look on his face—like someone coming home and finding fifteen guests tramping over the place, helping themselves to whatever they wished. Good breeding and manners conquered the urge to ask what the hell was going on, and it seemed that he suddenly realized we were all investigators—of different stripes, but investigators nonetheless. "I thought it would be over by now," he said.

Lake came from the dining room into the library. "Bax's still upstairs if you would like to see him."

Oliver got very still like his body and mind had been shifted into idle. Perceptively the firmness in his jaw eased and his shoulders slackened. He looked at Lake. "I suppose I should."

"No one would think poorly of you if you didn't," Lake said. "Some people prefer not looking at their dead."

Immaculate as expected, Oliver wore tan slacks and a black polo shirt. He said, "Let me think." He walked to a chair and settled into it, his knee tendons popping. "All the way here—it's so unreal. Joe said he was with the dolls."

I dry-swallowed. Lake asked, "Did you talk to him during the day?"

"Twice," he said, rubbing a hand over the crown of his head. "I recollect the conversation, not that it's anything memorable. We talked about the menu. We would have a shortage of artichokes for the salads—the truck didn't deliver because it went off the road. A party of ten wanted to have their meal served family style, so we had a discussion about how to cost it out." His bleak eyes stared at me. "He was looking forward to your coming here this evening."

"Did he say who else was coming?"

"No, I asked, and he ignored the question. If Baxter ignores your question, you don't ask again."

"What was he preparing for dinner?"

His chest swelled, his eyes brightened. He would be tackling a subject dear to his heart. "Red pepper olive-oiled roast pork tenderloins that would be finished with apricot cream that I had prepared ahead and he brought with him. A wilted salad with champagne vinegar; asparagus almandine. Petit roast garlic white potatoes. I prepared cherry tarts, which he also brought."

All of which Lake had seen in carry-out containers in the large refrigerator, then sighed and closed the door on possible evidence.

Joe Hagan had come in and leaned against the door frame.

"The tenderloins are raw in the refrigerator," Lake said. "How long would they take to roast?"

"Twenty minutes in a four-fifty oven. Barely pink in the center. He would have had his girl put them in the oven when the last cocktail was served."

"Was his housekeeper going to act as cook?"

Without hesitation he replied, "No way."

"What can you tell us about her?" Lake said.

Oliver gave a dismissive wave. "Nothing to tell." He looked at Joe Hagan. "How long will my—will Baxter remain here?"

"We're going to move him pretty soon. Do you want to go up now?"

"I've decided not to at this time. Where will you take him?"

"To the Georgia crime lab for examination."

"A nice way to say autopsy. Then what happens?"

"Are you his executor?"

"I am. I have a Power of Attorney also."

"That gives you the authority to make final arrangements. Show us the papers and then you can tell us what those are—

the mortuary, the cemetery, etcetera."

"He'll be cremated," Oliver said.

That surprised me. Baxter seemed a man for a sarcophagus with winged angels floating over his tomb.

Oliver directed his questions at Joe while Lake, standing at a window, jangled change in his pocket, apparently deep into his own thoughts.

Joe asked, "Did Mr. Carlisle own a dagger?"

Oliver's eyebrows rose. "Not that I know of, but I don't think so."

Would a man who collects dolls also collect knives?

Oliver asked, "Any idea who?"

Joe shook his head.

Lake spoke up. "You told Joe you had never met Inger Petersen. Tell us what Baxter thought of her."

Oliver scrunched his shoulders at a question he thought he had successfully dodged. He answered that Baxter was fond of her, he supposed, although she wasn't much of a housekeeper because Baxter had someone come in and do the rough work. Oliver added that he knew this because he paid the bills. Other than that, she was a cipher.

I said, "I understand she's an artist. Do you know where she works?" I was careful not to use the past tense because Oliver apparently didn't know that he was speaking of the dead. If he used the past tense suddenly, it would make me wonder.

He contemplated me like he wondered who I was. "If Baxter told me the name of the place, I don't recall. Artists rent spaces in the back rooms of galleries."

"What else can you tell us about her?" Lake asked.

His daze deepened, became torpid. "As I've said, I write checks. Some are for her art materials. Baxter supported the arts and artists. Do you think she stabbed him?"

Both Joe and Lake shrugged. Joe asked, "Did Baxter and Inger have an intimate relationship? Sorry to be so frank."

Oliver bucked up, apparently knowing these questions needed answers and from him. "At first, I wondered. Then I realized that Baxter took his pleasures far away from his domiciles. Anyone who knew him would never believe him to be enamored of Cho Martine." He stared at me, maybe five, six seconds before he said, "I'll settle up with you. I paid his bills when he was alive. As executor of his estate, I'll be continuing in that capacity."

He'd dismissed me. But I wasn't going. "Baxter hired me to find Damian Hansel. I'll continue until I do."

Oliver's eyes shifted. "The goal, as I understand it, was to find Damian to clear Baxter of suspicion in his disappearance and to prove the stalking charges against Cho Martine false. That goal has ended."

"Not really," I said concisely. "Martine has disappeared. Damian is still gone, Arne Trammel is dead, and so is Baxter. Arne may or may not have hung himself, but someone put that dagger in Baxter's back. There's a lot of work to be done by the police and by me."

Joe spoke up. "You will learn this from the morning media so I'll go ahead and tell you that Inger Petersen was found dead on the Canal Towpath."

Oliver's face paled to artist white. "Oh my God." Horror seemed to seep from the very pores in his face. "What is going on?" He twitched. "Was she stabbed, too?"

"Poisoned."

Hanging, stabbing, poisoning—all we need is a shooting. I looked at Lake and wondered if he'd begun to connect dots.

Joe was explaining to Oliver that the billiard room, as the crime scene, was off limits for use, as were the stairs, the elevator, and the tower room when I heard clumsy footfalls on the stairs. They were bringing Baxter down bagged on a backboard.

226

Oliver stood and went to the French doors to watch his father being carried into the foyer. He took several steps to meet the attendants carrying the stretcher. They paused, and Oliver nodded for them to unzip. He winced at the eyes still open in the face, and then hovered a trembling hand over Baxter's inert chest. Finally lowering his hand to touch his dead father, he used his other hand to bring a cross from beneath the polo shirt. He put it to his lips. After lifting it over his head, he laid it on Baxter's chest and whispered, "God speed."

Joe said softly to Lake and me, "Crime folks will be here all night. No need to hang around." He looked at me. "Dru, relay any information your computer wiz comes up with. We need to find Damian Hansel and Cho Martine. They're key."

We hung around another half hour talking to Oliver—who alternated between periods of resilience and languorousness— hoping to learn something of consequence. We didn't, and it was nearly four o'clock when Lake and I found ourselves on the driveway of the Italianate mansion. Looking up at it—artificial lights sculpting it—I thought it fretted in the cold fog, like it was cross that death had come into it. I liked that about it. One day I would come back. That would be the day I found the cold-hearted son-of-a-bitch who brought murder into its walls and gardens.

"I'll follow you," I said to Lake.

"Waffle House or the diner?"

It would be awhile before I had an appetite. "You choose."

Chapter Twenty-One

We'd checked into a cheap motel to shower, change clothing, and snooze for a couple of hours. At six we caught the news. Reporters were abuzz over the murders of Baxter Carlisle and his housekeeper, Inger Petersen. Already they insinuated an intimacy between them, but, like Oliver, I believed that Baxter had learned hard lessons long ago: you don't mess in your nest. You go to a land where the birds are different than those that live on your continent.

Lake and I agreed that I should try an immediate soft approach regarding the artist community, and so after a hearty—for Lake—breakfast, I found myself walking down Broad Street where revitalization in Augusta first began. Most of the shops didn't open until ten or noon, if at all, on Sunday. Some had signs saying they unlocked their doors by appointment only. These were the high-class galleries, gold-framed among the brown earthy types. I came to a narrow single-windowed gallery called Art by Curt Miles. Peering into the window, I saw a moving shadow by an easel. It appeared real art was being created. There were no signs on or near the door, so I instinctively turned the knob, recalling how I had done the same to the knob on Ammezzato's front door. *Bad habit.* The door gave way. Inside, the shadow became the skinniest human being I've yet seen. He turned to gape. The pale blue eyes in his skeletal face were alien huge. He gave a gay wave and said in a swirly voice, "Oh my, I left the door unlocked. We're not open today."

I walked further into the room, the walls of which were a riot of abstraction and colors. "I'm looking for information."

His head cocked on his long neck. "Oh?" I thought of Road Runner as he darted toward me.

"It's about an artist who you may or may not know."

His hands fluttered. "If he's a true artist, I would know him."

"What about a her?"

"Her, too. What's her name?"

He didn't look like the type to tune into news first thing in the morning, or last thing at night. "Inger Petersen, although . . ."

"How twisted are we going to be?" he said, flitting away from me. "I'm Curt Miles, and you are?"

"Moriah Dru. Call me Dru."

"Likewise. Why are you after Inger?"

"Not *after*, Curt." I showed him my identification. "I want to learn about her."

After several gazing seconds, he said, "Inger is hardly a child. If you don't know that, I can't help . . ."

"I do know that. As far as I know she's not in trouble." *She would not be in trouble ever again.* "I'd simply like to get an idea about her work and friends. I know she's an artist and works around here. Can you tell me where?"

"Miss Secretive works at the International Gallery. She's from Sweden."

"What's her specialty?"

"Nordic Art. But her real specialty is getting exhibitions for her studio."

"What else can you tell me about her?"

He zipped toward the back of the gallery. "Water's on for tea. Do you care for tea?"

"Yes, and I'd love a cup."

"Nothing like green tea to brace for the morning."

The back room was small and crowded and smelled of turps—goes yum with green tea. I told him that I was sorry to interrupt his morning ritual. He looked at me like naughty me had snuck in, but said he was happy to share tea with a pretty lady.

He flickered over the boiling water, making me nervous. He spilled more loose tea on the small cabinet than went into the china pot. His teacups were lovely and the handles too delicate for my fingers, although not for his long spindly sticks. Lord, how thin he was.

He placed cups, teapot, and accompaniments on a tray, wavered it into the gallery, set it on a small round table, and sat. I sat, too. He fussed with the pouring ritual, then said, "Now tell me truly, what's up with Inger?"

Telling this nervous bag of bones she was dead was out of the question. "I'm looking for a woman who might be a colleague of hers, someone you might have met."

"Oooh, more mystery."

You don't even know. "This woman is Oriental, or I should be more politically correct and say Asian."

"We have several Asians in the community, male and female. Does this Asian woman have a name?"

He wasn't a newsy, but he might have heard of Cho Martine. "Yes, but I'd prefer not to say. I wouldn't want to defame her."

"I'm not understanding this. I wouldn't want to defame Inger, either, although . . ." Handsy talker that he was, he flipped one back.

He'd defamed a bit by not continuing. "As a private investigator I'm careful and discreet. What you say goes no farther."

He leaned back and grinned. "Am I ever blessed *this soppy Sunday morning!*" The long muscles of his face gave him a macabre aspect.

"I find missing people. I don't do divorces or spy for insur-

230

ance companies or lawyers."

"Your dropping Inger's name gives me pause. Maybe this Asian girl wants to be missing." I nodded to indicate that that could be true. "Where is she missing from?"

"The University of Georgia."

He rubbed his sparse beard. I'd seen goats with more chin hair. "There is someone who was here—yes, she was an Asian girl—for a short time. She wasn't at International, but Inger palled around with her for a while. A tall Asian girl."

"The girl I'm looking for is tall and graceful. Long hair."

"Yes, all that," Curt said, excitement in his eyes. "She didn't stay long, a couple of weeks and then she was gone. Inger said she left for New York."

"When was this?"

"In the summer."

"What else did Inger say about the Asian girl?"

"Just that she left for New York." He leaned close, his hands agitating. "If you're in for a bit of gossip it looked like Inger took a liking to her boyfriend."

Damian and Cho. My blood pumped up. "Did it upset the Asian girl?"

"I wouldn't know." He sat back. "I'm not her confidant, but these girls, they change partners like hair color. First with Tom, then Harry, then back with Tom. Poor Dick on the outside looking in." He picked up his teacup, and on the way to his mouth, slopped tea on his whiskers.

"Is this man a Tom or a Harry?" I said, smiling.

"I don't know his name," he said, wiping his chin. "I saw the three of them together twice, at the café across the street, but Inger and the boy were almost indecent with their hands and lips, if you know what I mean, while the Asian girl looked on."

"Did the boyfriend disappear about the same time as the Asian girl?"

231

"I've seen him since, but I can't recall where. I haven't seen the Asian girl since she left for New York. If she left for New York. You never know in our world."

I told him the Asian girl was an artist but not the watercolor and oils kind, but the Performance Art kind.

He blinked like a manic. "Intervention is it?"

"Not so much intervention as performance. Like in Atlanta, where I'm from, an artist shoved himself into a tree to show how man should be at one with nature. That kind of art."

"I'm not a ritual conceptualist. It's usually unorthodox. They use devices meant to shock their audience."

"Like the general public?"

"If they can. Artists aren't all of one mind, understand." He spoke like an elitist. "The idea is to make people rethink their notions. We are a divergent community. I express myself with oil on canvas. A ritual artist uses his body and time and space to express himself."

"Are there any conceptual artists in Augusta?"

"Troops is the name of their gallery. They go places. A group went to Wall Street dressed like bankers and brokers of olden days and threw Monopoly money in the streets. They left before the cops got there. They often have run-ins with the police."

"Has anyone been killed doing Conceptual Art?"

He stopped his hand movements to contemplate for a moment. "Now why, I wonder, would you ask me that?" He'd spoken a whole sentence without hand gestures.

"I imagine most artists think of death like all people do. However, some might like society to change its concept of death."

"Death, yes. But you said *killed*. I don't know of anyone who died during a ritual performance, but I've heard of death ritual acts like slashings and drinking blood and urine."

"Where is Troops?"

"On Washington Road. I'd caution you to use *extreme* tact."

"What? I haven't been tactful?"

He laid a hand on one cheek. "Even though they're used to being made fun of, they're very touchy."

"Do you know anyone in the group who might know my Asian girl?"

"Oh, we're back to the Asian girl. Is Inger in trouble, is that why you're asking me all this and not her?"

He was sly-smart and loved to talk, otherwise I'd be getting nowhere. "Inger is not in trouble and I need to find the Asian girl." My cell phone rang. "The world interrupts," I said. "Mind if I take this call?"

"Go ahead." He jumped up, bouncing his bony knees against the table, upsetting the teapot.

I stepped to the front of the studio and answered. Lake asked, "Where are you?"

"I found an art studio on Broad open—well the door wasn't locked."

"You didn't . . ."

"I didn't do anything. I've been having a nice chat with Curt Miles, an excellent artist, who probably saw Cho and Inger together with a young man he called the Asian girl's boyfriend. The two of them are not around any longer. The Asian girl's been gone since last summer."

"Great," Lake said. "Joe is looking for you."

"He wants to pick my brain and then tell me to go home."

"You're psychic."

"I'm not leaving until I find Cho and Damian. They can't make me."

"I know that, my darling girl, but you must not poach on their territory."

"They rounding up artists yet?"

"Not that I know of. Meet me at the Coffee Haus." He

clicked off, Portia-style.

Curt Miles had disappeared behind an easel with a canvas on it. I called his name and he reeled around it. "Yes, Dru. Did I help you?"

"I've got to go. Give me a name from Troops."

"Baby Talk."

"Baby Talk?"

"If anyone met the mysterious Asian girl, it would have been her. She gets around with her conceptual idiocies. Lately, it's been to dress like a baby and ride buses to get people thinking about how happy they were when they were small and innocent, and just when she's got them hooked into her act, she draws black and brown lines across her face. She's very nihilistic."

"Sounds like it. You, Curt, are a prince. Thanks for your help and the tea. Delish!"

"Hope you find your girl if she wants to be found," he said, dashing back behind the easel.

If she wants to be found.

"That's the last thing she wants to be," I said to Lake while he chewed a buttered scone.

Swallowing, he said, "I'm halfway with you on this art concept theme. It's crazy, but, hell, people dream up crazier things." He buttered another scone. "How many nutcakes artists are in this scheme?"

"Damian, Arne, Cho."

"You forgot a couple. An Augusta artist dead, and a rich restaurateur-slash-doll collector dead and displayed. How did the Augusta artist get involved with the Athens bunch?"

"Through the restaurateur, but I think her connection to the Athens artists is tenuous." When Lake looked unconvinced, I said, "Let's say it began with a conceptual performance. Nature trails—meaning an emotion, say fear, is natural." Lake grinned like I'd said, *once upon a time.* "Stay with me while I muse. A boy is missing for a few days. His cell phone shows up on a trail by a river in Atlanta. The community is perplexed. Then clothes are found on a trail. The uneasy community wants to know more about the person and starts to form theories. Then the oars are found on a trail in Athens, and people fear a diabolical killer is at work. When his bicycle is found, they lock their doors and hound police. That's when Damian and Cho and Arne show up to explain their concept and take a bow."

"And answer to the authorities."

"But it got bollixed and Arne was killed before the oars were spotted and the still-missing bicycle found. According to Baxter, Damian and Arne came into his bar and argued. Arne said he wasn't *doing insanity.* That phrase stuck in my head. *Doing murmurs of insanity.* It sounds like the title of a project." Lake's lips twitched meaning he had his doubts. "Then Arne is hanged in a closet. Baxter is stabbed and draped with his dolls."

"Ah-ha! So Arne is gotten out of the way because he's objecting to the project. Baxter is murdered because he overheard a couple of words?"

"No, no, not unless Baxter told other people what Arne said. I wish I'd asked him. Inger was killed because she knew the whereabouts or possible whereabouts of the creator of the project, Cho Martine."

"Why put Inger's body on the trail; the project was already thrown off track—trail."

"Placing her in a fetal position seems to suggest that they morphed the project to make sense of the interrupted concept, all to satisfy their insane minds—birth, fear, death."

"The concept has holes." With an index finger, he made a hoop in the air. "Big holes."

"You are very literal, my love. And you are right."

"I might buy it if Arne was hanged on a tree on a nature trail and Bax was stabbed on one. Then there's those damned dolls."

"Cho and Damian sure as hell won't be showing up to take a bow if that's their finale."

"You think it isn't?" he asked.

"We're assuming Damian's alive because we haven't found his body. But he might not stay that way. He doesn't seem cunning enough to hide for the rest of his life. He's wealthy and has access to money. When he accesses that access we'll find him. If he's with Cho, we'll find her. Therefore, I conclude Cho will kill him to protect herself."

"I already thought she did." He twisted his coffee cup in his fingers. "Let's say you're on to something. It's a stupid idea; fraught with risk and risk happened. But here's where I go off trail. Bax is as far from the arty crowd as I am. If this had something to do with polo ponies, he might go along."

"He hired an artist housekeeper. Oliver said he bought materials for her, his way of supporting the arts."

"She's cute. Was cute."

"And," I answered sarcastically, "Bax was killed by her boyfriend. Find him, find the murderer."

"You need complications, like your theory."

"Baxter innocently intervened."

"By stalking Cho?" His voice had risen with disbelief.

"We both know better than that. Let's look at possible reasons why she stalked him. Cho and Damian were friends. Damian and Baxter had public disagreements over the art at Carlisle's. She set Bax up to take the blame for Damian's disappearance."

Lake looked like he was considering this muddle of thoughts and words. "What about Arne's death?" Before I could answer, he said, "I know you hate the idea, but Damian is dead. Arne figured out Damian was not just missing, but dead and so he was murdered, too. For his part, Bax wasn't taking these silly accusations from a teenage girl and hired you because the police weren't doing anything."

I took up the thread. "Baxter wanted me to come to Augusta to meet with someone he thought might lead me to Cho. That was Inger. By the time I arrived, Baxter and Inger were dead. Made to look like part of the whole concept . . ."

Lake interrupted, "You're still stuck on the art thing. I'm still not sure what the whole concept means."

"Try this on, then. Murder is common in the hood and among certain segments of society, but murder is shocking when it happens at happy places, like nature trails and in doll houses."

"Man," Lake said, shaking his head. "This is creepy."

"Poor Damian. He went along with being the faux murder victim in the original concept. He disappears to Atlanta, hides his things on trails. After the public is suitably fearful and the cops looking for a body, he shows up and says, 'Hey folks, our art shows you how unsafe you are in the beautiful places you've made for yourselves.' "

Lake gave me a long, assessing stare. "You got imagination, I'll say that."

"There an artistic symmetry to it, you have to admit."

"I wish I didn't," he said, brushing his hands together, a signal to change the subject. "Call Webdog and see if he's gotten anything on the Martines. Joe's not overjoyed that a computer geek is outfoxing him."

"We've gotten use to it. So can Joe."

CHAPTER TWENTY-TWO

"Can you get hooked up with Skype?" Web asked.

"Why?"

"A transatlantic conference with Viktor Martine."

I told him that if I found a computer with a camera and the software here, the cops would want in on it. He said that Paul Ardai had a conversation with Martine and Martine said that he didn't want to talk to the cops until he talked to me—that he wanted a full briefing first.

"Hold on," Web said. The cellular air between us hummed with expectation. I heard him rattle the keyboard. Seconds later he said, "I just got an email from Paul. Back at you in a sec." After another interval of key tapping, Web explained, "Viktor Martine's on flight number two, three, eight, five, six, Brussels to Atlanta, Meet in Bronze Room near international gate. Noon. EST."

"I got goose bumps, Web." Just what a grown woman, a killer at that, should say, but it was true. My neck hairs were standing on end. "He knows something important or he wouldn't be dropping everything. Get a message to Martine that I'll meet with him. Lake will probably be with me, whether Martine likes it or not."

"Gotcha."

"Scope out what you can on a group of Augusta artists called Troops. They do Performance Art. One woman's name is Baby Talk."

"Cool."

"Cool?"

I heard Web typing as he talked. "Baby Talk. You know, Dada, as in what babies say for daddy? That's what the Dadaists called themselves when they founded their movement back at the turn of the century—the twentieth century, back before World War One. Their antiestablishment art was supposed to be nonsensical like the babble of babies."

"So Dada Art is nonsense?"

"Except it established all kinds of serious art movements, like Avant Garde, Pop Art, Performance Art—the thing your Troops are all about. Postmodern Dadaists are quite serious."

"So am I."

Web stopped typing. "Baby Talk's name is Gina Lindsey. She's an occasional guest of the Augusta police. I'll find out more."

It was Joe who helped me find Gina "Baby Talk" Lindsey. He was feeling especially grateful because I'd told him about Martine and his plan to come to Atlanta. There was no way I was going to keep that vital interview for myself. I like being a private investigator. My agency is doing very well, and I have employees to pay. Joe agreed that I should meet with Martine alone, but I would tape the conversation, letting Martine know that I was doing so.

It was four in the afternoon. Gina "Baby Talk" Lindsey was where Joe said she'd be, at the Push-Pull Café on Washington Road. A big girl, you might conclude she was dressed for a performance at the Commedia dell'Arte. Her thick, dyed-black hair sprung from all points on her head; her eyes were so encircled with black lines they dominated her face, which was painted in red and white harlequin diamonds. She sat at a table with a thirty-something couple who resembled relics of the sixties hippie movement. Joe had told me that the man also was a frequent guest in Augusta's jails. He may have been an artist, but he was also a drunk. The woman had a peace sign tattooed on her forehead.

When I introduced myself, the man snarled, "Fuck, Baby. You got the dogs on us while we're eating."

"Dogs?" I said, and looked at Baby.

Baby smiled and flicked a hair spike. "Law and order."

"I'm a private cop, trying to find someone."

"I don't rat out," Baby said, giving Peace Sign a foxy grin.

"Haven't you heard?" I asked.

"Heard what?" Baby said, lifting her bizarre face and batting her eyelashes.

"Your friend and colleague Inger Petersen is dead—murdered last night."

"Yeah, I heard. Mr. Baxter, too. Some shit-kickers cross town broke in." She motioned her head toward her companions. "It may not look it, but we're in mourning here."

"I don't know about shit-kickers across town," I said.

Baby Talk stood and looked at her friends. "Ciggie time. I'll be right back." She motioned me to follow and led outside. She reached into her costume and pulled out a cigarette pack. She didn't ask if I minded and lit up. I'm happy to report she turned her head to blow the smoke away from me. "Look," she said. "Inger had her own crowd, and I have mine."

"I get it, but I heard you were friendly."

She nodded, drew in an ample lungful of smoke, and released smoke rings through her folded tongue. That takes talent. "Inger's in the morgue," she said. "That's all I know."

"I'm looking for an Asian girl who was here for a couple of weeks this summer, who was seen with Inger a couple of times." She shook her head no, her expression that of the cross-eyed, care-less harlequin. Despite that, I went on, "Inger told someone the Asian girl had gone to New York."

Baby Talk stuck a finger where a dimple would have been if her face wasn't so round. "I know who you mean. When I went to New York, I couldn't find her."

"When was this?"

"August. We were there to install an exhibit against the crap art at the Towers. We strung dog tags through cardboard bombs."

"That's making a statement."

"Yeah. They pulled it down. But they see it, they get it."

"Did the Asian girl give you an address in New York?"

"Sure. It was fake."

That sounded like Cho. "She had to tell you her name."

"Aneko Hattori."

"Japanese."

"Duh," she said, flicking an ash from the tip of her cigarette.

"Why had she come to Augusta?"

"Why?" she asked and pooched her lips. "Are you asking because it has something to do with Inger getting killed?"

"I don't know. Did she see your art performances?"

"Once. She raved and called it atavistic. She said it gave her an idea."

"Who was her male companion?"

"All's I know is Aneko and him came from New York. Inger joined up with them. They had some kind of thing going."

"A thing—as in sex?"

She tilted her head and twitched her mouth. "Doesn't have to be sex, does it?"

"With two girls and a man, it most times is."

She shrugged and said that the man was older, maybe in his thirties, even forty. You can't always believe descriptions, but she said he was tall and that she hadn't seen a man stand that straight in her whole life. Like he was in the army. She said he wore shades and a hat all the time and his clothes were like a hiker's.

"Did you know Baxter Carlisle?"

Perking like a peacock, she said that Mr. Baxter invited her to his house once when he was here with the Masters Golf Tournament. She persuaded him to let the Troops performers do their antiwar act for him and his crowd. She was proud of the fact he applauded, although most of his guests were drunk and hooted at them.

I asked, "Was his son there?"

She said that Mr. Oliver kept to himself when he was in Augusta. She mentioned that he had a partner from overseas come down sometimes, but that she'd never seen him. They were never at the house when Mr. Baxter was. When I asked how she knew this, she said Inger talked about them, how good-looking they were.

"If I email photographs, will you see if you recognize anyone?"

She hiked her shoulder. "Sure, why not?"

While I was making notes, Joe Hagan and Lake walked into view, Curt Miles between them. Curt and Baby Talk eyed each other. "Babes," Curt said, bouncing on his heels. "They caught up with you, too."

"I wondered how she knew about me," Babes said, her tone accusing.

"Too bad about Inger," he said, his hands flapping against his sides.

"Yeah," Baby Talk said. "I don't know what *these people* . . ." she looked at me and then at Lake and Joe ". . . think we had to do with Inger and Mr. Baxter."

Curt turned his blinking, alien eyes on me. "You didn't tell me she was dead. You didn't play fair."

Joe cleared his throat to get their attention. "Thank you folks for helping us."

Curt sputtered out, "We're all different, but we're all the same, and we don't kill each other."

Walking away, between Joe and Lake, I said, "He's right. They're all different, but they're all the same. Children. Then one fine summer Cho and some unknown older man comes into their midst. Big cats among the baby pigeons."

"To do what?" Joe asked.

"To plot and plan," I said, taking out my cell phone. I called Webdog and asked that he get me a full bio on Darla Gilmeath, Oliver's mother, and have Pearly Sue collect photographs of Damian, Arne, Baxter, Oliver, Henry Hansel, Cho Martine, Kirin Littlefield, Elena Littlefield, Perry Thomas (without uniform if possible), and Ludlow Parsons.

At the same time, Joe got a call from the state's crime lab concerning the official autopsy report on Arne Trammel. The medical examiner concluded that Trammel had been strangled before his body was hung by its neck. It had to do with furrows and the braid pattern of the rope. The rope used to hang him was soft and didn't make braid patterns while he was hanging from it. However, the killer strangled him with the rope, thus marking his neck straight across. If he'd been strangled or suffocated by hanging, an inverted V pattern would have shown a diagonal across the neck with its high end where the knot was located.

Joe asked if I'd gotten anything useful from the *artistes,* and I told him that the plot was a lot older than I thought. His eyes held unrestrained doubt while I explained that an art scheme was conceived in the summer, that it didn't include murder, but murder intervened.

"That means everything," Joe said in a snotty-statey tone.

Lake said, "You need to keep on her good side."

I'd gotten to my car and pressed the unlock button. "Maybe Martine can fill in some blanks."

If eyelid movement was a meter for brain activity, Joe was thinking rapidly. "Where are you going now?"

"Baxter's house."

"For your information, Oliver never left Athens yesterday."

I understood that Oliver would be the first he zeroed in on. "Can you be a hundred percent certain?"

Joe wasn't a hundred perfect certain because he hadn't eye-balled Oliver every hour, but he didn't think he could make it to Augusta, play a little pool, stab dear old rich dad, and get back to Athens between the times Oliver had last been seen by him and the sheriff. That didn't even take into account Inger's murder. I agreed that Oliver had not traveled to Augusta yesterday, but as the benny in the will, he was a tempting suspect. Joe said, "You can't have it both ways, Dru. The murders are the work of mad artists, or for gain."

I raised and lowered my shoulders and maybe even looked a little smug because I thought I could have it both ways.

"See you in Atlanta, tomorrow, noon," Joe said. "It will be interesting."

Not for Viktor Martine. "Are you planning on busting into our meeting?"

He waved, walked away without answering, and got into his car. Lake asked, "Where to?"

"Baxter's."

"You mean Oliver's?"

"Funny, the turn of things," I said.

"Yeah," he answered. "But you're not going to get anything out of him."

"How much you want to bet?"

"I never bet against you."

Chapter Twenty-Three

The state forensic wagon was parked near the carriage house next to a police cruiser. A new Cadillac SUV had been nosed into the rose bushes. It had stickers that said it was from Clarke County and the owner was a member of the Georgia Bar Association.

The gardener was blowing leaves off the path as we walked up and pressed the bell. Good to keep to a schedule.

Oliver was not happy to see us. Oh, there was the manner and the smile and the handshake, but also evident was that little something that says you've intruded where you're not wanted. He led us into the library. Oliver must have been busy with the cleaning supplies and gadgets because when we'd left at dawn it had been in disarray. Now it was immaculate. But that was Oliver.

"Crime lab's taking it's time," Lake said.

"They've finished this floor but still working in the tower room," Oliver said. "I wanted to be here until they finish, then lock up. I've got to get back to Athens. The restaurants."

"Who's minding Bax's businesses?"

Oliver hadn't expected the question phrased like that and looked annoyed. "The staff. The restaurants are closed until after a viewing service, nonetheless I must look after special needs that always arise."

"Of course," Lake said genially. "Here in Augusta, you'll need to find somebody to take Caspar's place until he recovers

245

and hire a housekeeper, won't you?"

"I intend to hire a full-time guard and come back when I can. That is until I decide . . ."

Already making decisions before the will's read. I asked, "You thinking of selling this place?"

He struggled to hide his irritation. "Premature."

"Is Anthony DuPlessy your attorney, too?"

"As a matter of fact," he said. "Tony's here."

"Fabulous," I said. "It saves me a trip to Athens to talk to him."

"Why would you want to talk to him?"

"He's the attorney of my deceased client."

"I don't see . . ."

"What Dru is getting at," Lake said, "is that there are certain activities she's undertaken for Baxter that might need clearing through an attorney."

I didn't know what Lake alluded to, but I liked his interruption. It gave Oliver time to reconsider his petulance.

Oliver said, "He's using the study. I'll fetch him."

"I'll go with you. I saw computers. I'd like to borrow one to check my emails."

He nodded. "Of course."

Anthony stood. He'd been sitting in a leather chair behind the lovely inlaid desk. He came around to the front to shake hands. "Mr. DuPlessy," I said. "This is Detective Lieutenant Richard. . . ."

"We met at the Athens Police Department," Anthony said, appearing distracted, not looking at our faces, but at piles of papers on the desk. Obviously, he was in the process of going through Baxter's desk, piling record books and file folders on top of it. He'd been reading an unfolded document of three or four pages, but it wasn't dressed in will blue.

"You have a job ahead of you," Lake said.

"Mostly old stuff, before Baxter kept computer records," Du-Plessy said, drawing his hands apart and going to sit behind the desk. "It's necessary that we compile what comprised his personal and business life."

"Any business life here?" I asked.

"Not that I can see," he said. He laid his hands on a stack of jacketed papers. "Insurance policies here." He waved his hand over gray and green old-fashioned record books. "Gardening receipts, going back before he lived here."

"Was this house a family home?" Lake asked.

Oliver and Anthony exchanged uncomfortable glances like they didn't know certain things and were trying to find records like deeds and other important papers, even the will.

"That's a private matter," Anthony said.

"You might like it that way, but it's not," Lake said. He looked at Oliver. "Have you gotten in touch with Linda Lake, Baxter's half-sister, about succession?"

Oliver answered, "I have not. Mr. DuPlessy has consented to do that for me." Gone was the nickname, Tony.

DuPlessy looked like he'd like to show us the door. "Time enough to sort through inheritances."

"Have you found Baxter's will?" Lake pressed.

"I have a copy in my office," Anthony said. "I believe the original rests in a safe deposit box at his Athens bank. It takes time to get into that box."

"If you don't have a key," I said, looking from Anthony to Oliver. "Did you know how Baxter was leaving things?"

Oliver said, "He intended to sit down with me and our attorney, Mr. DuPlessy here, and go over his properties and put me on the deed to this house."

"When?"

Anthony interjected, "No set time. Obviously, he didn't foresee his demise. You can inform his *half*-sister that she has been named in the will, but I can't say now what the nature of her inheritance is."

By the look on his face, Oliver didn't like what he was hearing. His glance at Anthony seemed to warn against saying more.

But Anthony went on, "The Athens properties were in an estate trust, the monies to accrue to the estate and dispersed in a specified amount of time to his heirs and assigns, which includes a number of charities. Mr. Carlisle was a very charitable man." *I just bet. Wonder who's on the boards of these charities?* "It was his intent that the restaurant operations would go to Oliver and this house would be deeded to Oliver, also."

"Have you found the deed?" Lake asked.

"No," Anthony answered.

Oliver's face was a rictus of controlled antagonism. "It will surface. In the meantime, I feel it my duty to act as caretaker until we sort through Baxter's holdings."

"As Bax's blood son?" Lake asked. "Your name is Oliver Gilmeath, is it not?"

I'd never thought he was anything other than Baxter's son and fastened on his face. There was some resemblance in the coloring and the shape of the chin and nose. But unless there was a clear and concise Last Will and Testament that included Oliver Gilmeath—not simply as a generic son, but as a named individual—there was going to be a DNA analysis in Oliver's future. Trust Linda on that.

Oliver stood stiffly, his hands balled at his sides. "If you have any notion that I'm an imposter, get over it. I am Baxter Carlisle's son. He acknowledged me without question. He supported me from the cradle. I am a legitimate heir."

Lake lifted his shoulders and lowered them in a *we'll-see* gesture that further annoyed Oliver. Lake said, "I wouldn't go messing around with records, insurance policies, deeds, etcetera, until the court and all relatives and interested parties get hold of a copy of the will and the trust agreements."

Anthony cleared his throat. "Life goes on. As the estate attorney, I will see that everything is done strictly according to the law, the wishes of the deceased, and the heirs and assigns. I can do no more. That is my duty as an officer of the court."

Oliver looked my way. "Changing the subject to the matter of your contract with Baxter, have you calculated your expenses and other monies owing?"

Gee, he was sounding more like Anthony DuPlessy than Anthony DuPlessy. "I will when the job's finished."

"If you are going to continue your inquiries along the line of your theories, I'll continue to pay you," Oliver said. "How much do I owe you so far, and would you like payment now?"

"You don't owe me. You didn't hire me. My client is deceased and any money owed will be paid by Baxter's estate when I hand in my statement. Correct Mr. DuPlessy?"

"Pursuant to court approval," Anthony answered.

"Bullshit," Oliver said, raising my eyebrows at such unexpected language. "I'll hire you to find out who killed Baxter." He stared at me. "Close your account with Baxter and open one with me."

I checked my emails, then called Web. What he had dug up on Darla Gilmeath wasn't much, and I told him to dig deeper, get Pearly Sue to help with Oliver, too. Then I totaled my per diem and expenses. Oliver paid me, using his new check-writing privilege, which was granted to him as the executor of a will that was not yet proved. I executed a new contract that authorized me to investigate the death of Baxter Carlisle on behalf of Oliver Gilmeath and the estate of Baxter Carlisle to a reasonable conclusion. I would be paid whether or not the murderer(s) were charged and convicted.

We left Oliver and Anthony in the study and walked ourselves out of the house. "That was a neat thing for Oliver to do," Lake said quietly.

"Makes him look good."

"Innocent, you mean?"

"He's got the perfect motive."

"Motive isn't everything," Lake said.

"I go on it."

"I look for alibis and timelines."

"Looks solid for Oliver."

"If he even entertained the idea of offing dear old dad, he was premature. You heard—they don't know exactly how Bax left things."

"I learned from Bax that Anthony recently took over his grandfather's practice. The old man probably knew things that never got on paper. And I do believe you're right. What you're saying is, Oliver needed more time to get dear old dad to put things on paper and thus acquire more inheritance. Or it all. The hell with the charities."

"That's how I read it."

"Did you see the beneficiary on the insurance policy that lay open?" I asked.

"I don't have enough eyes to study suspects and roam over private papers."

"Susanna Lake."

"Hey, that's my girl."

"Half a mil."

"Daddy can retire."

"In trust."

"You're kidding. You saw a trust provision in the flick of an eyelash?"

"No, but it's always that way." I tapped his shoulder. "So parents don't buy Lamborghinis with kiddle-dee-dee funds."

We'd come to our cars when the wheels of another crunched

on the pavement. Halfway up the driveway, the car halted. By appearance, it was a rental nearly identical to my midsize. However, the windows were dark, and I couldn't make out the driver. For sure, it wasn't law enforcement.

The driver, apparently seeing cars on the pavement with two people ready to get into them, backed down and turned onto the street.

"That must be the accountant," Lake said. "With the prince in the counting house, needing help to find his money."

Watching the car, I said, "He could have parked behind the Caddy. I sense something furtive."

"You and your intuition."

"Sixth sense. Try and get a look at the driver."

The car idled at the curb as we drove out. Lake turned right and I went left. The silhouette in the seat showed the driver to be tall. I got his tag and county in my rearview mirror before he pressed the gas and swerved onto the driveway. The academy teaches recruits how to read tags from all angles. Academy training comes in handy.

Up the street, I turned around and called Lake with the number. "Fulton County. Want to bet the airport?"

"I'll call Joe, get him up to Baxter's."

We started the trek to Atlanta, me following Lake. It's a hundred and forty-five miles to downtown Atlanta from Augusta. Halfway into the drive on I-20, near the Eatonton exit, Lake called my cell. "Car is a rental from Fleetwood, picked up at the airport and signed for by Uli van Uum, a London address."

"So Oliver calls his boyfriend to come succor him."

"Get you around a bunch of intellects, and I have to get out the thesaurus."

"Did Joe go to Baxter's?"

"In his capacity as bureau chief in charge of the case, he

questioned van Uum who provided proof he flew from New York to Atlanta and rented a car. He provided addresses for his homes in London and Prague voluntarily. He said he doesn't know a Viktor or Cho Martine."

"How long has he been in New York?"

"A month. He has a six week exhibit. He had planned to visit Oliver after his exhibit. No need to get Webdog on van Uum, Joe's contacting NYPD."

"NYPD has nothing else to do."

"They'll check him out. See if he's taken any trips south since he got to the U.S."

"How well does Joe know Anthony DuPlessy?"

"Enough to say there's nothing dodgy about him."

"A job for the Webdog," I said.

Lake observed, "Webdog's got nothing else to do, either."

CHAPTER TWENTY-FOUR

The Atlanta Airport is a hideous mess. Didn't used to be when I was a young girl. For the last ten years it has boasted being the world's busiest airport by the number of passengers, landings, and takeoffs. If the goal was to be the world's most muddled, then Atlanta wins that prize, too. Its very name is busy. Hartsfield-Jackson Atlanta International Airport. Atlantans call it the Atlanta Airport or Hartsfield, after the first mayor in the name, Jackson being the second.

I found my way to the international gate and entered the Bronze Room. Taking center stage was a horseshoe bar with plates of finger sandwiches, veggies, fruits, yogurts, nuts, juices, coffee, and lots of teas. Behind it a fully stocked booze bar had been built. White-coated barkeeps were eager to serve the thirsty. To my right were custom club chairs and coffee tables for travelers to read or people watch. On my left, computer stations were ready to serve those who couldn't stand being unplugged.

I scanned the room. Martine must have been on the lookout because a man stood and came forward. I met him halfway. "Mr. Martine?" I said quietly.

"It is I," he said, extending his hand. After the shake, he waved to a door near floor-to-ceiling windows that overlooked a runway. "I have arranged a private room for us."

The spacious room was set up like an office with a bar off to one side. It had a small under-counter fridge and fixings for coffee and tea. He went past the bar and the desk, and I followed him to the windows where a fat jet was lumbering into the air. "I still marvel," he said, "that those flying hotels can lift into the sky. I'm a ship man myself."

"I'm more comfortable on terra firma," I said.

Martine was tall and muscular, silver-haired and tailored after the European style of business dress, which meant flashier than the average American mogul. It was his face that captivated me. The face of a man of the sea, deeply tanned, with the bluest of eyes set in crinkled lines. Sometimes you just like someone instantly. You trust them to take care of your baby while you go to the restroom or hold your bags containing thousands of dollars. Were it not for my deep love of Lake, I would have fallen for this man the instant he smiled.

"We must get to the point, I fear," he said. "I have to travel to London shortly."

Good luck with that. I'd seen Joe and Lake come into the Bronze Room just before Martine led me into the private office. "You came all this way to talk personally about Cho Martine, your daughter?"

He nodded curtly. "Yes."

We sat in barrel chairs facing each other. In between us was a tray with Perrier, juices, biscotti. He reached for a water and I for an orange juice. We uncapped and drank; him glancing toward the plane lifting off, me feeling a tug of unease. When we'd placed the drinks on the tray, I said, "Do you mind if I audiotape this conversation?"

His marble blues met mine. "I do not. You may share it with the police. You do intend to do that, do you not?"

"They allowed me to talk to you in private, as you wished, but I couldn't keep them from knowing of this meeting."

"I understood that."

"They will want to talk to you also."

"I think I can clarify adequately."

"Regarding your daughter?"

"That is so."

"It's funny," I said, without a hint of laughter. "I thought she was an imposter. I had my assistant look up likely places where she could build an identity."

"That likeliest place is where you exist," he said. *An enigma, no less.*

"Your daughter is missing," I said.

"That is true."

"Do you know where she is?"

"Not exactly."

"When did you last see her?"

"Two years ago."

"A family estrangement?"

"I am not deliberately deceiving you, Miss Dru. My daughter is dead. Her ashes were scattered on the lake near our Swiss home. So you see I am not exactly sure where she is."

I felt like I'd been tested and found wanting. "Tell me what you need to say."

"My wife is still distraught. That is the reason I don't want the police questioning our family. I will lay out the situation."

"How old is, was, your daughter when she died?"

A blur of pain dulled his eyes. "Eight years old. She and her nanny and her dog, Yettie, went to the lake that day. Her nanny and Yettie came home. Cho went to the morgue. She had drowned."

Drowned. Hanged. Poisoned. Stabbed. Shot to go.

He said, "You look visibly shocked, Miss Dru."

"I am. And I'll tell you why in a bit. Was it an accident?"

His features seemed to close in a guarded way when he said it could have been an accident and that the nanny didn't admit to being negligent. It could never be proved that the nanny had

255

purposely done anything to cause Cho's death. Cho, he said, was an excellent swimmer, having swum in the lake since she was a year old. She was found in six feet of water with an unexplained small bruise on her neck.

"What is your nanny's name?"

"Aneko Hattori."

My mind had made the leap when he said that Cho was dead, nonetheless I felt an involuntary tic in my right eye. "Tell me about her?"

"She came to take care of Cho the year before. Aneko presented a sweet disposition to us. My daughter worshipped her. They were both Japanese, you see, as is my wife. But my wife is very delicate, and she wanted someone to take care of Cho, someone who would understand her. Europe is not the States when it comes to discrimination, particularly in the upper classes, but Cho was self-conscious about being different than the other children in her school."

"How old was Aneko?"

"I had my secretary look it up. Twenty-three years of age at the time."

"That would make her twenty-five now."

"Yes."

"We know that Cho Martine, the imposter Cho Martine, falsified records in the Savannah, Georgia, school system in order to attend the University of Georgia. She did it with a computer. Did she use computers when she was with you?"

"We called her a genius. She taught our Cho to play the games and many different aspects of the computer. We were quite happy about her work with Cho."

"Did you do a comprehensive background check on her?"

He was adamant that his wife and secretary had vetted the Japanese woman thoroughly and that his wife had final say for the nanny of what was to be the only child she could bear.

"Where was Aneko from?"

"Born in Tokyo, studied in London, having attained a degree in fine arts there. I have in my briefcase a copy of the materials we had on her. I have a copy for you and your associates."

My associates, the cops.

"Did you ever get a call after your daughter's death that concerned Aneko Hattori? Someone asking for recommendations, that kind of thing?"

"No. I asked my secretary who has been with me for twenty years, and he said that after that terrible day, he never heard from her or anyone asking about her. She didn't come to the funeral service. She must have perceived our suspicion and must have known she was not welcome. The police couldn't find her after she gave her initial statement. My wife will not hear her name."

"Now that you've learned Aneko appropriated your daughter's identity, do you think it possible that she deliberately killed your daughter to do just that?"

"It's tempting, but in honesty, I can only accuse her of being careless. She was sunbathing on the dock, she said, with a magazine, but she swore she kept her eyes on Cho. Then Cho went under. Aneko went in after her, but could not find her."

"Is the bottom of the lake treacherous?"

"It is not. It is a clear mountain lake. It is always cold, but clear green, and you can see the bottom. I don't know how she overlooked seeing Cho's struggles, or finding her, or bringing her to the surface. She claimed on her application that she could swim, but later said that she wasn't a swimmer. She had lied and our daughter died."

He was a man still tormented, still trying to understand the tragedy that had come upon him. The tragedy named Aneko Hattori.

"I came here for my wife," he said. "I do not want her

disturbed by this inquiry. She is fragile. She often finds she has no reason to live, and for that reason she always has attendants."

"I'm terribly sorry for your loss and for her unhappiness."

"You are kind."

"Did Aneko have a boyfriend?"

He hunched his shoulders. "A friend that is a boy, or a lover?"

I smiled. "Either."

"When we would travel, in her free days she visited with art people, particularly in Rome and Paris and Prague. It was mere weeks before we lost Cho that I saw her in a Rome café where she ate and drank with two young men. They were happy and drinking."

"Americans?" I asked, thinking of Damian and Arne.

"I am not sure. I passed by them but I did not stop to talk. I am an English speaker, but I do not speak or hear like a native. They spoke English, but I could not tell if they were British or American."

"If I showed you photographs, would you know these men?"

"I could not say. They were typical young men, not old, or fat, or bald."

I rose. "Let's exchange documents." He followed me to the desk where I had deposited my briefcase. I removed the photographs that Pearly Sue had collected. Since my initial request, I'd added a few more. I laid them out on the desk top. Baxter Carlisle, Damian Hansel, Arne Trammel, Oliver Gilmeath, Perry Thomas, Ludlow Parson, Joe Hagan, Henry Hansel, Uli van Uum, Curt Miles.

After several minutes, he shook his head. "I can't be sure." His brow furrowed. "You understand, I'm sure, the seriousness of pointing an accusing finger." I bobbed my head to show that I did understand. "So I do not accuse, but one of these men is very like a man I saw with Aneko." He picked up the photographs and arranged them so that the picture of Uli van Uum was on top. He had lingered a moment on Hansel's photograph.

He handed me the photos and said with sly merriment crinkling his eyes, "Young men look alike to old eyes like mine."

I took out the school identification photograph of the woman I knew as Cho Martine and handed it to him. "Is this your nanny?"

His eyelashes batted feverishly. "It is she." He paled and I thought he might faint.

"Are you all right?"

"No I am not. This has upset me greatly. My wife must not hear of this."

"What else can you tell me about Aneko Hattori?"

He took a long leather wallet from his breast pocket and handed it over. "Her resume." He went back and sat in his chair. Another jumbo jet crept into the sky. He said, "When all is accounted for, I do not know much other than what was on her resume. She did say she is of Samurai blood. Very proud, she was."

"I saw fierceness in her face."

"It could be more fiction than truth with an imposter like that," he said, looking at the photograph that he'd laid on his knee. "It is how you make it; how she made it. She acted a sweet girl, but I have come to think of her as a she-devil."

He reached out with the photograph. I took it, saying, "I believe that she is evil. That she was evil when she was in your employ, even before that. I believe she may have deliberately drowned your daughter."

"To assume her identity?"

"It isn't unusual for imposters to take the identity of deceased children." I held up Damian and Arne's photographs. "These young men were students at the University of Georgia. As artists, they may have met her in Europe on one of their jaunts. Let's say Aneko wanted to come to America, but not as Aneko

Hattori. Perhaps she couldn't enter on her own name; we don't know yet. When she met these young men she may have called herself Cho Martine and claimed she was your daughter. That would give her cache in the eyes of the rich American students."

He rested his back against the easy chair. "Yes, I do see. She had access to all of Cho's records, even her passport—any identifications she needed. And I must admit forgery is an art form in some of our countries."

"As an artist and computer expert, she may have forged them herself."

"It is reprehensible, these people."

"Last summer the fake Cho showed up at an Augusta, Georgia, artist enclave claiming to be Aneko Hattori. It seems she retained her real identity when it suited."

"What a tragedy this is," he said. "She is poisonous. A spider waiting in its web."

I handed Damian's photograph to him. "She became friends with this man. We believe they were hatching a Performance Art scheme to occur after she enrolled at the university."

He shook his head and handed the photo back. "There are idiots who do this in Europe. The scourge. They call themselves artists. They are nothing but pigs at the trough, garnering funds for their disruptive performances. In Copenhagen they drenched themselves in the blood of small animals and stuck needles in their skulls. What is artful about that?"

"It's the kind of art that's supposed to make us think differently about our values and culture and way of thinking. The object of conceptual Performance Art is to shock. I think we're in the middle of the performance right now. The shock is still to come. So far, one of the Americans"—I handed him Arne's photograph—"is dead from hanging." I offered Baxter's photograph. "This man was found stabbed to death in his home, and his housekeeper, an artist herself, was found poisoned. I don't want to upset you any further than you are, but your daughter's death by drowning might have initiated the performance, its beginning. Each death is by a different method."

His throat emitted a guttural, "Vile." He handed the photographs to me. "Aneko was gifted enough to have conceived this grand scheme."

"And she was a very patient spider in spinning her web." I heard the door click and look over my shoulder. Joe Hagan and Lake walked inside and closed it.

Viktor Martine looked at me. "They have come."

"It is necessary," I said.

"I do not want to be in the newspapers. My wife . . ."

I rose. So did Martine. Lake held out his hand and introduced himself.

Joe said, "I'm Special Agent Joe Hagan with the Georgia Bureau of Investigation. We need to talk."

"I have a plane to catch," Martine said.

"Unless it's tomorrow, it will be leaving without you."

Martine looked at me, resigned. "I knew this when I came. I am not stupid about Americans."

Lake said, "We'll make this as brief as possible and get you on your way."

"I do not want headlines," he said. "It will kill my wife."

"If we can avoid reporters, we'll be more than accommodating," Joe said. "I don't like headlines either."

I gave the photographs to Joe. Lake knew it was the proper thing for me to do since Joe was in charge of the case, and Lake was on admin leave. To further Lake's non-involvement, Commander Haskell opened the door and walked in. I opened the leather wallet with the Hattori resume and scanned it while listening to Lake. He said, "I suggest Mr. Martine leave with Dru and myself. We'll check him into our safe room in the hotel, away from prying eyes and ears. I suspect half the staff here is in the pockets of reporters on the lookout for famous people traveling through."

"I am not famous," Martine said.

"Lucky for you," Lake said. He looked at me. "You recorded?"

"Yes," I said, removing the recorder from my jacket pocket and handing it to Joe, along with the resume.

Joe said, "We'll review it here while you get Mr. Martine settled."

At one of the nicer hotels near the airport, Viktor selected a green bottle of beer from the refrigerator, and I water. We spoke about the case, going over the same facts, and then he reminisced about his daughter and how good Aneko was with young Cho. "They both loved Prague. I did some work there for a couple of months and Aneko took Cho all over the city. They had a lovely time. I recall the time Cho wanted to go to the art institute with Aneko. When she came home, Cho had a hard time explaining the exhibits." Viktor smiled at the memory. "She tried to explain a symphony of gas bubbling and people that looked like microphones. She told me that the exhibit was called *The Unreality of the Real* and tried to explain what it meant. I thought then that it would take her several more years to understand it. I will always regret she never had those years or that understanding."

Joe and Commander Haskell arrived. Lake was unhappy about not staying for the questioning, but he was on leave from APD until the church massacre—as the press labeled it—was resolved.

I bid Viktor goodbye and God speed and wished such awfulness didn't visit the truly kind-hearted so often.

It was three o'clock. I had time to go home, shower, and dress for dinner with Mama. I hadn't planned to remind Lake, but he said, "What time do we need to be there?"

"You don't have to go."

"Let's not go over it again." I didn't blame him for the somber mood.

"Four-thirty is the first seating. Mama likes to eat early."

"Me, too," he said. "Then I can eat later."

"If you have the appetite for it," I said.

CHAPTER TWENTY-FIVE

Mama can walk, but an attendant wheeled Mama off the elevator. When I asked, the young woman said she'd been in bed all day. I nearly went on a rant, but didn't with Lake listening. I generously tip attendants to keep her out of bed during the day. I don't want her sleeping her life away. Apparently—if it's a conscious thought—Mama's all right with it.

I bent to kiss her forehead and looked into her dazed eyes. "Sleepy head. It's about time you rose and dressed."

"Moriah, my pet," she said, patting my cheek. Mama's not a kisser, but rather a toucher.

"Good to see you, Mrs. Dru," Lake said.

"Where have you been?" Mama demanded, looking up at him.

"Getting ready to see you."

"It's about time," she said, ruffling her shoulders. "Somebody needs to scrub the floors around here."

Lake pushed her chair into the dining room.

The round tables were set for six. The wide place settings accommodated wheelchairs.

The three of us sat uneasily and listened to the mother and son opposite, something we couldn't avoid since the elderly woman was nearly deaf. She shouted, "When is supper coming?"

Her son smiled and touched her hand. "Mother, we're about to be served."

"They lost my glasses today," she said.

"But now they're found," he said, soothingly.

"Yesterday they lost my teeth."

"Your teeth are in your head."

"They're not mine. They belong to that whore."

"Mother, quiet, please."

The salad came—a lime green jelled creation with cream cheese on the bottom and shredded carrots on top. I'm not fond of jelled salads or desserts; neither is Mama.

Lake said to Mama, "This is festive."

"You can have mine."

"Mine, too," I said.

Lake looked put-upon already.

We got through that course with little conversation from the mother and son. Except that the woman ate sloppily, the slick gelled substance bounding down her chin and onto her breast to carom onto her lap. Her son flashed us an occasional apology.

"Griselda had a birthday party today," Mama said. The only Griselda I knew was a neighbor who had a cat my daddy hated. Big yellow, nasty tabby.

I said, "How old is Griselda now?"

"Six."

"Six is a nice age," Lake said.

"Six is a stubborn age," Mama said. "Cats are so independent."

"Yes they are," I said.

Lake said, "What are you reading, Mrs. Dru? I know you're a great reader."

"*Cat on a Hot Tin Roof*," she said. "Cats are so independent."

"What else?" I asked. "Have you finished *The Shell Seekers*?"

"Never heard of it."

The woman piped in. "Dumbest story every written."

The son said, "Mother, don't intrude on others' conversations."

"Go to hell," she said.

Lake turned to Mama. "Would you like to go for a ride after dinner?"

"I'm not going anywhere with that cat."

"We won't take it," Lake said.

"I'm tired, I need to lie down."

"We haven't had our entrée," Lake said.

"I have."

"You haven't eaten a thing."

"I'm finished. I never liked steak."

A waiter brought in plates of Chicken Divan—shredded chicken, tiny bits of broccoli in a cream sauce. It looked like something that cats eat. I hoped Mama didn't get on that wavelength again. The waiter laid separate servings of carrots and peas before us and added a saucer with a roll and butter. I snuck a look at Lake, who'd been expecting me to. He gave me a tight-lipped smile and said, "Chicken and broccoli, one of my favorites."

Mama said, "I don't eat cat food. Some do, but I don't."

The woman across the way said, "Don't talk like that at the table." She brought a forkful of the viscous chicken mess to her mouth. Half of it slid off the fork sending waves of nausea through my stomach.

"No salt, no pepper?" Lake asked.

"Can't have it," the woman said. "Blood pressure."

"I see," Lake said. He'd actually taken two bites of the goop.

I played with a piece of roll. Mama's folded hands never left her lap.

"Ouch," the woman yelled. "That's about enough from you."

Her son dropped the napkin with which he had wiped her face. "You've got casserole everywhere," he said.

"Leave my fucking mouth alone," she said.

My mother straightened. "I beg your pardon, you don't talk that way in church."

The woman leaned toward her. "You go to hell."

An attendant came, spoke softly to the son. He rose and wheeled his mother away.

"Such a ta-do," Mama said. "I'm stuffed. It's past my bed-time."

We sat in Mama's parlor and watched her watching out of the window. Just looking down at people and cars on busy Peachtree Street.

Lake said, "It's a fascinating street, isn't it, Mrs. Dru?"

After several moments, she answered. "Mr. Dru said it was the most famous street in the world. I told him it was not. Twenty-One-B-Baker-Street is." She looked at Lake. "Don't you think it is, Mr. Dru?"

"I think you are correct."

Ten minutes later we left. I went through the revolving doors in tears. On the sidewalk, Lake said, "We'll take your mama away from here. She's rotting away." He'd thrown me a life raft. "Let's go get a steak. And if you ever make me broccoli and chicken, I'll dump it in your lap."

We drove separately to Longhorn's, the original of the chain that began on Peachtree Street. It was good to sit in the rustic booths, crack shelled peanuts, and listen to country music.

Joe called Lake and said that they'd kept Martine until his story checked. Most everything he and Commander Haskell got was already on the tape I'd recorded, except they'd pumped him on the identity of the other man with Aneko at the café in Rome. He suggested it might be Damian Hansel, but he wouldn't swear to it. He seemed pretty sure about Uli van Uum.

He swore he'd previously never seen a photograph of the artist because he didn't care about the art world.

I stayed with Lake but had too much on my mind to be a good lover. Discerning this, in seconds he was fast asleep. At the window, I rubbed my arms, disquieted, looking at the stars and the waning gibbous, desperate for inspiration. Cases are unique, except for the period where the pieces should come together, but won't. Oliver couldn't have killed Baxter; he was in Athens. Uli was in New York, but private flights could get him into Augusta and back to New York in a day's time. Baxter knew Uli so he would invite him into his home. Did the artist stick an ornamental dagger into his partner's father's back? Then there was the Arne-Damian-Aneko aspects. Uli was from Prague so he might have met Aneko—I'd begun thinking of the imposter by her real name—on one of her trips to the art institute with or without little Cho. In Europe, had Uli and Aneko connected with the American vagabonds, Damian and Arne? Before I realized it, clouds had massed, hiding the stars and the moon. Now the night was as dark as a tomb.

Tomb. Why was Oliver reducing Baxter to ashes?

When I finally fell asleep I dreamt of dark places—catacombs and crypts and black cascading water.

I awoke when Lake got up at four-thirty. He dressed, hugged and kissed me, said to get more sleep, and that he would be back and we'd go to breakfast.

When the door closed, I called Webdog; he who seemingly never sleeps. His voice was throaty with sleep when he said, "Paul will get back later this morning on Uli van Uum."

"Sorry if I woke you."

"I grabbed a few Z's having put the Mac on autopilot to search out Anthony DuPlessy's background."

"Anything useful?"

268

"How's fraud."

A giggle escaped my throat. *Imagine that—a fraud for a lawyer?*

Web said, "It happened when he was in law school." *So that's where they learn it.* "It was a commodities futures Ponzi scheme where they got investors to pool cash and bet on pork bellies and such. Eventually, profs vouched for their otherwise upstanding character and excellent grades. Judge ruled youthful indiscretions on the two defendants. Money returned, probation for two years, clean from then on."

"You said 'they.' Who else? Baxter?"

"Close. Oliver Gilmeath."

"Oliver?"

"College classmates, although Gilmeath was in accounting, not law."

I rolled over and slept like the drugged until Lake came back. I felt his fingers caress my cheek. "You don't wake up, you'll sleep through the performance."

I propped on an elbow.

Lake explained, "Baby Talk left a text message."

"About?"

"The artists at Troops are eulogizing or ridiculing—take your pick—the Augusta art murders today at three. I'd be there if I was you."

While I conjured images of this ghoulish vulgar event, Lake said that Oliver was in Augusta presently and that the restaurants would open the day after a service for Bax, one being held for the citizens of Athens on Tuesday where they could file past his open coffin. It gave me chills thinking about open coffin viewings. There were many who could attest that it was Baxter Carlisle in a closed coffin.

I threw the covers aside. "Geez, it's cold in here."

"The heater gets fixed today," Lake said. "And, by the way, Arne and Damian went to Prague two years ago. Paris and

Rome last year. Henry said that Damian never mentioned having met the imposter Cho nor Uli van Uum."

I mumbled, "Rich people go to Europe like we go to Florida, in winter, to get warm," then wrapped the quilted robe around my body as I told him about Web's info.

He said, "Some youths—as my daddy called delinquents— shoot out street lamps or get skunk drunk every night and screw what'll lay still for them. Oliver and Anthony, however, go into the commodities business."

"Add Uli van Uum to the mix and what have you got? An artist, a lawyer, and a restaurateur. I hope to meet the artist today. And you can be sure, my sweet man, I'll be careful about accusing Oliver of not being Bax's son."

Lake grinned. "I thought I was rather clever. Got his blood up. Are you going to mention the Ponzi scheme?"

"I might, just to rattle them," I said, heading to the rack where my clothes hung. "Aneko links the players in the scheme. So which of those evil geniuses will give me the clue?"

"When you get it, will you tell me in understandable sentences what came first—the murder plot or the art escapade?"

I made for the shower. "I can't wait to see Troops's mockery."

"Do us a favor, Dru," Lake called.

I turned and stuck my tongue out at him. "I know; don't become part of the performance."

CHAPTER TWENTY-SIX

There were no cars on the mansion's driveway, but the carriage house was big enough to hide at least eight cars, not to mention bikes, trikes, cycles, wagons—and a small wingless plane.

Not surprising, no one came to the door. No need to rap until the knuckles bled, the door wasn't going to open. Oliver wasn't going to appear. Intuition and logic said he was inside. I'd called his cell three times and got the answering option. My new client was being elusive.

To aggravate him if he stood at the window, I sat in my car on the pavers and dialed Web. "Any luck with Interpol?"

"A few emails from Paul telling me to keep my chemises on. Van Uum apparently travels between the continent and the U.K. frequently. It's harder to trace someone's moves now that they don't automatically ask for visas at border crossings."

"Did you call Joe with the Anthony DuPlessy information?"

"Yeah, but he already knew it."

"Bastard. He didn't share that with Lake."

"Drinking buddies at night, territorial rats during the day. There's someone wants you to call her."

"Who?"

"Kirin Littlefield."

"This case is so busy, I overlooked her. Got a number?"

"Here 'tis."

We rang off and I called Kirin Littlefield. She was with a patient and would call me back.

Cruising Broad Street, past the James Brown statue in the median and across from Augusta Common, I could feel the buzz along Artists Row. There were posters on every corner—nailed to sticks in the ground, tacked to telephone poles, plastered on brick buildings, posted on glass doors. The title of the exhibit was *Dolled up for Death*. The letters were superimposed over a likeness of Bax in a hard hat, like polo players wear, lying among dolls.

Curt's shop was locked up. The only store open in the district wasn't a gallery or art studio, but a card shop. I walked in. Nobody out front. "Hello?" No answer. I walked toward an open door at the back of the shop. "Anyone around?"

A woman came out. Stout, thirty, brass blond hair, plucked eyebrows, but pretty rosy cheeks. "You need help?" she asked, her voice a drawl.

"Where is everyone? All the shops are closed."

"Most always are on Mondays. After weekends."

She said she was locking up early so she could be at the exhibition. When I asked what the exhibition was about, she asked if I was a tourist. I said I was from Atlanta and she told me about the *big bug* that owned a mansion and his maid. She said the exhibition had music and the artists were *real good*.

I called Kirin Littlefield again.

"She'll be right with you," her receptionist said. And she was. She said she'd spoken with Baxter twice in the last couple of days and felt she knew me.

"I'm truly sorry about Baxter, Miss Littlefield. He was a fine man."

We agreed to first names.

Kirin said, "Baxter called me the afternoon of the day he died. He planned on coming to Savannah the next afternoon and we would have dinner. The reason I called you is that he was very mysterious. He spoke of the girl, Cho, who has disappeared with another art student. And then there was their friend who was killed. He was excited but not very concise. He was confident you would untangle the whole jumble."

I filled her in on the case that began with Linda Lake asking me to help Baxter out of a jam and ending with Aneko's identity.

Kirin spoke about Bax's being a comfort all these years. "We grew up together. It's hard to think of him gone."

"He told me he wanted to marry you."

"Bax was a little older than me. Of course, back then, that *little older* meant a lot more than it does now. How much did Baxter tell you about us?"

"He loved you, but you were too young."

"Back then, he never fondled me or anything like that. When we grew up, with all our dinners and travels together, we never had sex, never so much as touched a private part. We just had fun."

Women are lucky when they have a friend like Bax. I said, "I know that you've written about your abusive stepfather."

"I hated him until I gave birth to my beautiful daughter. She's very special, so I've come to accept that sperm providers deserve a nod even when they're bastards."

I doubted I could feel the same way, but I would never know. "How's your daughter with it?"

"She doesn't care how she got here, just that she's here and having a wonderful life."

Time to get to the mystery. "In what way was Baxter mysterious?"

"First let me say Baxter would never stalk anyone. He's not interested in people, if you know what I mean?"

I told her I did and when she mentioned his overblown sense of proper behavior I couldn't help smiling. She continued, "Here's the mysterious part. Baxter said his housekeeper knew something about the Japanese girl who stalked him, then turned around and accused him of stalking her."

"That would be Inger Petersen."

"Now the housekeeper's dead, too," Kirin said.

I asked if Bax told her what Inger Petersen knew.

"It's all so confusing, Dru. She apparently had two names—this Japanese girl. Someone recognized her is what Jeannie told Bax. He was anxious for you to hear what Jeannie had to say. He thought you might be able to find the Japanese girl from that. Then you went ahead and found her on your own." She sighed. "Poor Bax. I'll always remember how excited he was."

I would, too. "Kirin, you keep saying 'Jeannie.' The girl's name was Inger."

"Well, maybe. But he said Jeannie's name a couple of times. I could have misheard. It happens in my line of work when you see so many strangers."

Kirin didn't know who the *someone* was that recognized the Japanese girl and told Inger—who she called Jeannie. I figured it was Uli van Uum, a man I hoped to speak to soon—here in Augusta.

Then my mind stuck on Jeannie. "Kirin, you said Bax said Jeannie's name several times. Are you sure he was talking about his housekeeper?"

Dead air hung between us, as if Kirin were pondering. "Well," she said, "He didn't say that his housekeeper's name was Jeannie, but he talked about a Jeannie. Believe me he was as excited as I've ever heard him."

Jeannie. Genie. Lake had said Bax told him he'd found a genie. Couldn't be the housekeeper.

"Anyway," Kirin went on, "after that Bax reminded me that he left the dolls to me and Elena. Elena was the only one he would let touch the dolls. He told me many years ago that he collected them for me. I think he got the idea when I gave him my Raggedy Ann doll. I didn't want her seeing what my stepfather did."

Her tranquility had me wondering if she'd gotten psychological help. Maybe writing the book was cathartic. "Did Bax bequeath the dolls to you in a will?"

"I didn't ask, and he didn't say anything about a will. You know Oliver, right?"

I said somewhat.

"I called to ask him about the dolls. He hasn't called back. Anthony DuPlessy is his attorney, and I called him a couple of times, too. He must sleep at the courthouse."

"When attorneys don't want to talk to you, they're in court."

"The news is out that Baxter was killed among the dolls."

"Technically not, Kirin." I told her he was killed in the billiard room and posed in the tower room with *some* of the dolls.

After an interval, she said, "Could you get the word to Oliver or his attorney that if the dolls are mine, I'd like to keep *those* dolls in that room separate and bury them with Bax. Is that reasonable to ask?"

"Oliver said Bax wanted to be cremated."

Her intake of breath wasn't surprising. "You're kidding me. Baxter bought a cemetery lot to build a crypt for him, me and Elena, plus three others. I'm on the deed with him. Above all, though, Bax couldn't stand fire. He was the only teenager I knew that didn't play with bottle rockets and cherry bombs."

"Does that make you suspicious, too?"

"Well, yes, but he *was* murdered, wasn't he? No doubt about that?"

"True, and until the murderer is discovered, the body is evidence. As are the dolls."

"You don't think Oliver . . ."

"Oliver didn't kill Baxter. He was in Athens, unless he could get back and forth from Augusta in under an hour. It's eighty miles, one way."

"Oliver can fly a plane."

"The Carlisle plane wasn't flown that day."

Kirin said that Baxter sometimes flew loaners and suggested Oliver might have done the same. I asked if she thought Oliver capable of killing his father.

"I don't know him that well," she answered. "Rather stiff, but good-looking. He lacks Bax's charm, but then—you know that story."

I said I knew the story, but that I'd never met Darla Gilmeath. Kirin told me that Darla lived in Savannah now, and that she, Kirin, was her neurosurgeon. "She has a bad back from an automobile accident. You'd never know her origins were rather—um—humble. Speaks the Queen's English better than the Queen. Baxter did right by her. After she divorced that pig she married instead of Bax, she and Oliver did very well. Bax was proud of them both. Darla practically lives in church now. I'm assuming Oliver is Baxter's major beneficiary."

"I, too, assume. Oliver said nothing about the dolls. Neither did Anthony DuPlessy."

Kirin hummed. "Maybe Baxter didn't name us in his will. That would be unlike him—to remind me, then leave things to my word against anyone who wanted the dolls."

I wound up the conversation by telling her to watch herself and Elena until we found Baxter's killer. She remarked that if she and Elena were in danger, there must be something funny going on with Bax's estate.

I rang off thinking, *no doubt about it.*

CHAPTER TWENTY-SEVEN

Lake didn't know what Bax meant by finding a genie, so I called Webdog. He was more than happy to locate any genie that might pop into our case.

I didn't have much trouble finding the *theatre*. The cop tape wrapped around trees on the trail, and the audience was some fifty feet away from where Inger's body had been found. A young man with a large cooler on a strap around his neck sold water and Cokes for two dollars. Young people made up most of the audience—students in jeans and anoraks, those with babies had them strapped to their backs or fronts, motorcycle freaks in leather. Others happened upon the scene, like dog walkers, runners, and boaters on the river who'd been attracted by the crowd. All eager to catch the show. In my work clothes—dark slacks (hiding my gun), dark turtleneck, peacoat—I looked as much in uniform as the cops who patrolled the edges, hoping perverse enthusiasm didn't get out of hand.

A horn blew and the crowd noise halted. The artists from Troops—I assumed—wearing doll costumes emerged from the trees and arranged themselves as stage props. A figure darted from the towpath. The half-masked female wore a white body suit, fitted to every crack and crevice, mound, and indention. In front of the cast, on the dirt, she laid and curled herself into the position in which Inger had been found. Apparently the Troops artists didn't know Inger was found fully clothed, but heck, naked is better when drama calls.

All of a sudden a recording of the Rolling Stones pierced the cold, eerie air. "Start Me Up" blared out. I love the Stones. I know the lyrics of every song they've ever sung. Mama loved rock, so I grew up on the Stones and Led Zep. Daddy used to gripe that such crap was going to ruin my impressionable mind. Maybe it did, but I'm here to say that not all Stones songs bring Satisfaction—like the last line of the current offering. Poor Bax, being parodied in death about his love of young women. It's enough to make a grown woman cry.

A male figure rushed out from the trees dressed as Sugar Daddy Ken, Barbie's aging boyfriend. The silver-haired, fake-tanned Ken wore a green-and-white patterned jacket with a pink polo shirt and white pants. He had a stuffed white dog on a pink leash. Ken also carried a bottle labeled in big black letters: POISON. He drenched the girl on the ground with viscous black sludge. The crowd went crazy. The girl rose, held out her arms, and cried, "Thou hast poisoned me."

"Nay," Ken called. "All here poisoned you." He turned to the cast. "Show what you are."

The cast raised signs and led the crowd in chanting, "We are poi-son, poi-son. We slay you, we slay you. Die for money, die for nothing." Not exactly the stuff of poets.

Ken grabbed the girl and they disappeared into the woods to the hoots and applause from the gathering.

I felt eyes searching my face before I saw him. Lake. I wondered what he saw in my unsuspecting expression. I couldn't recall when my mind went from appalled to amused. *Of course I wasn't amused.*

Lake stood beside me. "Nice presentation, huh?"

"Lovely. Hi Joe."

Joe Hagan said, "Lo. Your computer geek is true to his word."

"He tell you he's getting a line on van Uum?"

"NYPD says van Uum shows up on one flight manifest leaving New York for another state in the last six months. We know about the recent flight to Atlanta. However we didn't know that he'd cancelled his gallery exhibit ten days ago. He neglected to tell me that when I questioned him earlier."

I mused aloud. "Oliver can fly a plane; maybe van Uum can, too."

"Fine and dandy," Lake said, "We'll find out if he can or has, but Oliver hasn't flown or driven anywhere since this whole thing started. You serious about him?"

"Oliver didn't kill anyone."

"Someone did it for him. Van Uum can certainly drive a car and get around quite easily in ten days."

I said to Joe, "It's possible Arne, Damian, Aneko, and van Uum met in Prague. They'd all been there two years before the Performance Art scheme got rolling at UGA. Prague is a community of artists and artist wannabees."

Joe raised his eyebrows and asked if someone was supposed to be murdered in today's performance.

"I think all along the plan was to murder Baxter for his money and use the art performance as cover."

Lake darted his gaze between me and Joe, and I grasped that he'd laid out my Conceptual Art theory to Joe. Lake said, "You've worked up a different hypothesis, *suddenly.*" Evidently, he was aggravated that I didn't run it by him first.

Joe said, "Okay, they hatched a plan called 'Let's Kill the Rich Guy and Blame it on'—who?"

"Damian and Aneko."

Lake's eyes narrowed. "You got them as victims now?"

"It's an idea," I said.

Joe said, "There's something about little Cho Martine's lake drowning that Viktor Martine didn't tell you, or us. He may have been too distraught to learn of the aftermath. According to Interpol reports, Aneko was seen in the street with a man that fits van Uum's description. Witnesses report seeing her leave with him—never to return. The thing is Damian and Arne were in the States at that time."

"Van Uum then," Lake said. "Kill Baxter so his partner, Oliver, inherits Bax's zillions."

The music box fired up again.

"Oh! You Beautiful Doll, You Great Big Beautiful Doll" blared from the speakers. The cast of dolls danced out in a can-can line. Neither poets nor dancers, still the artists got the point across. Then a male doll in formal attire and wearing jester shoes staggered from the woods swigging from a champagne bottle. He doffed his top hat. An ivory-faced, vampire doll rushed up behind him and stuck him in the back with a collapsible blade knife. I hoped it was a collapsible blade.

The crowd stilled as if holding their breaths.

The male doll went down. The line-dancing dolls looked stunned, their eyes wide, their mouths forming big Os. Then a Barbie doll and a Kewpie doll picked him up. He hung limply between them while the dolls sang the refrain: *Oh! You beautiful doll, You great big beautiful doll! Let me put my arms about you, I could never live without you; Oh! You beautiful doll, You great big beautiful doll! If you ever leave me, how my heart will ache, I want to hug you, but I fear you'd break; Oh, oh, oh, oh, Oh, you beautiful doll!*

The actors formed a bunny-hop line and took to the streets of Augusta with a large portion of the crowd following.

"Oh boy," Joe said. "Well, they're not our problem." He glanced at me. "I don't see Gilmeath or van Uum here."

"Nor I," I answered.

"Maybe they weren't invited," Lake said.

Suddenly a Harlequin clown doll broke from the line and heaved herself straight toward me. Baby Talk.

"Enjoy the show?" she asked as if we'd attended a New York musical.

"Not bad," I said. "Given the ghastly nature."

"Yeah, well, it was a special for Mr. Baxter."

"He'd be pleased, I'm sure," Lake said.

She stared at Lake. "I'm talking to her." Meaning me.

"Okay," he said with a grin. "Talk."

She quickly lost her peevish posture. "I wanted to tell you," she said breathlessly and glanced back to where her troop hopped farther away.

"Where are they going?"

"Mr. Baxter's house. Anyway, I wanted to tell you that I saw the man that the Asian girl was with."

"When?"

"Yesterday."

"Where?"

"At Mr. Baxter's house."

"Why were you there?"

"Mama always said when there's a death, you take a casserole. I don't cook, but Mama made one for me. Long time ago, she did housework for the Carlisle's. She drove and I went to the door."

The old Southern tradition comes through. "And?"

"Well, he was coming from the garden. Just walking and talking with Mr. Oliver and another man I didn't know. They came from around back and when Mr. Oliver saw me, he signaled to the two strangers that they should go back the way they came, and then he came up and took the casserole. He's so handsome, I'm not surprised he has two boyfriends making him feel better about losing Mr. Baxter."

"What did the man look like?"

"Tall. He was wearing the same hat and shades as with the Asian girl."

"What kind of hat?" I asked. "Baseball?"

"No, a hat with a wide brim, a bucket or a boonie, I don't know exactly."

"Are you sure it's the same man?"

Instant miff. "I'm a trained artist, and I recognize people by their bodies and gestures. His head cocked a certain way and I remembered his long face."

His photograph showed van Uum with a distinctive head cock. I asked Joe to show her the photos I'd given to him. He said they were in his car. Baby Talk said she couldn't wait for him to fetch and return, but she would look at them after the performance. She went on, "I don't think Mr. Oliver was happy to see me. But he took the food and thanked me, and I went back to the car." She looked to see the line dancers a block ahead. "Must go," she said, laboring away.

"She could be wrong," Lake said.

Joe said, "Damian Hansel is not tall and is what you might call a red man. Sunburned fair skin, round face."

Lake, Joe, and I separated and each drove to Baxter's house. If the line dancers were serious, and it looked like they were having too much fun to quit, it would take them a couple of hours to bunny hop to Bax's.

Chapter Twenty-Eight

I pulled in behind Joe. The only car in the driveway was van Uum's rental. I walked between Joe and Lake up the path to the front door. Maybe it was my imagination but the Italianate wore a worried expression. Its very ironwork fretted like a cranky child—or doll. Silk draperies hung like shrouds from the tower window.

Oliver answered the doorbell. His aspect was sober, like a manored butler's. "Miss Dru. Detective Lake. Agent Hagan."

As case chief, Joe took a step forward. "Is Uli van Uum with you here?"

"Why do you want to know?" Oliver asked.

"We'd like to speak to him."

"Would you please tell me what this is about? He is my guest, my *invited* guest."

"Just a few questions, that's all."

Oliver appeared to reflect on that statement. "I hate bothering my friends over my personal problems. We've been treated to a sorry show at Canal Towpath."

"I didn't see you there," I said.

"Parts of the insane spectacle were videotaped for television. We're in mourning, and preparing to leave this evening for Athens. My father's farewell viewing is scheduled for tomorrow and I have much to do."

I bobbed my head in understanding. Joe said, "A few questions is all."

"I think I should ask Uli first."

"No need to make a big production," Joe said.

"Three of you look like a big production," Oliver said, looking at Lake and me like we were holding weapons and handcuffs.

"We happen to come together from separate places at Canal Towpath," Joe said. "If it would be better for Mr. van Uum, Miss Dru can wait in another room or out here."

That brought a spark to Oliver's eyes and eased the tension in his jaw. "Miss Dru might object to being left out." He nearly winked when he looked at me.

I said, "I'm not the authority here."

Without hesitation, he said, "I hired you to find my father's killer. I think Uli would rather talk to you than a special agent and a homicide detective."

Joe huffed like an impatient bull. Oliver held up his palm against the temper stream, and Lake said, "Simple questions."

There was movement behind Oliver. An accented voice said, "I hear my name." Van Uum stepped beside Oliver. "I'm always curious when I hear my name. More than once, especially, and spoken by a committee."

I'd seen van Uum's photographs, but standing before me he appeared leaner and more intense. He had narrow shoulders, keen gray eyes, and thin lips. His skin was evenly tanned either by the sun or tanning bed. He wore his blond hair shorn up the sides but long and upswept on top. He had several diamonds in his ears. I'm not fond of facial hair, but his thin moustache was nearly unnoticeable because it was the color of his skin.

Oliver said to him. "These investigators would like to ask you questions. I take umbrage at their coming here to question my friends at this time and in this manner."

"Oliver, Oliver," van Uum said with a smile. "You are too, too correct. Let them come in, sit, and we'll answer what we can." *The royal we.*

Oliver stepped to one side. We went in flanked by the self-declared resident and his guest. Anthony DuPlessy stood beneath the mezzanine looking like an officer of the court. A faint but curious odor made my nose twitch—the combination of alcohol and other forensic chemicals. There are luminol preparations that smell of alcohol and hydrogen peroxide, and I noticed that the billiard room door was fully open.

Joe said, "Anthony, how are you?"

"I don't know yet," Anthony answered. "Depends on why you're here. Your warrants are no longer good."

"No need for warrants," Joe said. "A few questions need clearing up."

Anthony said, "We'll go into the library."

"Lieutenant Lake and I would like to speak to Mr. van Uum alone," Joe said, looking at van Uum.

Van Uum shrugged as if that was fine with him, but Anthony said, "I think not."

Oliver spoke up. "I'd like Miss Dru involved. I'm paying her to investigate my father's death." Ah, Baxter had become *my father. Where there's a will . . .*

We moved chairs and arranged ourselves in a semicircle. Joe looked at van Uum and began, "Notice I do not have a listening device on me." He spread his coat. "But I will take notes." He removed a pen and notebook from his inner pocket. "Your name, please."

"Uli van Uum."

"How long have you been in the United States?"

"This visit?" van Uum asked.

"Yes."

"A month and a day. I can show you my passport and visa."

"It won't be necessary now," Joe said. "How many visits have you made to Augusta, Georgia?"

"Do you have a time frame?"

285

"Include your first visit."

"Hmmm," he said, pausing to think. "Not more than half a dozen. I'm not sure. Again, my passport will confirm."

"How many visits have you made to Athens, Georgia?"

Touching his fingertips to one another, he looked at the ceiling, then spoke, "Nine, maybe ten times." He looked at Oliver. "To visit my friend."

Oliver said, "I told Miss Dru about your work on the Bulldogs' mascot."

"For the late Mr. Carlisle's sports bar," van Uum said.

"Were you in Augusta this past summer?" Joe asked.

"Augusta? This past summer? No, I was not."

"While here in Augusta, at any time, did you become acquainted with Inger Petersen?"

"My God. Inger." He made a sad face and shook his head. "Yes. I met her. Right here, in this house."

"Was Baxter here at the time?"

"No, I came to visit Oliver. She cleaned the house that day."

Oliver had lied about having never seen her. I looked at him; he glanced away.

"Were you ever out in town in her presence?" Joe continued.

"Not at all," he said, his mouth turned down in a baffled frown. "What is this? She is dead."

"When you were in Augusta, did you make the acquaintance of an Asian woman called Cho Martine?"

"The missing Martine woman?" He appeared genuinely surprised. "Of course not."

"What about an Asian woman called Aneko Hattori?"

"Aneko?" His mind seemed to be stuck in neutral for a moment. "Was here?"

"You know Aneko Hattori?"

"She introduced herself a couple of years ago in Prague." He blinked his glacial eyes. "She was in Rome once when I was

286

there." He paused and looked at Oliver. Then Anthony. It seemed something of appalling significance passed between them, but maybe it was my imagination. He looked again at Joe. "What has Aneko to do with any of this?"

"We're not sure yet," Joe said, waving a hand. "But you say you were not with her in Augusta?"

"No, I've never been with anyone here but Oliver."

"While here, did you visit an area called Artists Row?"

Van Uum's index finger waggled between himself and Oliver. "We have gone together. I have never gone alone."

Anthony cleared his throat. "I advise my clients to speak with caution."

Van Uum looked at the lawyer as if a scorpion sat on his shoulder. "I am cautious, and I tell the truth."

I said, "Most artists are truthful because obfuscation and deception are anathema to them."

Van Uum stared at me. "You are correct. The first caveat, be true to oneself. Falsehoods show in one's work."

Oliver rose. "I think we're finished here." He looked at van Uum. "Don't you think, Uli?"

Van Uum looked at each of us. "Any more questions?"

I asked, "Have you met a young man named Damian Hansel?"

Van Uum's head turned from Oliver like I'd asked an absurd question. "The man who accused Oliver's father of spying on his girlfriend?"

"I don't know that that's a true statement, but he is the man who first disappeared. The case started with him. He traveled in the art circles of Europe, including Prague and Rome. He fancied himself an artist, but most believe it was wishful thinking on his part."

"I have heard of him," van Uum said, looking at Oliver. "But I have never met him. The only reason I would wish to is to clear the fog around the deaths of two men—Mr. Carlisle and the student who hanged himself."

Lake spoke for the first time. "Let's not forget Bax's housekeeper, Inger Petersen."

"I would never forget her," van Uum declared. "I am appalled by her death. She had talent and ambition. It is a waste. Whoever killed her should forfeit his own life."

Joe stood, so did Lake and I. Van Uum remained seated. Artists have run-ins with the law or critics or patrons, and it toughens them, but van Uum looked profoundly appalled.

"Have you found Bax's will?" I asked Oliver when we turned to leave the library.

He seemed distracted like he was trying to recall where he mislaid it; then he shook his head. "I guess you consider it your business since I hired you, and you believe it might have a bearing on his death. But, no, we've not found where Baxter kept the original."

I looked at Anthony DuPlessy. "But you have a copy, correct?"

"That is correct."

"Is there a provision for who inherits the dolls?"

Anthony's nostrils widened like they'd encountered a sour odor. "I suspect there's a reason you're asking that question?"

"Kirin Littlefield. The name mean anything?"

"If it does?"

"I spoke with her. She said Baxter promised her the dolls. Something left over from their childhood. He collected them for her."

"I can tell you that Miss Littlefield will be notified at the proper time."

I remembered the polo luncheon where Anthony had looked like he wanted to eat me whole. That was when he was *Tony*. It must have had something to do with the fabulous suit Baxter kept for guests in need of appropriate attire, because now he stared at me with extreme distaste.

"One more thing," I said, holding up a finger. "She wishes that the dolls found with his body be interred with him."

Oliver said, "My father will be cremated as soon as the police are finished with his body."

"What about the cemetery lot for his fancy aboveground tomb?"

He swallowed like something unpleasant clogged the back of his throat. "We spoke about that. He changed his mind. He'd become more in tune with the environment. It will be sold."

Maybe not, if Kirin Littlefield had anything to say about it, I thought, but just nodded.

I looked at Oliver. "Baxter promised to show me the dolls. I only saw those that were arranged with him. Is it possible that I can see the fabulous ones he told me about?"

His eyes shifted like he thought he was being had. Anthony quickly intervened as if Oliver might come undone. "I'll show you the doll rooms. It's a bit hard on Oliver."

"I imagine."

"I'm leaving you folks," Joe said. "I've got a case report to write and a wife that expects me home before the kids go to bed."

When Joe left, Anthony motioned us to follow him. He intended to pass beneath the staircases and use the elevator at the back of the house. I stopped and said, "Anthony, I'd like to go through the mezzanine if that's all right with you. I may not get another opportunity. I'm a fan of mezzanines and this one is exquisite."

Anthony considered a moment, and then said, "It won't hurt to indulge you."

He remained on the top step while Lake followed me onto the mezzanine floor, his foot falling more heavily than usual.

Walking to the center of the arched balcony, I looked down to see Uli and Oliver staring up. Moving and positioning my stance on the rose-patterned carpet, I called down rather giddily, *"All the world's a stage,* and I'm on it." Uli had enough good humor left to grin. I moved like an actor while quoting the Shakespeare passage. *"All the world's a stage, And all the men and women merely players: They have their exits and their entrances; And one man in his time plays many parts."*

Uli van Uum called up, "And all the world plays the actor. Bravo."

Anthony clapped twice and I could hear the sarcasm in the staccato. When I walked over, he asked, "Satisfied?" I smiled, and he added, "This mezzanine is a unique architectural feature."

"Worth preserving," I said, suddenly instilled with a notion. Had he purposely given me a hint?

On the third floor, Anthony took a key from his pocket and opened the first door we came to. The enormous room consisted of floor-to-ceiling glass cases. Every doll you could imagine or want stood, or lay, or sat, or cavorted. Some stood with their faces in corners or against furniture. These were, I knew, chastised dolls, time-out dolls. They had no faces, which was kind of creepy. The collection in this room was indeed from every country on the globe. I was drawn to a singular glass case with a rather strange-looking doll. She stood eighteen inches tall on a wooden stand. Her face was polished brown wood; her eyes were round button rings. A coarse string of beads, bangles, rings, stones in materials from ivory to metal hung from her neck to her waist. Inside the case, a mounted plaque told me she was a South African Marriage Doll. Turning away, I looked back at the doll as if she held a special message or meaning—maybe illustrating Bax's obsession with a marriage never to be.

The second and third rooms were much the same, dolls of

manmade and natural materials ranging from plastic to carved marble. I noticed there were no fabric dolls. I said to Anthony, "Cloth dolls were placed in the tower with Baxter."

Lake said, "For the squeamish. To wash before playing with."

Anthony cracked a smile. "If Kirin Littlefield has her way, and I'm not sure that she should or will, she wants them buried with Baxter. That would be a shame."

"Well, so far we know who gets the dolls," I said. "Now, we need to know who gets the house."

"I don't know that you need to know that," Anthony said. "Unless you think it will be you."

"No, but Bax did give me an open invitation."

"Is that so?"

"Otherwise I would never have walked in, felt something amiss and called Lake."

He gave me a *we'll see about that* glance.

"Could we go up to the tower room?"

He rubbed his lower teeth on his upper lip in distaste. "The dolls there have been boxed up. I don't know if the police are finished with them yet."

"I'd like to see the room before it was . . ."

"Follow me."

In the tower room, the expensive rattan furniture had been placed willy-nilly. Fans were whirring in the four corners and the portal doors stood open. I stepped outside, onto the narrow railed porch that hugged three sides of the house. When I turned the corner at the back of the house, I scanned the gardens. It was so high up, if someone wanted to take a suicidal leap that would do the job on the stones below. Beyond the garden, in the woods, deciduous trees had lost their leaves, and through the bare branches I could make out what looked like a little tree house. I noted that the elevation culminated in a bluff. The view was truly spectacular.

Before going back inside, I took in and released large lungfuls of clean crisp air so as to clear the stench from my olfactory passages.

My cell phone played the concerto. It was Web.

"Tell me you've found genie."

Web laughed. "Several actually. There's the famous garage door company. Don't think that's applicable. There's the obedient spirit of wish granting, which could apply if Baxter found himself a magic lamp. Also the Genie Café right here in Atlanta, GA."

"Web get to it."

"That brings us to Open Sesame from the Genie Spy App Company. There are many companies out there. I never heard of this one, but Dirk's has used it. Download the app on the phone you want to monitor and the target never knows it's there. If it's an iPhone, you have to jailbreak it. There are ways to detect the security breach in the firmware with the chmod command. Just copy the su binary in the PATH. For example. Slash-system-slash-xbin-slash-su, and . . ."

"You're doing that on purpose, Web."

He laughed. "The main reasons companies lock their phones is so only their proprietary carrier has access and the owners buy the maker's approved software."

"How are they monitored?"

"By a control panel on the spy's internet connection. Open Sesame steals the target's texts, emails, his calendar, people in his contact list; it hears his chats and can GPS him. It could even wipe out his data."

"Let's say this is what Bax meant. That means he found out he was being bugged."

"Be my guess. He could have found the control panel on the spy's computer or overheard something, or maybe suspected he was being spied upon and laid down a false trail. He could have bought an anti-spyware app that would show the Open Sesame icon in the bootloader. Some cause the open source app to un-install, and . . ."

"That's all I need, Web."

Lake and Anthony hadn't made friends while I was outside.

"Everything okay with you?" Anthony said.

"Sure," I said and looked at Lake. "You?"

Lake addressed Anthony with a frown. "I can't help but wonder why Bax's will hasn't turned up. He was an everything-in-its-place kind of guy."

Now I knew why it hadn't turned up.

"I can't answer for a man who's dead," Anthony said, "but I can tell you that we have a notary in our office and she witnessed his will along with a secretary who's been employed for many years. Mr. Carlisle provided the notary with a copy, according to the law, so I have access to it. If we can't find the original, that copy will become valid if the court orders."

"I thought that was the case," Lake said.

I have no idea if Lake thought that or not, but it satisfied Anthony, and we trooped down the steps.

On the first floor, Oliver and Uli were seated in the library. They rose. Uli looked distracted, as if he'd withdrawn interest in our visit. Oliver adjusted his tie and said, "I trust you've satisfied yourselves."

I gave him a calculating stare and nodded.

He folded his arms across his chest. "Are you making progress in the quest to find who murdered my father, and should I understand your interest in this house?"

"Where death happens is always of interest."

Lake intervened. "She was once a cop. A very good cop. A very good cop never stops asking questions about who, where, when, and why."

"Like reporters," he said, with a small smile.

"Exactly. Now, Miss Dru and I will leave you to your travel plans."

With thanks and goodbyes, and my asking after the recovery of the caretaker, who was still in the hospital, we left the house. On the path, I looked up at the façade and felt like weeping. The tower room. In it Baxter had been carefully arranged with dolls that weren't so much beloved by him but collected as penance for his innocent interest in a child, interest that he well knew was wrong even if he'd not taken the disastrous action for which he would never forgive himself.

"Devices and desires," I said, and watched Lake's face screw up. "By airing out the tower room—a device—they desired that anyone smelling decomp would attribute it to Baxter's rapidly rotting body."

"My dearest darling, your way with words and phrases is quite astonishing."

"They also used electronic devices to spy on Bax."

I was in the middle of explaining about Genie when Lake cocked his head toward the south. "Do you hear what I hear?"

As I've thought so many times, we are a great team. I can smell, he can hear. I concentrated with my ears and heard the refrain: *Oh you beautiful doll* . . .

"They couldn't have gotten here so quickly," I said.

"Cars," Lake said. "I heard doors slamming."

Hurrying toward the driveway, I said, "And the inmates here think *we* were a nuisance. Question, do you think they'd come out, maybe wear hats and shades, and form a lineup for Baby Talk to pick out the mystery man?"

"Devices and desires; rhetorical questions? I'm just a lowly cop here."

"Here's a literal question. If it wasn't Uli van Uum with Aneko, who was it?"

"Looking like van Uum. Artists are flakes, but lest we forget, it's Joe's case." He opened my car door. "Where to?" he asked. "Atlanta?"

"The hotel here. Shower. Change. Food. I'm starved."

"Hey, that's my line." He canted his head to one side. "What's that look for?"

I wriggled my nose. "Odors."

"Crime scene cleanup."

"They didn't get the death out."

"My nose isn't as good as yours, but I can already smell the country-fried steak and gravy."

It looked like all the Troops artists, plus about thirty citizens, had made it to Baxter's house. We turned into the street as the line dancers headed up Ammezzato's driveway.

CHAPTER TWENTY-NINE

They didn't get the death out.

I smelled decomp and Baxter wasn't dead long enough to decompose much before he was taken from the house.

"Lake," I said, around a mouth full of cornbread, "Baxter gave me permission to enter his house. Told me the alarm code and where the key was hidden. It fits all doors to the house, so . . ."

"You've said, and I know where you're going with this. So does van Uum, Oliver, and Anthony. The answer is: No, you can't . . ."

"Why can Oliver camp out? It's not his house, officially."

Lake pointed his fork. "Without invitation, you would be breaking and entering and if you took anything away, it would be burglary. The precedent was set when we left the house in his care after Baxter was removed."

"Precedent was set when Bax asked me to be his guest. I'm still his guest, *in absentia.*"

Lake chewed and shook his head. "Death voided that."

"And, don't forget, Oliver hired me to find Bax's murderer."

"Well, I was not invited, and I wasn't hired, and I'm on admin leave, so I'm not going in."

"Chicken."

At daybreak patches of ground fog made driving perilous especially if one didn't know Augusta streets. We figured that if we visited Ammezzato in the middle of the night that ramped up the breaking and entering problem; at least that's what Lake figured. But if we waited until dawn, well, we were paying an early visit. That's what I thought while maintaining my right to enter by invitation of the deceased owner.

Lake turned through the gates and stopped suddenly. "That's van Uum's rental." He reversed gears and backed into the street. "Appears he stayed behind."

"Don't think he would," I said. "Probably rode with Oliver."

"Nonetheless, we're checking it out prepared," he said, angling against the street curb. "Don't make noise. If he's here, we leave." That was our deal. We agreed we weren't going in with people inside. He opened his door and shut it gently.

Lake looked over the gear inside his trunk. Although it's his personal car, he carries guns, ammo, and several Kevlar protective jackets. He wasn't carrying one for me particularly, but most cops carry at least two protectors if they can afford them. Some like concealables, others tacticals.

Lake whispered, "Stab or ballistic?"

"I think this guy likes up close and personal, so I'm going for the stab."

"Remember what I said. If he's inside the house, we're leaving." He held up two choices. "Groin protector or neck?"

"Not *that* personal," I said, and reached for the side and neck protectors.

I opened the door to the carriage house, stepped inside, and let my eyes adjust to the night-light plugged into a socket on the far wall. I looked for the old Model T. It wasn't hard to spot. Nothing looked older than the fifties Thunderbird that must have come straight from the showroom. The black car, the object of our search, perched on blocks. I headed for it, Lake behind me.

"On the floor mat," I said when we reached the black antique.

Lake shined the light inside the car and opened the door that was so well-maintained it didn't creak. He lifted a mat that wasn't a standard feature on old granny. "It's here," he said, picking up the key and backing away. He handed it over. "You sure you smelled decomp?"

"I'm sure," I said. He'd told me ten times that all he smelled was chemicals. "And while you think I was simply spouting Shakespeare, I was moving my feet. The hardwood was uneven."

"Uneven doesn't mean someone's buried under the floor. Your smelling decomp in a house where a murder occurred and was discovered isn't going to get a warrant to rip it up."

We went through all this last night. I said, "We'll see when we raise the carpet."

The long carriage house ran parallel to the house and a portion of the backyard gardens. We would avoid the front garden even though its hillside trees and shrubs made the front door invisible from the street. The plan was to enter the house through the conservatory.

At the rear of the carriage house, there was a door that led outside. At least I presumed it led outside.

It wasn't locked and Lake turned the knob and drew it in.

My God! I almost shrieked.

"We're out of here," Lake said, shutting the door.

The door didn't lead outside, but instead to a modern garage where Oliver's and Anthony's cars were parked. They hadn't gone to Athens last evening after all.

I said, "They'll be going to Athens some time this morning, so we'll check out the house after they're gone."

"It's a plan to consider, but right now . . ."

Even I heard the scraping sound outside. Perhaps, I thought, the gardener came to work this early, but knew in my heart it wasn't a working sound.

The windows facing the house and conservatory were shuttered. Lake went to a plantation blind and raised a slat. "Jesus!"

"What? I can't see."

He stood aside. Two men had emerged from the conservatory and reached the flagstones. They were dressed in camouflage, like soldiers or hunters. Those two weren't soldiers. One was Anthony. He held a shotgun and the other was Uli. He was handcuffed and Anthony dragged him along the ground by the cuffs toward the woods.

"Drugged," I said.

"Or dead," Lake said.

I grabbed his arm. "It was a deer stand I saw, not a tree house. I bet . . ."

Lake understood immediately. "We go."

I reached for my ankle bug. Lake drew his standard issue Beretta since his Sig was in police custody, as was my 17.

"You ready?" Lake asked. "It'll be quick."

"Better be. Yep. Let's go."

Lake ripped open the side door, took a shooter's stance just as Anthony let go of Uli's body, and whirled. He was quick at racking the shotgun, a hunter no doubt. His finger found the trigger housing as he raised the gun.

Lake called, "Don't do it, Anthony."

"Get the hell out of here!" His aim was over our heads when he pulled the trigger. The boom echoed eerily through the light fog. He brought the barrel down. Depending on the pellet pattern, one of us could get a chest full or worse.

"Put it down," Lake called.

"You son-of-a-bitch," he yelled, lining his eye on the sight.

I pulled the trigger on the Glock twice and got his right arm. At the same time, Lake's one shot pierced the middle of his chest. The long gun clattered to the stones; he fell on it.

Holding his handgun out and down, Lake hurried to the man and felt for a pulse. "None."

When I got to Uli, he was coming around. Dazed and blinking, he might have thought he was dead and that I was an angel looking down at him. "Were you hit or drugged?" I asked.

"Uh," he said.

Lake turned him gently. No blood, no marks.

"Hunting accident," he groaned. "That's how . . ."

Lake felt his wrist pulse. "Slow." He unlocked the handcuffs while Uli continued to shake the fog of drugs from his head. It was a struggle but he propped himself on an elbow. "I confronted him," he said, his mouth working like a man in a trance. "I figured it out. Aneko and Anthony. In Rome. What was up. After the fact."

"Save your strength," Lake said, cell phone in hand. "Help will be here soon."

"My beautiful Oliver . . ."

Uli eased his body to lay full-length on the pavers. Splayed, he looked as flattened as Anthony.

Betrayal will do that.

I walked up the path and inserted the key in the lock. No need to check the alarm.

In the study, Oliver sat in a high-back wing chair facing away. I couldn't see the back of his head, but I could see his hands on the leather arms.

He asked, "Is it over?"

I walked toward the chair. He didn't move.

"Is it?" he said.

He leaned forward. I came to the side of the chair. He didn't look up when he said, "Damn Uli. Why the hell didn't he stay in New York like I told him to? Tony, you're too fucking smart for your own good." He flung himself back in the chair. "You shouldn't have called for him to come . . ."

Turning his head, his eyes met mine. The fright of not seeing

Anthony, but instead me, couldn't counteract his total defla-
tion. I've never seen a man so full of himself completely col-
lapse.

"You," he said. Seconds went by while he accepted what was
to come, and what had occurred outside. Then his fingers picked
the studs in the leather of the chair arm. He couldn't resist asking. "Anthony?"

"Dead."

"And . . . and . . . Uli?"

"Alive."

"Where is he?" Jumping up, he nearly knocked me down. "I
must go to him."

I grabbed an arm. "Sit. The paramedics are on the way. So
are the cops."

"Let me go . . ."

"No," I grasped harder. He yanked away. I grabbed again,
spun him around, and got his neck in a vise grip. "I said no."

He gasped and pawed at my crooked arm. I squeezed a little
tighter. He wouldn't strangle, but he thought he would.

"Ho-hokay," he whispered.

"I'll let up, but you'd better sit or I'll shoot you, Oliver.
Between your greedy, frigging eyes."

Rubbing his neck, he collapsed into the chair. He looked at
the ceiling and croaked, "Uli's alive. It shouldn't be—been like
this."

"You planned it. Kill your father, get his wealth for yourself.
Patricide, as old as rich fathers and avaricious sons. You were in
a position, by virtue of your father's money, to round up cohorts
who were dumb enough to play out a scheme that would
obscure the age-old money motive."

"I did it for Uli," he countered, like that made all the sense in
the world.

"But you failed to see that Anthony wanted it for himself.

Administering the estate would be his ticket to a full-time job and eventually getting the entire Carlisle estate for himself."

He kept his eyes trained on the ceiling. "I wanted to create something fine for Uli and me."

"Baxter would have given you . . ."

He threw up his hands and yelled, "You don't understand. I was going to be his Man Friday for the rest of my fucking life, or his!"

"So it was to be his."

Anger subsided quickly into self-pity. "He never loved me." The bastard stared up at me, his eyes imploring pity. None from me, though. "I wanted my own life, my due."

"You're getting it, Oliver." His lips tightened. "You knew Uli wouldn't plot a man's murder. Like you said, Uli isn't supposed to be here, but in New York at his show. But you knew someone who was as capable of murder as yourself. Your old college buddy."

He snorted. "Anthony wanted to hire a hit man. For God's sake! Hit men are notorious for getting caught and blabbing."

"Time went by, and then happenstance gave you a better idea. Through Uli, you met some nutty artists in Prague and hooked up with Aneko after she was suspected of drowning Cho Martine. What happened? Did you become lovers and did she confess to you?" He smirked. "And did you confess to her that you wanted your father dead so you could inherit?" He wagged his head like I would never understand. "She had already taken Cho's identity and had met Damian and Arne— innocents in the murder plot. You told her about Baxter's past and she used it to stage whatever concept she had in mind. She got poor besotted Damian to fall for her conceptual performance scheme, with himself as star performer."

He sat straight and smoothed his pants legs with both hands. "It started out perfect. They'd stage scenes. Then Cho would get Baxter involved by accusing him of hitting on her. The intent was to disorient, confuse, make him feel guilty about his perversion. I wasn't sure where she was taking the plan, but she said it would end with Baxter killing himself. His self-destruction would end his moral dilemma, a metaphor for the weakness of the moral man, something like that. And if he didn't kill himself, there was Anthony."

"But it didn't end up perfect because Aneko teamed up with a more devious partner, Anthony."

He shook off that truth. "Baxter gets spooked and hires you. You got him thinking outside his usual fog. Aneko tries to blackmail Anthony over Damian. I planned none of it."

"Then Bax changed his will."

"I saw it coming."

"You put spyware on his cell phone and read his communications with his new lawyer. But Bax got onto you, Oliver."

He laughed. "You can't tell those things are on your phone."

"Bax was obsessed with the phone spoofing that was getting him in trouble so he went on the Internet. He learned about spyware. He took his cell phone to the iStore and they found it had been jail-broken."

From some of the clues he dropped on me and Lake, I inferred that Bax's cell phone was to be the mystery guest at dinner. I believed he wanted to tell me what he'd suspected about Oliver and Anthony and what he was doing about it. It had nothing to do with Inger, but she was killed to keep the murder an arty concept.

Oliver said, "His manner toward me changed. Anthony saw it, too. We needed more time."

"While you narcissists were setting up Baxter to kill himself over his weakness for young women, Anthony and Aneko were using Arne and Damian to dupe you. Anthony would murder Baxter and make it look like you did it. There was no subtle in

Baxter's death, no suggestion of purifying suicide."

His hands clutched the chair arms. "But you're wrong thinking Anthony was going to frame me for Baxter's murder. He couldn't. I was in Athens. I'm no one's fool."

"In a few days, you were going to be charged with murder."

He doubled over with fake laughter. "You're nuts."

"There is a dead body in this house. The smell will soon lead to its discovery. There will be evidence with it that you were the murderer. When is the new cleaning lady due in?"

Oliver looked like he was trying to solve a math problem in his head and couldn't quite work it out. "Today, while we were in Athens. Anthony hired her to do a thorough . . ." He stopped. He looked like something awful had crawled into his windpipe.

I said, "Uli started asking questions and making deductions so he had to die in a hunting accident. Whose body is in this house? Aneko's or Damian's?"

As if all was lost, he conceded, "Aneko is in her car in Lake Oconee. I had nothing to do with that."

"Where was Damian before Anthony moved him here?"

"Wrapped in plastic in a storage cooler at Carlisle's." *Wait until Athens's diners hear about that.* "We planned to bury him in the woods when everything was over."

"That was not Anthony's plan."

He took a deep breath at the implication, at what authorities would assume, at all Anthony might have done to set him up for the murders.

"With tons of money, you wouldn't go to trial for killing Damian for a long time. You certainly wouldn't get the death penalty. But you would be under suspicion for the rest of your life in the deaths of Arne and Aneko, if Aneko was ever found. Uli's hunting accident was to happen when you and Anthony were in Athens for Bax's service, but hunting accidents and suicides are hard to stage, so you would have been a suspect in

Uli's murder, too."

His eyes were skittish with fear. "Uli's alive, that's all that matters. He'll see that I had no choice but to go along. I never killed anyone." He spread his hands, smug, assured now. Typical narcissistic mood swings. "I never knew what they were going to do next. I didn't want to know. After Arne . . . It was supposed to be easy, but that crazy woman kept changing things after Arne . . . Anthony, my God, when he killed Arne . . . It was like he'd fallen in love with killing. He killed Inger with poison in her wine. He told me how he got Baxter shooting pool. And when you came in, he itched to kill you, too. You see, I know what happened. I can clear myself with the police. I did nothing illegal."

Lake walked in with Joe and the local cops. Oliver jumped up. Suddenly every cop in the room had his gun aimed at him. He faced Lake, palms held up and out. "I'm fine. I didn't do anything wrong."

I held my breath, afraid some trigger finger would fire off.

Oliver laughed genially. The brink held. Joe removed handcuffs from his pocket. Oliver looked as if it didn't matter one bit. He said, "The world is full of excellent lawyers and you will soon learn the name of my new counsel." He grinned at me. "Everything I said here is a lie. I'm a known dissembler, but I am not a killer." He looked at each of us in turn. "Now, if you don't mind, I have a viewing scheduled for my father later today, and there are a few things that need doing."

They removed Damian's body from the mezzanine floor, and when I surveyed the Italianate façade for the last time, its windows gleamed as if an arduous burden had been lifted. Turning to walk away, I heard the sigh, a whisper of relief. A tour of homes was in Ammezzato's future. Baxter had bequeathed it in trust to the Summerville Historic Society to be nominated for a place on the National Register of Historic Places. The caretaker recovered from a head injury he didn't remember receiving and retired.

For three days after Baxter's interment, authorities searched for Baxter's new will. His Atlanta lawyer came forward and confirmed that he'd executed one, but no one had a clue where Bax had stashed it. Finally it was found lying alone in a safety deposit box at his Augusta bank. I'd awakened in the middle of the night in a brainstorm. The next morning I told Joe where to look for a key. He found it hanging around the neck of the South African Marriage Doll.

Baxter bequeathed Power House to Oliver. That's all. The rest of his estate will be in probate for years. Oliver's lawyers are angling for an insanity defense on the charges of murder and conspiracy to murder all those who died.

Webdog had discovered the Open Sesame spyware control panel on Oliver's computer and told Joe.

Lake was exonerated in the deaths of Big DD's bangers, and I got my 17 back.

M.C. continues to heal after his beating, and Devus Dontel McFersen sits in jail charged with murder and conspiracy to commit murder—plus lesser charges—in the gang shootout witnessed by Johndro and in the deaths of his thugs at the church. Pearly Sue charmed witnesses, and Johndro, currently in a safe foster home, is set to testify against him. As yet, there is no new drug lord in the Bluffs.

Last weekend I brought Mama home for the weekend. She fretted and fussed and demanded to return to her *real* home. When I gave in and settled her into her assisted living suite, she giggled like a kid with a new kitten.

ABOUT THE AUTHOR

Gerrie Ferris Finger is a retired journalist and author of several novels, three published in the Moriah Dru/Richard Lake series: *The End Game, The Last Temptation,* and *The Devil Laughed. Murmurs of Insanity* is the third in the series published by Five Star. Ms. Finger lives on the coast of Georgia with her husband, Alan, and their standard poodle, Bogey.